Joseph V. Sultana

Unsceptred Isle
Three of a Kind

PERCY
PUBLISHING

Inquiries should be addressed to
Percy Publishing
13 Ivy Chimneys,
Epping,
Essex. CM16 4EL.
England.
www.percy-publishing.com

FIRST EDITION
First Printing February 2012

Printed By
The Atlas Print Group
Sophia House,
28 Cathedral Way,
Cardiff. CF11 9LJ
Wales.

ISBN : 978-0-9571568-0-7

Cover Design Copyright © 2012 Joseph V. Sultana

Dedicated to all of you who have shown an interest, helped as proof readers or sounding boards. I thank and salute you. I also want to thank Ruth Killeen for her belief in the novel and me, as well as gaining a deal so quickly.

Mostly, to my wife and children for their

un-wavering support.

Mum and Dad

To Paul
You have been a
great champion for
me mate.
Take Care
Joseph V.

Joseph V. Sultana is a safety assurance manager with a 22 year experience in the UK rail industry. Unsceptred Isle – Three of a Kind is his first published work which is the initial instalment of the Unsceptred Isle series.

Joseph V. Sultana

Prologue

In 2034, the England that was once part of the mighty United Kingdom is now fragmented and impoverished. Scotland, Ireland, Wales, even Cornwall, now known by the ancient and historical name of Kernow, have all become separate and independent countries in their own right.

During the opening ceremony of the 2012 London Olympic Games, the detonation of a bio-nuclear bomb occurred, almost killing every living thing in London.

They called it the double whammy, or the old one two. A term used in boxing, meaning a jab with one hand followed by a cross by the other. It was the perfect description for what had happened.

The dying, ancient city was the first to be surrounded by a barrier and it had taken the authorities just four months for the first wall to be built. The barrier, constructed from razor wire, lined with gun turrets circled London, taking the route of the old M25 motorway. It effectively turned the city into a forbidden zone with no-one being permitted in or anyone allowed out.

In the two years that followed, the construction of a solid wall was finally completed and standing at thirteen metres high and six metres wide, the smooth concrete erection was constantly monitored to ensure its sole purpose of security was not compromised.

London, once the centre of an Empire that stretched around the globe, had perished and was now becoming just a memory. The poor bastards who had survived the aftermath were left to die an exceedingly painful and agonising death. Some caught the plague, via the airborne biological agents that were scattered in the attack, while others, those who were lucky enough to be immune, became sick through radioactive fallout. Over time, rumours spread that now and again chilling screams and gunshots from the guards could be heard.

The whole of the British Isles had suffered as a result, with countries around the world, all turning their back on their one time ally and friend. Fearing for the safety of its own population, the French Government decided to fill the Channel Tunnel with a plug of reinforced concrete more than two miles thick at their end, while the rest of the United Kingdom's neighbours closed all their borders, with the penalty being death, if you were caught trying to get in.

The British Monarchy, those that were not killed in the attack, moved to Switzerland in a self-imposed exile, where, to this day, they remain. The Government transferred to the north, with power initially being shared between all parties to work out their next move. They all decided to impose a state of Marshall Law on the people, which was harsh, but necessary and it worked for a few years, with people beginning to rebuild and life went on.

However with the defining of one border, the construction of other walls began soon after. In 2016, Scotland became the first to declare its independence and immediately her government began to stop oil and gas supplies south. The Scottish wall was the second wall to be built and they decided

6

to construct it on the foundation of the original wall built by the Roman Emperor, Hadrian. This too became a method of control, a way of keeping out the unwanted, while making Scotland a fortified country, self-sufficient on fuel, food and now with its own armed forces.

The Midlands became an Islamic State, a 'no-go' area for most non-believers, with a select group allowed within the city walls.

Up and down the country, the changes came quickly, changes that mainly affected the poorer people of society.

Work for the most part was non-existent and the breaking of whatever laws that happened to be in place, in what remained of towns and cities were dealt with by new local enforcement patrols governed by Elite Enforcers.

This robust regime was the remnants of an imposed and forgotten Marshall Law but despite that, crime was the career of choice for many with the trafficking of drugs, contraband and people out of England and into its thriving, neighbouring countries.

Those who were caught, or who were stupid enough to try and take more than they should, were dealt with quickly and inhumanely, as courts and juries were outdated and considered 'a thing of the past'.

These judicial processes were replaced by a system of capital punishment, which had become a form of sickening public entertainment, as well as being a deterrent.

Such were the remains of a corrupt system of laws, that grew more corrupt as time moved on that by the end of 2034, what was left of England looked more like a thirteenth century godless wilderness, than a land of the twenty-first century.

With the establishment of the Celtic Kingdoms, people of England tried to migrate there, however, the authorities had put a stop to allowing just anyone to cross the border and only the wealthy or corrupt managed to get in.

Those that were left behind began to set up small communities around these new seats of power, with some communes growing into large towns or small cities.

It was in these places that the businesses of trading stolen goods, gambling or prostitution openly plying their game was carried out and corruption at almost every level of this new 'civilisation' was the norm.

The rest of the country was left to rot into a god forsaken wilderness that had no resources, no money and no laws except the law of survival.

Farms were left untended, villages were abandoned and society devolved, reverting to the past. Bows and arrows became the weapons used, guns were held only for the authorities and horses were used to pull modified cars. Even though technology was still around, there was little point in having it, as there was no power for it to operate, also nobody to service and maintain it.

As time went by, things came to a head and many civil wars had been fought and over the next seventeen years, it became irrelevant who was responsible for the carnage and in 2034, survival was the only thing left for them.

Chapter One

Jon Maitland held his grip on the Punisher's throat, pressing harder each time he felt the thrashing beneath his vice-like hold. Maitland's five feet ten inch mastiff like build helped him, in the not so easy job of, strangling a man while holding him off the floor. Both men and for different reasons, were struggling for breath.

As a civil engineer, Maitland was unaware of the science behind this particular method of slaughter. For instance, he didn't know that crushing the trachea alone was not enough to ensure death. He did not care that he also had to stop the flow of blood getting to this, the latest of many victims' brain, by applying pressure to the arteries in the neck.

All he knew was if he pressed long enough and hard enough with his giant hands around a person's throat, that person died, but only once had he heard and felt the cracking of a bone from somewhere inside the throat.

The killer was devoid of all emotion, except that of the raging anger that flowed through his body, as he found himself killing yet again.

Here was one man, dangling in the air terrified and choking for breath, while the other was looking into the eyes of his victim, wanting to make sure he knew who was responsible for his death. It was a habit he had picked up the first time he was in a situation where he had to kill.

The engineer managed to ignore the numbing ache in his fingers as the pain shot up his arms, as he dug harder and deeper into the flesh covering the now crushed windpipe of the gasping low-life.

The pressure of his grip did indeed halt the flow of blood on its journey to the brain and this poor excuse of a human being was denied his own blessed life for crimes against his fellow person.

It was life being cut out, just as a cancerous tumour would be, in an attempt to save a sick patient. That patient was society and in these lawless times Jon Maitland had become the surgeon who was prepared to do what he must.

Somewhere along the way, he somehow managed to almost become a callous cruel killer with little or no regard for human life. He was very nearly no better than the animal he was now disposing of.

There it was; he heard and felt a bone crack as his thumbs conducted the sensation of whatever it was that gave way.

It made Maitland blink.

The breathing and the struggles of the man died off, as did his body and Maitland allowed himself to inhale the very air that was denied his victim.

With this sharp intake of breath, Maitland began to notice the racing of his own heart and his jaw was clenched just as tight as his grip had been. He saw that the dead man's blood was no longer being pumped by the pressure of a once beating heart, it oozed and flowed, mixing with Maitland's sweat as it trickled down his hands from the puncture wounds that his fingers had made in the neck of the lifeless body.

As Maitland released his grip on the dead weight, he watched it fall to the ground.

It thumped loudly onto the bare floorboards throwing up clouds of grey dust that had lain hidden of any attempt of cleaning.

The particles descended in a futile attempt to bury the corpse where it had just been dropped and remained lifeless on top of the waste that the victim had involuntarily expelled while in the throes of death.

Panting to catch his breath, Maitland crouched to check the body for any signs of life remaining. He found none and once again he was successful in the art of execution.

Tired, he lifted his head twisting it about to look around the room. His sweat-soaked long hair clung to his face, with his cold, hazel eyes peeping from behind the matted grey and brown strands.

The vile, gut wrenching smell of human waste, filth and decaying food filled the room and his nose. The stench acted on him as smelling salts would on an unconscious person, re-engaging his senses and with a shake of his head, Maitland suddenly became completely aware of his surroundings.

The window had been covered with a jade coloured curtain that was lazily placed across the dirt encrusted panes of glass.

The thin opaque material gave a warm, greenish hue as the summer sunlight managed to get through. It showed off the ageing, floral wallpaper which, through the years, had become damaged and tinged with brown discolouration.

In places there were parts that just managed to cling to the wall, in a futile attempt at retaining some aspect of respectability. On the ceiling, a solitary grey light bulb gently swung in its dust covered, plastic pendant fitting, that had yellowed.

It was then he saw the woman, she was lying on a metal bedstead, bound hand and foot spread eagle and naked.

She looked terrified out of her wits.

No surprise really, she had just witnessed the cold execution of another human being and god knows what else by the look of her.

It must have been her screams that flicked the switch inside Maitland's head. It was a switch that once activated, turned him into a cold, callous and merciless killer.

***

'Would it be my turn next? Is he going to kill me?' she thought as the murderer turned and looked at her.

Celeste had lost count of how long she had been shackled to the bed and today, she woke trying to work out how many days it had really been. She decided it was perhaps the fifth or sixth day of being secured.

'Had it really been nearly a week of not being allowed the dignity of using the bath, or the use of a toilet even?' She asked herself.

Twice a day the Punisher would bring her a tray of food and he would sit on the bed spoon feeding it to her, but always in a childish manner.

If she ever refused to eat, he would force it into her mouth, which of course, made her vomit.

Laying in the bed listening to the silence, she had no idea what time it was when he returned to the room. Today he was drunk more than usual and still taking great swigs of an open bottle of whisky as he entered.

'Well now my delicious Celeste, here we are again. Tell me something, how does it feel? You know, not to be in control for once, eh?' he was laughing at her, 'not so superior now are you? lying there, in the shit of your own making. You see it does stink after all.'

He pointed at her while laughing once more. He then replaced the metal screw cap on the glass bottle and allowed it to drop out of his hand. It hit the floor, with a bang and the fragile glass container somehow remained intact.

Over the years the house had suffered a slight subsidence which caused an incline to the floor and made the bottle roll away from his feet.

Its short journey however, was abruptly halted when it came into gentle contact with the skirting board that once had a high gloss pure brilliant coat of white paint.

The sudden stop made the amber liquid slosh about inside the bottle and the glass vessel began to rock gently back and forth, creating a soft tapping sound as it knocked against the old wooden fascia, flashing its label off to the world.

Just like the bottle, the Enforcer swayed unsteady on his feet and he was still giggling when he began to loosen his belt. Trying to focus his vision he looked at her and allowed his un-tethered trousers to fall about his ankles. He placed his hands on his hips and winked at her before he started to kick them from around his feet.

It was then he stumbled, he fell to his knees and then onto his hands. Strangely enough and even under these circumstances, seeing this drunken slapstick routine with him ending up on all fours, like the dog that he is, Celeste could not halt a smile appearing across her sad, beaten face.

He looked at her and immediately became aggravated.

Eventually he managed to stand, he staggered toward her.

'Are you laughing at me you bitch?' he shouted and without giving his helpless victim a chance to answer, he clenched his fist tight. He threw a punch in her direction.

'Let's see if this wipes the smile off that pretty face of yours.'

Closing her eyes, Celeste looked away preparing for the moment when two separate pieces of flesh and bone would meet to make a sudden, loud and very painful impact.

The knuckles on his right hand almost buried themselves into the socket of her left eye. The sound of her face fracturing, the bright sparkles of light shining in the darkness and the pain instantly rising in her face made her gasp just before she blacked out.

Celeste slowly began to regain consciousness but her mind was fuzzy and fogged. Her smashed eye had swelled up and remained closed and she could feel every agonising throb that hurt like hell.

As her reality dissolved the fogginess, the throbbing seemingly turned to movement as the mist further cleared from her senses.

Then with the realisation this disgusting man had finished yet another invasion of her body. He was now dressed and sitting in a chair waiting for her to regain her senses.

As her mind cleared, Celeste screamed loudly and then thrashed about as hard as she could in another futile attempt to break free. It did no good though and he just continued to laugh, while her screams grew louder.

Suddenly stopping, just long enough for him to jump up and cover her mouth with his hand; he moved his face close to hers.

'Scream all you want you bitch, no one is coming; there is no one out there to help you now.' His laugh became harder after which he ran his vile tongue over her cheek.

The whiskey on his breath did little to disguise the halitosis caused by the rotting of his teeth.

In this society Celeste knew about the punishment squads and she knew full well that this sort of tactic was only one of the tools at the disposal of these monsters.

Just like others in town though, she had always ignored it, little thinking it would ever happen to her.

The tears of her pain, anger and humiliation poured from her eyes, but these were ignored by the laughing animal.

Then all hell broke loose.

The door to the room was suddenly smashed from its hinges, followed by the entry of a filthy, deranged man exploding into the room. He pulled the attacker off her by grabbing at his throat and lifted him clean off the ground.

There was no fighting or talking, no time even for the drunken sod to react in defending himself. He was simply hoisted into the air and in that moment she saw the same fear on her abusers face, that she had felt every time he entered the room drunk and violent.

Nevertheless, by watching the sickening and terrifying action quickly unfold in front of her and somewhere deep inside she began to feel a small spark of justice was being served. But with everything that had happened to her she was in no real state of mind to fully comprehend what was really going on.

These new events only served to increase her confusion and terror, as she watched the lifeless body of the Punisher being carelessly dropped to the floor.

When the intruder, with his cold eyes peering at her through his curtain of long greying hair, turned to face her, she knew she was going to be an easy target for him.

His face was still contorted with anger and his jaws remained clenched so hard that the sinews on his neck protruded under his skin.

She moved her remaining open eye to focus on the dead body to stare at the flaccid pile, watching the blood seeping from the open wounds, dripping into the red pool beneath it.

The man's heart was no longer beating, but hers was racing as it had never raced before and Celeste was finally shocked into silence.

***

Maitland slowly made his way over to where she was shackled. He saw her naked and that she was trembling with fear, cold and anger and as he tore the curtain from the window he allowed the blinding light of the summers day to flood the room.

The brightness forced him to squint as he gently placed the material over her, covering her naked and beaten body. It was an attempt at restoring a small amount of the dignity which had been so cruelly stolen.

Remaining silent, it was a gesture she ignored; completely unaware of the unusual kindness this particular rescuer was showing. She simply carried on staring at the dead body, hoping it would not get up from where it was.

As he placed the curtain over her, he saw her whole body was covered with cuts and bruises; injuries which were both old and new.

He looked at her face and saw her left eye had swollen shut and was surrounded by black bruising. Her hair was matted with dirt, blood and semen, he could not tell what colour it was, she was so disfigured and filthy he couldn't tell her age. Finally, he clearly understood that she had suffered a prolonged, degrading attack.

It would seem this was the weapon of choice these days and it was a weapon he had seen used before, far too many times.

Maitland slowly began to reach out to release her shackles of the thick leather bracelets that were held into place by rusting metal buckles.

Lying on her back and still in her own urine and excrement, the source of the putrid smell, Celeste saw from the corner of her open right eye, his bloody hands coming toward her.

The sudden movement so close to her, made her start to scream and thrash about again. She became so hysterical, it made it impossible for Maitland to get hold of the buckles so he moved away a little and for the first time spoke to her.

'It's OK, I'm trying to release you.' He said while attempting to make his tone as sympathetic as he could, but he was far too out of practice to be effective.

She did not respond but continued to struggle while still screaming and crying.

He pulled back a little more.

'Fine, have it your way, but if you don't let me help I will leave you here like this. Is that what you want?'

The words fell from his mouth with such a cold and uncaring tone it made her think he would actually leave her. It seemed to have worked; his words appeared to sap her energy. Her screaming and thrashing instantly stopped, her chest erratically rose and fell beneath the green curtain, as she was now the one who was trying to catch her breath.

In resignation she threw her head back onto the filthy pillow with a growl and settled enough to allow him to start releasing her from her incarceration.

As he worked, Maitland knew he was being studied, that every inch of his muscular frame was being taken in by her. He decided it would be best if there remained no eye contact between them. He made sure no gestures of reassurance were given by him for her to misconstrue. There was not so much as a smile on his face as he restarted the rescue.

She watched his movements closely and saw he was by no means a good-looking man and his face was unshaven and scarred. It was a face bearing the marks of many past encounters. His eyes seemed cold and lifeless to her; they looked as though they had sunk into his olive shaded, leathery skin and even though he did not look ill, he did not look well either.

An uncomfortable Maitland did his best to ignore her stares, but that putrid smell refused to be forgotten and even though he knew she was not to blame for the situation, his body automatically reacted and before he could free her completely, the retching got too much for him.

Maitland quickly pulled himself away from her, just before he promptly vomited where he stood, adding to the existing human debris in the room.

The orange, yellow colours of the sick, wet with thick sticky saliva, stuck to the whiskers of his eight-week old beard, while his stomach muscles contracted to pump more vomit over his feet.

He bent himself over a little and breathed deeply trying to regain a little control and when his puking finally finished he moved towards her, again reaching out to remove the final shackle that held her arm.

She was still watching his every move, still silently studying his face while trying to figure out just how far this, seemingly her saviour, could be trusted and what would happen once she was freed.

It was only when he retreated from the bed to the window that she realised he had finally released her and Celeste sat bolt up. It was then she noticed the curtain that he had placed over her body and frantically she wrapped it around herself and then quickly moved like a trapped, frightened animal, into a corner of the room.

Celeste settled down pushing her back hard into the wall, trying to place herself as far away from Maitland and the corpse, as quickly as her achingly numb limbs would allow.

From here she glanced at Maitland, he had just wiped the remaining vomit from his face with the cuff of his black, filthy duffel coat as it dribbled down his mouth.

Maitland looked in her direction.

'How many of them and how long?' He asked and as his rage subsided, his tone was still cold. He spat on the floor, clearing the bitter taste of bile from his mouth.

She looked back at the half naked, bloodied pile of skin and bone the corpse had formed on the floor. His dead eyes remained open and they were seemingly focusing on her. 'How does it feel now that you're lying in your own shit?' She thought to herself and turned her head to Maitland, but kept her good eye on the dead attacker.

'He is dead isn't he?' she was pointing at the body and her voice cracked as she spoke.

Maitland looked at her uncovered neck, there were the marks of where she had been throttled during the frenzied attacks, they looked painful and he wondered why she was not flinching at all.

She was stronger than she looked, he thought.

'Yes,' he replied, 'he won't be causing you or anyone else any more trouble. Was it only him or were there more?'

Maitland took the shaking of her head to mean it was only him.

'So, how long have you been here?'

'About a week I think, I'm not too sure really. What day is it?' she replied without taking her eyes off the body.

He crossed the room in complete silence, without pity or concern for either the corpse or the woman, or in fact what day of the week it was.

As Maitland walked he had to step over the body on his journey toward the broken and splintered doorway.

He went through it, leaving the woman alone in the room with her dead tormentor and by the sound of it, her tears.

Chapter Two

'What the hell do you mean Baker didn't meet you!' Exclaimed Lattimer as he stood to his full six feet, four inch height, towering over the five feet six inch Robert Garforth. The leader was livid, his gaunt face twisted as he shouted and his jet black hair fell out of place from its normally immaculate sweptback style. The whites of his piercing blue eyes were bloodshot and became wider as his rage increased.

'That little piece of rubbish had better not be screwing with me. You! Garforth,' saliva erupted from Lattimer's mouth, showering his subordinate as he shouted his instructions at the man, 'go and drag that sorry excuse for an Enforcer here to me.'

The terrified Garforth nodded, saluted and ran from the room. As he did, the feeling of Lattimer's stare was burning into his back as he knew the leader's eyes would follow him until he was completely out of the room and out of sight.

Russell Lattimer, the Elite Enforcer of Launceston and surrounding area, turned to face the others who were in the room. They sat in an uncomfortable silence after witnessing the vicious altercation between the leader and one of his favourite students.

It ensured Lattimer had their complete attention and with deep frustration, he rubbed his face. The abrasive action of his hands chaffing caused flakes of dried skin to detach from him, leaving tiny white dots of powder dry skin cells to float in the air and begin their dance on the warm rays of sunlight that made their way through the gaps in the heavy curtains.

The light interspersed by shadows created a misty church like effect from the windows.

Lattimer breathed deeply, trying to calm down.

'People, people, people. How many more times do I have to make examples of you? and for what? just to ensure that we survive?' As he spoke he felt himself calming down, though he could hear his words were being spoken through his still gritted teeth as he addressed the audience of uniformed Enforcers.

Each person seated represented a town or city, a garrison or just a presence for which Lattimer had control or interest. His power was extreme, his grip lethal and his reach far extending beyond that of Launceston.

'You all know we have a common unity here, you are all aware that we are the only ones who can bring stability, not only to this town, but to this part of the country.' He slumped down in the red padded, throne like arm chair and looked around the room again.

He searched the eyes of his audience, wanting to see if anyone was prepared to show dissension before continuing.

'But perhaps you can tell me,' his voice became louder and he smashed his hand down onto the table in front of him. Several people jumped, 'how the hell can we do that if we let ourselves down time and time again?'

He stood and walked around the room in silence.

'We all have a part to play and you know I am not a tolerant man, you know my temper sometimes gets the better of me, for which I make no apology,' he made an exaggerated hand gesture while he once more scoured the room, 'and you also know how much I really hate unreliability.'

He bowed his head, listening for some response, any response, but silence was all he could hear and his rage finally subsided. He was back in control, not only of his emotions, but more importantly, he had regained control of the audience in front of him.

Still with no response from anyone gathered, he thought how good it was that he intimidated them and with a smile he raised his head and continued.

'No, I am not sorry for getting angry, because just like you I feel passionate about what we are doing here.'

Lattimer knew he could play the people, it was a trait in his personality that gave him the idea he would make a good politician, once he had established himself over the Celtic border that is.

That is exactly where his plans are going to take him and no one, whether through fear, belief or respect, seemed to disagree.

'Well then,' Lattimer said, with a smile, 'is there anything else I can help you with today?' He held out his arms, his mood had now returned to normal, his voice was now soft and gentle, almost charming. Everybody shook their heads in silent unison as they all knew it was not a good day to give him further bad news.

'Good, good, then off you go and remember, everyone is guilty of something, it's the level of guilt that counts.'

The audience stood and left the room.

Lattimer was alone with the noise of footsteps diminishing into the distance from behind the closed door. He stood, looked at himself in a mirror and ran his hands through his hair so that once again it was swept back.

Almost satisfied, conceit brought a huge smile to his face and as he crossed the room, moving towards the French Doors, arrogance and over confidence radiated in each and every one of his footsteps.

The Penthouse was the nerve centre of Lattimer's operation. He had the suite of rooms decorated obsessively in white. It helped to camouflage the snow globe of dust his skin ailment caused.

Lattimer's slim, but athletic, build was all thanks to the vigorous exercise regime he put himself through every morning. He was nearly fifty-five and so very proud that he had remained as well toned as he was at this age. He might have even been considered handsome by some, had it not been for the affliction of chronic psoriasis plaguing his body and today he was suffering with it terribly.

This was partly to do with the stresses of office, but more to do with there being little or no commercial medicines available. He had to resort to using homoeopathic creams, which were made for him by local herbalists.

Lattimer found them to be of little help and made him a martyr to the condition. The psoriasis caused him some pain, discomfort and embarrassment. Once, his best friend had made the mistake of brushing off some flakes of Lattimer's skin which had fallen onto his dark uniform, while still in the presence of the Elite Enforcer. That friend now has a stump where his hand used to be.

It was a condition that made people even more wary of him than they would normally have been. Having been cursed with the skin complaint since childhood, other children teased him.

They made fun of him. Calling him names and not wanting to be with him, Lattimer played alone. Oh yes, throughout his life, it had affected him.

It eroded what little confidence and self-esteem he had had.

This affected his ability to interact socially with his peers and he became unable to talk to the opposite sex. No girl would ever date him, not with that skin disease.

He remained single and alone and as he reached his adolescent years, he accepted the situation. In adulthood he began to use it to his advantage. Lattimer did any work that would take him away from people or jobs which meant lone working and eventually he reasoned that without this cursed affliction, he would not have been able to reach the position of Elite Enforcer. He would have been just one of the weak, just another of the oppressed he was now ruling over.

Lattimer was completely aware he was a bitter, twisted and lonely individual, but they are the key ingredients making him the man he is today and besides, he came to like the power more than the hatred of himself.

He smiled with great pleasure in seeing the fear he instilled into Robert Garforth. However, in his mind his one and only regret remained. Women still found him just as repulsive as they did when he was younger and there was no way around that.

On opening the lined white curtains, a twisting tango of dried skin flakes became visible and danced on the warm sunbeams.

He walked through the French Doors and out onto the sun drenched, scaffold balcony overlooking the public square below. He had to use one hand to shield his eyes in the bright sunshine while with the other he reached into his top left pocket, pulling out a pair of scratched sunglasses. He gently thumbed the word 'Police' embossed on the silver metal arm.

The glasses were a remnant of a more materialistic, decadent age and as he placed them proudly on his face, his darkened vision disturbed a memory from behind his consciousness and he thought he could hear yelling in the distance.

Three of a Kind

He looked up at the sky and saw the yellow sun had dissolved into a silver, half-moon that shone down through the clouds.

He shivered as he could swear he could feel the rain as it splashed on his face.

Returning his gaze down, the memory finally helped him recall how both the square and balcony were constructed some years back, after the last major civil unrest.

His attention became distracted and he watched the ghost of a crowd walking towards him in the distance.

He was now standing in a cold, wet November evening and the group of protesters gathered to march on to the town hall. The people of Launceston were complaining about yet another unreasonable increase in what they were expected to provide, all they wanted was a fairer system in place.

If Russell Lattimer was nervous that day, he did a great job of hiding it, even though it was his first time in heading a team in the field.

Admirably, he leads by example; refusing to let his inexperience show to the others as they stood, strong and proud, ready to repel the oncoming mob.

When the chanting protesters marched along the dark streets, Lattimer took five steps to put himself ahead of his team.

He pulled out the wooden handled kitchen knife he had hidden beneath the soaked leather raincoat. Suddenly and with a loud cry he began to run headlong towards the leader of the group.

He jumped into the air and Lattimer came crashing down onto the shocked protester, sinking the ten-inch blade into the chest of the troublemaker.

They both fell to the ground, rolling around in the rain soaked street and the crowd fell silent.

Lattimer was the only one to stand up from the scuffle. He was covered in the blood of the fallen freedom fighter and he roared, pointing his blade at the crowd, leaving them helpless to watch as their leaders' life ebbed away.

A wild-eyed Lattimer held the blood soaked knife skyward and he roared again. It was the first time he had killed anyone and he felt more empowered than he had ever had.

'Go home people, your business here is finished. You have five minutes to leave this place or my men will make sure you never return.' He turned his back on the hushed crowd and returned to his team. Since that night, he had decided one day he was going to be the Elite Enforcer and he would rule over Launceston with an insatiable and unreasonable iron grip.

However that was a long time ago and today, standing on the balcony he was looking down on the very place that, for him, was a monument to that night.

The armed guards stationed at a gated entrance at one end of the courtyard, ensured there was no way out or in for anyone without being seen. He stood dressed in his usual white linen suit, his arms crossed over his bloated chest. He was an imposing sight to the people gathering to listen to his daily speech.

Lattimer continued to look down at the people, his people and it was indeed a brilliant manifestation of his power, they seemed almost to worship him, just as they would have a deity.

The Enforcers ringing the congregation ensured this particularly demented idea of his became a reality, but what he had achieved in bringing together this ragtag mix of the lost and the worthless, was to his mind, nothing short of a miracle.

Everything was under control, his control and the system worked well. It worked very well, in fact, but for a small group of resistance fighters who, every now and then, caused a slight irritation to him. But who better to handle irritations than a man who has had to live with them all his life.

Of course, there were those living in the community who were hard working and honest, there were those who believed in the charismatic architect of their new society. These were the farmers, bakers and market folk, but even they didn't escape the whims of Lattimer and his cohorts.

He had made sure they were treated well enough, with things like a fair tax system in place; at least it was fair for him. However, once Lattimer's demands had been satisfied, the corrupt lower ranking Enforcers would choke the people further, in any way they could think of.

In this forgotten country, crime lords operated freely and everybody wanted a piece of the action. In this part of England, Lattimer was the one who controlled everything, while oppressing everyone and while he was presiding over things, gambling, drugs and prostitution were all allowed to continue. With only Lattimer making sure everyone paid their dues.

Then there is the on-going negotiation between him and his contacts in Kernow, these talks were progressing well. The start of legitimate trading was in sight and the next fortnight was going to be critical to his plan.

Russell Lattimer was not going to let anything, or anyone stop his dreams from coming to fruition. He wanted this trade route to go ahead. No, he needed it to go ahead, not just so he could control the traffic which would be generated, but also it would enable him finally to leave this hell-hole called England for a new life in Kernow.

Like everyone else in England, Lattimer wanted to make a better life over the wall. Kernow is a place where he would have access to proper medicines and maybe have a chance to do greater things with his dull existence.

The Elite Enforcer did not realise he was toying with the gold pendant hanging around his neck, a nervous habit he had developed whenever he was stressed about things, like addressing the crowd. The dented, small gold locket was a reward given to him for a job well done when he first started

Enforcing, he hadn't opened it in years and now didn't even try to remember the details of its history, only that it was handed to him by the then Elite Enforcer.

He recalled that it was a defining moment, an epiphany for him. It was when he knew Enforcement was the only choice open to him if he were to not merely survive, but to become someone in this new world order. It was the first time in his miserable, lonely life he was accepted and that made him feel good.

Lattimer moved to the edge of the balcony and opened his arms wide, as if to embrace the crowd below, waiting patiently for the chattering to quieten.

He began to speak and his voice reverberated around the square, reaching the ears of everyone assembled.

'People of Launceston, it has been a long journey for us all and you have all worked extremely hard, making so many sacrifices to get us to this point.'

Lattimer stopped talking for a moment, watching while the heads of the people were clearly nodding in agreement.

'Our journey will soon be at an end when the promised land of Kernow will open its gates to us, their people open their arms and welcome you, their lost brothers and sisters, their forgotten family, back into their lives.'

He scanned the distant faces.

The Elite Enforcer wasn't looking at anyone in particular in his captive audience, he was using their reactions just as a pilot would slide his vision over the dials in his cockpit, allowing him to gauge how well he was flying.

He proceeded with his sermon.

'However, it has come to my attention that some of us are not as reliable as they should be, some of us are not as trustworthy as, perhaps the rest of us are. We do not have the luxury of being able to carry these time wasters along with us. They should be reported to the Enforcers immediately, regardless of who they are.' The crowd began looking around at one another as if to search out the miscreants.

Amid the noises of disbelief he heard, Lattimer continued. 'The weak, the lazy and even the sick, whether they are neighbours, friends or family, all of these people are a drain on your resources.'

He stopped talking again, allowing a moment for a reaction and as expected the crowd voiced their disapproval as they looked around at one another, still trying to see whom it was he spoke of.

Lattimer allowed himself a small wry smile, he always enjoyed pitting one against the other and again he was doing it, this time to the people themselves.

'You should all be proud of the things we have achieved here as these are nothing short of a miracle, something that not even the almighty could do.' He pointed to the old Catholic Church, now disused and derelict since he banned and expelled religious groups.

The heads of the crowd followed where he was pointing. 'For you there has been no divine intervention. You have been forsaken by your Governments and by your Gods, but not by me.'

The crowd became more agitated as his voice became more excited. 'Now I ask you to pray with me and let your prayers be made for me. No, no, I want you all to pray to me, because this is my kingdom and I am your power, just as you are my glory.'

The crowd were roused to almost riot levels and they cheered wildly. Some people began to kneel, but Mike Spencer stood alone with a look of complete contempt on his face as he raised his eyes to gaze at the preaching Russell Lattimer.

The leader had to raise his voice to be heard over the cheering, applauding people below.

'I never asked to be your leader, but I have taken your burden and have pledged to you that we will be part of the living paradise that lies beyond this wall.'

He pointed to the crowd who again cheered.

'Now come, pray to me and give me the strength I need to finish what we have started, for only then will we all be able to enter the gates of Kernow as free men and women, to re-join our brothers and sisters in their promised land.'

The crowd roared so hard he felt the vibrations through the scaffold below his feet.

'I am truly a God amongst men,' he whispered to himself, while smirking. He pushed his arms out and began to shake them and wave to his flock.

After a minute or two of listening to the incoherent mumblings of the congregation he motioned them into silence and everyone fell to their knees.

Mike Spencer reluctantly started to join them a second or two after. Nevertheless, he was just a little too slow for one guard who walked up behind him and kicked his knees away, forcing Spencer down onto the floor a bit quicker. The guard had returned to looking around the crowd for anyone else, who may also be too slow and after a moment or two of silence, Mike Spencer heard Lattimer continue, but there was a softer tone to his voice.

'I want you all to now go about your business, make yourself proud, make me proud and remember to pray to me.' Just like the obedient children that they were, they did as ordered and all rose to their feet slowly to leave the courtyard.

Lattimer remained on the balcony standing in the sun, watching the struck man hobble out of the courtyard.

The self-proclaimed leader began to think back to, what for him was the beginning. He remembered coming to Launceston a few months before the double whammy of the 2012 London disaster.

'Was it really twenty-two years ago?' He questioned himself. Twenty-two years since he had taken the civilian job with the local Police Constabulary.

It was his job to advise people and businesses on matters of security, forcing him to interact with people on a personal level, something he wasn't used to and that made him uneasy. He had always kept himself to himself, rarely socialising and never made friends.

For him the job was a very difficult one.

Lattimer chose to lead a hermit like lifestyle and he bought a small isolated farmhouse, far enough away from Launceston but without giving him a difficult journey.

He was happy enough being alone, but the events of the old one two propelled him into the active arena of Enforcement. Only after civil unrest in the area, did his job change, he was enlisted to help secure Launceston and the surrounding area.

Lattimer worked hard and learnt a lot from his old mentor. His outlook altered, he became less introverted and moved up through the ranks quickly, finally becoming second in command.

However, after years of strong leadership, the previous Elite Enforcer started to show signs of dementia. He started to become soft with the people and this leniency annoyed the hell out of the now ambitious Lattimer.

One night the old man met with a sudden, unexplained and gruesome death. He was found with both wrists cut, strangely while he was still fully clothed in a running shower.

His skin was completely white, his lips blue, he was colourless where his blood had been washed away by the water.

No one could prove it, but everyone thought the responsibility lay firmly with Lattimer.

That afternoon, Russell Lattimer became the Elite Enforcer of Launceston and overnight he began his reign of intimidation and terror.

So he was right, well sort of. He had not asked for this job, he had taken it.

'Was that really ten years ago?' he thought.

It was a time when the town had lost its direction and back then, it remained just a collection of lost and aimless people. Since he took control, Lattimer had moved the town on; he had moved on and changed from being a shy, insignificant freak of nature into the most powerful man in this part of England.

Unless it is controlled and respected, power has an innate ability to corrupt even the nicest of people, but with Lattimer's sanity and mental stability eroding, he found it all too easy to let his darker side of himself come to the fore.

Although he was still a shy recluse, he now has a heartless and cruel nature.

Chapter Three

Maitland decided to look around the house for anything that may be of use to him. He stopped, just for a moment, outside the room so he could take in his surroundings while safely ignoring her sobbing.

He found he was on the upper floor of a farmhouse, the landing and stairs were covered by, what used to be, a beige coloured carpet and considering everything it looked to be in reasonable condition, except for the dirt that had been ignored during cleaning, forming a border around the edge.

Maitland thought for a second, trying to recall how he got up here. It was late in the morning, almost noon, as he walked through the wood when he stumbled on the house.

It had been very well and very deliberately hidden by the overgrown trees and well-planned bushes.

Slowly, he walked cautiously up the pathway leading to the front door. He was trying to find food and shelter for tonight as there were no signs of life other than the four or five feral cats on the outside, he decided to look through the letterbox for any indication of occupation on the inside.

That was when he heard the chilling screams of a terrified woman. He didn't remember coming into the house at all, only that he heard the screams.

The next thing knew he was dropping the body of the dead man onto the floor and seeing her tied to the bed.

His mind returned to the house, he took a peek over the banister of the stairs leading from below. He saw the tails of the cats walking around the hallway downstairs. He looked at the doors leading from the landing into what he assumed were rooms or cupboards.

He opened the nearest one to him.

Behind the door he discovered another bedroom, but this one was filled with unmarked, brown cardboard boxes, which had been neatly stacked

He craned his head around the door and saw a large antique pine, double wardrobe in the corner.

He entered the room.

It was a similar size and shape to the one he had just left and with the same jade curtain placed across the window. He found it came off just as easy.

The air in the room was stale and he could see the dust floating and tumbling in the sunlight. Dust disturbed by his entrance and the removal of the curtain.

He tried to open the window to let in the smell of fresh air from outside to replace the arid, dusty aroma but it had been nailed shut.

He opened and looked inside a few of the boxes and sneezed loudly as he disturbed more dust. Inside he found tinned food, cigarettes and whisky. All of which was clearly contraband and by the look of things ready for shipping.

He assumed the person now occupying the house was a supplier to someone in Launceston or maybe, even further afield, 'who knows?' he asked himself aloud, 'who cares' was his mental reply, besides it was hardly his concern?

The shrill cries of cats battling downstairs made him decide to leave the room to see if anyone had disturbed them. But it was clear, it was only a battle between them, perhaps a leadership fight but not one to the death.

Not like the battles he had fought and won.

Maitland moved to the final room and he smiled when he found it was a bathroom. He entered and the musty smell of damp replaced the dry smell of the previous room.

Quickly he looked around and noticed a hatch in the ceiling, allowing access into the roof space. He decided he would look up there later, just in case something useful was up there.

The mix of bright white and pale blue tiling was taken over by patches of black mould growing from the grout. He looked at the white porcelain sink and reached out to touch the hard, cold, lime scale covered chrome taps.

He thumbed the dark blue letter 'C', which was embossed onto the white plastic button covering the small brass restraining screw beneath it.

He turned the tap head clockwise without expectation and to his surprise water gushed from the open mouth of the glistening appendage. It had been a while since he had the luxury of indoor plumbing at his disposal, he thought.

He put one hand under the cold flowing liquid.

The freezing water began to hurt, it felt like his skin was almost burning, but it felt so good.

He tried the other tap, the one marked with a red 'H'.

This time the water that spilled out didn't just feel hot, it was hot. Steam soon rose up from the fast, down flowing column of sparkling clear water, misting the mirror fixed to the wall above the basin, distorting his reflection.

'Hot water,' now this was more than a surprise.

After wiping away the moist opaque coating, from the surface of the mirror, he saw in the water-beaded reflection that behind him was a bath. Above it a shower had been installed. He turned and on finding that the shower actually worked, another smile came to his face.

Again, he looked up at the loft hatch and the thought that perhaps the house had been fitted with solar panels at some time crossed his mind. But he didn't care how it worked.

The important thing was it worked!

He stripped from his rags and stood in the bath, positioning himself below the head of the shower. He looked up at the many holes in the white plastic faucet and then closed his eyes in anticipation of the warming, cleansing rain falling on him and he began slowly to turn the taps.

The water poured down on him, forcing his eyes to remain closed and he stayed like that until he needed air and it was only then that he lowered his head taking in a large breath.

At first, as freezing water drenched him, it made him shiver violently, but still it felt like he was in heaven, well almost.

The water then began to warm up until it suddenly hit full temperature. The change also made him again, or continue, he was not sure which, shiver.

The splashing on his skin, the sound of the water rushing from the showerhead, landing on his head, somehow felt comforting to him and from a dish fixed to the wall he picked up some soap.

He looked at the cream coloured bar, he sniffed it.

The smell of the infused perfumes and boiled up animal fats was a hell of a lot better than his odour. He proceeded to use it to wash and scrub at his bruise-riddled body. The bruising on his left side, around his ribs, was evidence he had recently been in a fight and it was only now, as he lathered the soap into the area, that it started to hurt again.

There were two puncture wounds on his right leg, old scars from taking a couple of hits from a very frightened but capable child of all things. They caused him little concern as he washed the hard skin that had grown over the holes.

With his head still bowed, Maitland began to rub the soap into his long filthy matted tresses. The inhabitant nits began to dig deeper into his scalp, resisting their watery eviction.

It made him scratch at his head harder with his filth-encrusted fingernails.

He rinsed and opened his eyes to watch the water, which had turned a dirty, reddish brown colour from blood and dirt, gurgle down the plughole.

Maitland placed one arm against the wall and took little notice of the white, train track scars that could have been a drawing of an old railway junction like Clapham. He used it as a pillow to rest his head on and in a wonderful moment he wanted to savour, he stayed under the streaming water, allowing himself to relax. He needed to gather his thoughts and reflected on what had happened over the last few hours.

It was only this morning he had arrived outside Totnes, a small town in the west of England not too far from Launceston. It was to here, where an encampment once stood, he was first brought eighteen years ago. With the help of a group of pagans, he recovered from the injuries he had sustained.

He remembered how all religions were being banned or abandoned in this part of the world, but some people had rediscovered and adapted the ancient pagan ways. Although not considered a real religion, it was tolerated but also frowned upon. A few hours ago, he was looking at the footprint of where the commune used to be.

Three of a Kind

It was eighteen years ago that Jon Maitland had been found wandering about, half-naked and completely crazed. The pagans had taken him in, they were kind and nursed him with their homoeopathic medicines and pagan potions.

As time passed, the wounds on his body repaired and healed, however, Maitland was not the man he used to be.

He woke each morning to find the normal fears that any man had inside of him were reducing. Until one day they had diminished to the extent that he reasoned he no longer had anything or anyone left to fear.

Everything he held dear had been destroyed.

Maitland had become fearless and not even death scared him, in fact, he welcomed her cold embrace. It was then he decided to follow a path of self-destruction, a journey of trying to commit suicide at every opportunity, but the pagans made sure he was constantly watched.

It wasn't enough though.

While in the encampment, he tried once more to invite death to visit him which failed and once more the self-inflicted wounds on his wrists healed. The pagans decided it was time for him to leave the compound forever. But today the camp had gone, it had either been destroyed or moved, it didn't matter to Maitland, he simply didn't care which.

This morning he was looking for shelter and when he found nothing he moved on and continued his journey back to the beginning.

He walked away remembering that when he had left the compound all those years ago, he had no particular plan or direction and embarked on a nomadic life to become a loner.

To his mind, if he ever got close to anyone they inevitably met with a gruesome end and he's had enough of feeling guilty for his own loss let alone anybody else.

Maitland recalled that he had chosen to shy away from society and not get close to people, and on his journey he somehow managed to constantly feel responsible for the death of his beloved Laura and Emily; he never wanted to increase that number.

At first he stayed completely away from people and communities, but it wasn't too long before he had little choice, he needed food and a change of clothes.

After he had been walking for several days he found to the east of Launceston, the town of Blandford.

It was a small community with only a couple of hundred people there, but they were friendly enough and welcomed him in, offering the food and clothing he needed. The only things they wanted in return was for him to help build a better, stronger barricade than the one they had cobbled together. It was yet another barricade, still more walls to keep people in or out of where they should or should not be. Reluctantly, the engineer agreed and set about designing something more sturdy using the materials at their disposal.

He stayed there for several months securing the town and his time there was almost uneventful and peaceful. Right up to the point when a group, of what used to be the armed forces based at an old military camp went rouge.

The base was a couple of miles away, but they raided the town now and again to replenish their food stores and take women. The twisted military were not happy at seeing the town being fortified and the frequency of the raids increased. Maitland also lent a hand in the fight to rid the town of the menace, but when he survived the battles and the barricade was completed, he decided it was time to move on.

On the eve of his departure, he was half-asleep, living the same nightmare in his mind when he heard a commotion from inside in the compound.

He got up to investigate what was happening, as he looked out into the night he saw the silhouette of two people in the distance. It seemed that a man and a woman were arguing with one another, he turned his back on them ignoring the situation and tried to go back to sleep.

The next day a woman's body had been found. She had been attacked and murdered and to Maitland's scrambled thoughts it was the second time he had failed to save someone.

The memories flooded back to his mind, they were too painful for him and again he suppressed them.

The water from the shower eventually ran cold, it's tingling brought his daydreaming to an end. Maitland turned the tap, stopping the freezing deluge. He stepped out of the shower onto the cold floor.

The chilled afternoon draught gently blowing through the house covered his skin in tiny white goose bumps and reaching out to the rail screwed to the wall he pulled at the towel. It rolled off the chrome bar and he began to dry himself.

His return to Totnes had made him realise that, for the last eighteen years, he had wandered around England in search of someone who might put him out of his misery. He had covered nearly all of England on foot and coming to Launceston was the last place he wanted to be. For him, this place was where it all began, but it might also be where it all ends by having the luck simply to die.

***

Launceston is a large town sitting on the border of Devon and Cornwall. It's a place, which for centuries has been known as the gateway to Cornwall. Today it's said to be the gateway, and whoever controls Launceston controls the gateway and the possibility of a new life in Kernow.

For Jon, his return to the area brought a renewed hope that the release he had searched for would finally be in his grasp, but it was also a chance for him to remember the past, no matter how painful that would be.

It was just another circle that life creates, he thought as he turned to the mirror at the sink.

He pushed gently on the edge and opened the door of the white medicine cabinet behind the silver glass.

Inside he found a pair of scissors and an old-fashioned straight razor. Taking hold of both implements and as he lifted them from the shelf he found they were slightly fixed through time and old soap.

He looked at them in his hand; then laid the razor on the vanity unit while keeping hold of the cutters.

The idea of using the razor to cut his own throat there and then quickly crossed his mind, but so fast was the idea, it did not have time to grab his attention, so Maitland looked down at the dull silver scissors that he was holding. They were about eight inches long and had loops at one end, one slightly bigger than the other.

The smaller of the loops had a sort of tail on it, the reason for which he had no idea and as he placed his fingers into the circles of metal, he operated the blades with a snap.

He found the small loops were tight and probably far better suited to a woman's slim elegant fingers than his own sausage-sized digits.

He returned the cutters to the unit and picked up the towel, using it to clear the mirror of the fog that had formed.

For a moment he studied the battle ravaged face reflected back at him. With a sigh he tried to decide where to start, by twisting his head left, then right. He pushed his head up while running his hand over his face.

Finally he pulled at the course, wiry facial hairs holding the longest ones out as he trimmed them short using the scissors, discarding the whiskers on the side of the unit.

Once that part had been completed and with no sign of a shaving brush, he had to lather the soap in his hands and then apply copious amounts of white, perfumed foam to his beard.

With the shower and the soap softening his bristles, it was more than enough preparation for the sharp metal blade to glide over his skin in an act of deforestation.

He picked up the razor and pushed down with his thumb on the dark metal tail and with a swish the blade slipped smoothly out of the handle. The sharp fin of metal looked like it would make an excellent weapon but first he needed it for another reason.

Maitland had never used this type of instrument before, but then there were many things he hadn't done before that day and so he proceeded in removing the eight-week growth of beard.

The sound and feeling of each hair being cut as he dragged the sharp, cold steel cutthroat down his face made him feel normal, though he always felt inhumane.

He watched as the blade reflected a spark of sunlight as he rinsed it under the cold running tap. Again the thought of the blade slicing into his skin, to open an artery in his neck entered his mind.

He was thinking how easy it would be just to use the blade and inflict a fatal wound on himself by delicately dividing the tubes that contained his blood as it circulated around his body.

He could easily bleed to death on the bathroom floor, the girl was in no shape to help or raise the alarm, but with a shake of his head, he once again dismissed the notion of suicide, well at this time anyway.

Maitland continued to shave until the sound of rasping turned into the pain of friction, making the skin on his neck feel as if it was glowing red hot. In the mirror he saw small spots of blood appearing on his face where the razor nicked his skin.

Finally he finished and replaced the razor on the vanity unit. He splashed cold water on his face and neck trying to cool his skin. How he longed for the pain of having some aftershave splashed on. The stinging pain would at least prove he was still awake and that this was not a nightmare.

Though he had no reason to carry out the grooming session, he continued, after all it's not as though his social life was exactly brimming with invitations. None the less, it did make him feel better and when he finished, he admired his handiwork.

Maitland felt the smoothness of his skin, it seemed the removal of the beard and the tying back of his long hair, rolled back some of the years. He somehow looked younger, but as he looked closer at the reflection, he realised he didn't know the man who was looking back.

Oh, it resembled him well enough, but behind the eyes there was someone different lurking, someone Maitland didn't particularly like, but had to live with anyhow.

He knew through that one incident all those years ago, most of his humanity had disappeared. It was a change that was completely out of his control, a change that turned a good man bad.

After using a small, frayed, hand-towel to dry his face, Maitland walked naked from the bathroom into the room where he had found the wardrobe. He searched the golden brown, wooden box for a change of clothes and soon he found some jeans and shirts, which although were a little too big for him, they had been laundered and that would be good enough.

He admired himself in the mirror. His face didn't reflect how good it felt to be clean, after which he continued to search the room, looking for some footwear. He found some old brown boots, the type that had a thick sole and light stitching around the edging, they too were a little big, but he put them on all the same and made his way out onto the landing.

Once more he puzzled about the house, it was obviously well stocked and self-sufficient and considering the environment they were all living in, it looked well maintained. But in these days of crime, squalor and filth, not many innocent people hid things. Maitland wondered how the house came into the hands of the man he had just killed.

Judging by the uniform the dead man was wearing he was definitely some kind of Enforcement Officer, but he did not rank high enough in the regime, affording him such a place to live. Maitland didn't think he was the type to be in a position to claim this house as his own.

Perhaps the girl would tell him, he returned to the room where he had left her alone with the body.

***

Celeste remained cowering in the same corner of the room just where he had left her, but she was now in the company of the ugliest cat Maitland had ever seen. It was a sphinx, a rare breed that was furless, with wrinkled pink skin and only one amber eye in its head.

He noticed how the woman, without thinking, was stroking it with only her fingertips as though anything harder would cause the feline some discomfort but, with skin against skin causing friction the cat seemed happy enough with the attention and purred.

The woman was calm and they both looked up at Maitland as he entered. Celeste was slightly startled by the difference in his appearance which at first had taken her aback and initially she thought someone else had entered into the furore.

The cat stood up from her arms and ignored Maitland. It was like she had a sense that he too was feral of sorts and that they were kindred spirits. The bald feline stood and regally sashayed across the room where she looked and sniffed at the dead body while licking her lips.

Celeste then recognised him.

'What now?' she asked.

For a second Maitland simply stared down at her, debating whether he should answer her question or just question her further on what happened.

He decided 'neither' in his head; 'it's no concern of mine' he thought and began to walk away.

'I'll go and fix us some food, there's a shower in there and some clothes in the next room, I think you might want to make use of them.' He replied indifferently.

She nodded in agreement rather than obedience.

He still showed no emotion, not even a smile of apparent concern.

Her stare followed him as he left her alone in the room.

Then Celeste stood unsteadily on her feet and she needed to lean on the wall for stability. There she waited for the room to stop spinning and her legs to become firmer and only then did she begin to move from the room, finally leaving the body alone with one-eyed Jack.

On the landing, she watched as Maitland's shadow continued down the stairs and once he was out of sight, she entered the bathroom locking the door behind her.

***

The farmhouse looked smaller from the outside and on entering the hallway, a living room was situated to the right, with the stairs he had just descended situated on the left.

Finally, he could see another door at the far end of the hallway.

This door was closed.

Maitland entered the rectangular box of a living room, he saw the large round mirror hanging above the beige tiled, Art Deco fireplace. It had its mouth gaping open waiting for some wood to feed it.

The mirror's gold painted wooden frame, had what was supposed to be sunrays radiating from the centre, the illusion was lost on Maitland. The convex reflective surface dominated the room, like the non-blinking, single eye of a Cyclops watching his every movement.

What with the cat and now this, Maitland began to feel as though he was being put under some kind of surveillance.

He approached the domed looking glass and watched his distorted reflection grow.

'Nothing to be big headed about,' he exclaimed aloud as he examined his bulbous headed reflection.

The room had been furnished with an old settee and two armchairs, which were covered in a brown cloth material and several cats. They showed him no fear, but some gave him a hiss, a warning that he was not welcome here.

He looked over at the windows.

They were dressed in old, discoloured curtains that hung sadly either side of the rectangular opening. He guessed the sash windows were nailed shut too.

Jon Maitland realised that him just being here, let alone killing an enforcer, put him in a hell load of trouble.

He philosophically shrugged and sighed, 'nothing new there then,' he said to himself and turned his back on the Cyclops. He finally walked out of the room leaving the cats to settle down again.

Out in the hallway once more, he moved towards the back of the house and opening the closed door he found the kitchen. He entered the room and revealed a large kitchen with an adjoining dining room and all around were signs that the current occupants lived to a high standard, indicating that they were either well connected to a local crime lord, or they had status within enforcement.

Everywhere he looked, he saw signs of a decadent, luxurious lifestyle.

The house had to have been like this since before the old one two had happened and despite its dilapidated appearance it was very well maintained; well compared to what he had seen in other parts of the country at least.

The kitchen had a large green and black enamelled wood burning stove; he could feel it was still hot from the days use.

Against one wall was a small dining table with a couple of folding chairs.

He imagined someone using it to prepare food, or sit in silent solace with their thoughts, while others busied themselves around the house and the farm.

Maitland found some food in a cupboard; tinned ham. The label had no indication of its origin, but it also confirmed the trouble he had just got himself into was, the deepest he had ever been in.

But with trouble, there was always a hope jumping into his mind. A split second thought that, 'maybe, just maybe my nightmare will end.'

The humming of the upright, white fridge freezer matched the purring of the cats and brought his thoughts back to the room. He walked over to the source of the mechanical noise and gently touched the white surface.

As the vibrations ran up his arm he snatched it away. He could still feel the tingle and rubbed his fingers together smiling to himself. It had been a while since the simple feeling of the vibrations of a machine brought back a sense of normality to him. It confirmed that some sort of electricity was being generated from somewhere.

He ignored the rust blown edges, as well as the dark dirty marks that unwashed hands had left on the handle as he opened the fridge door.

The internal light came on.

He had forgotten about this feature on such appliances and with childish wonder he opened and closed it several times, making sure it worked each time the door operated the concealed switch.

With the door open as wide as possible, it revealed a white china plate on one of the three frosted glass shelves. On the plate were two slices of red meat, swimming in their own blood.

He picked the plate up.

The coldness of the hardened clay ran up his fingers and continued up his hand as he lifted the plate to his nose and sniffed at the succulent, bright red, dead muscle.

'Yes definitely meat,' he deduced 'and fresh too, killed yesterday or the day before, either way they will be eaten today' he said to the cats that were now sitting on the floor by his feet.

Closing the door for the final time, he placed the plate on the table and began to prepare a meal of fried meat, with boiled fresh vegetables he found in another cupboard.

The two uninvited cats watched and licked their lips after which they gave a tiny meow.

He looked at them.

'Hungry guys?' He enquired and he cut a small piece off and threw it out the door into the hallway. They both gave chase and when he closed the door he heard the two fighting over the raw morsel and hoped they were not eating any type of relative of theirs.

He moved to the cooker and picked up the pan from the side, placing it on the hotplate. He started to cook the meat and the sound and smell of the flesh sizzling in the pan made his mouth water and his stomach rumble.

Maitland was no chef but the finished dish would be hot and edible.

He left the food to cook and continued to look around.

Dotted around the shelves were various photographs and as he scanned them, one in particular caught his eye. It was a colour image in a small wooden frame, showing five people who 'must have been a family' he thought as he plucked it from its resting place.

He looked at the man smiling back at him and the laughing woman who was sitting on a large, bright red and yellow tractor, and to the left of them were two children. One girl and one boy, both of them seemed to be no more than toddlers.

He moved his head to look out of the window, perhaps it was a picture of a family working in a field on a sunny day, all smiling and laughing, all playing but most of all he noticed they all looked extremely happy.

Jon Maitland assumed it was a photo of a previous and long departed occupant of the house, maybe pre 2012.

So there they were; the farmer with his family on their own land and in happier times.

A sudden twinge of envy slammed into Maitland's chest, his reaction was to angrily discard the thin wooden frame. He threw it back onto the shelf from where it had come. It missed and fell onto the stone floor, shattering the thin dusty glass that protected the photo.

Maitland didn't like looking at family photos anymore and with a feeling of regret that he had taken his frustration out on an inanimate object, he gently placed the picture frame back on its shelf and cleared the broken glass.

**

Celeste slowly entered the kitchen alone and sat gingerly at one of the two places he had set at the table; the skin covered moggy must have remained outside. He didn't turn, but even to him it was obvious she was in a lot of pain.

However she tried to hide it and fussed with her cutlery to pass the time in the awkward silence. First, she polished the shiny metal eating tools on her clean tee shirt and then moved them to a position that was more to her liking.

The room remained silent except for the hum of the fridge and the sound of cooking, so Celeste purposely sighed.

'Where's your pet?' he asked.

'Oh, One Eyed Jack is not a pet, she doesn't belong to anyone,' Celeste looked up at Maitland even though he still had his back to her, 'she lives with her colony in the woods. By the way I didn't thank you.'

Maitland continued to stare at the woods in the distance.

'You don't have to.' He replied without turning to look at her. Instead, he moved to the stove where the food was cooking. He picked up a fork and plunged it into the under cooked, browning slabs of meat and turned them over in the pan.

As the meat touched the searing hot, metal plate boiling fat and juices splashed about increasing the volume of the sizzling. It sounded to him almost like a small round of applause from a hidden audience.

He checked on the steaming vegetables by lifting a spoon from the worktop and scooping a little of the bubbling vegetables onto it. He sniffed at it and then blew across it, cooling it down enough to carefully place the edge to his lips so he could taste it.

His brow furrowed, 'Jon, you definitely cannot cook mate,' he complained out loud. He shrugged his shoulders and he began to dish up, placing one steak each on a plate to which he added some of the vegetable mixture.

'Not sure if you're going to like this,' he said to Celeste as he carelessly dropped the plate on the table in front of her. He joined her a moment later and sat, they ate in complete silence.

Maitland did not look at Celeste, either before or during the meal and his aloofness gave Celeste the distinct impression he wanted to be alone, even while he was in her company.

'Is that your name? Jon,' she paused to look at his response.

There was no response from him, not even a nod or shaking of his head.

'Well Jon, for a hero you don't seem to be overly interested in what happened here?'

Maitland still did not reply, but continued to eat.

'At the very least you could tell me who my hero is.' There was an unexpected air of authority in her sarcastic tone; it accompanied her slamming her knife and fork down onto the table.

'Maitland!' was his single word reply, spoken through a mouth full of semi-chewed food 'and I'm no hero.'

'The Reaper you mean? You're telling me that you're Jon Maitland, the vigilante? Wow, I've heard of you, who hasn't? Are you here to kill someone?' she seemed to get excited at the thought.

He still remained silent and could feel himself getting more and more agitated at her questions. He calmly placed his knife and fork on the table stood up and walked over to the sink.

Picking up a cup from the drainer that had been placed upside down, he released some of the cool, clear water from the tap.

He lifted it to his lips and drank slowly while her words, 'The Reaper', circled around his head. He stared back through the dirty window onto the garden; this reputation of his was so far from the truth.

Jon Maitland was an ordinary man, a civil engineer by trade but now is known as a killer, a murderer.

But, before here, before now, he wouldn't have got even a parking ticket, let alone break any kind of law. Back then, Maitland was almost obsessively clean and tidy, making sure that everything had a place to live, 'but now look at me' he thought to himself.

'OK, not my concern,' she added as her gaze followed him around the room 'tell me though Maitland, why is life so cheap to people like you and Lattimer?'

He did not recognise the name, but he turned his head slightly to her, though still not looking directly at her, to answer.

'Life isn't cheap, but then this isn't really living is it?' He replied bitterly and as he dropped the cup into the sink, he walked.

By the time the shattered shards of bone china and the splashing of left over water had settled, he had already made his way through the open door to leave and as he rushed past her, Celeste stood up trying to follow him.

'What about me? Maitland, you can't just leave me here. I've nowhere to go and others will come here, looking for him and me.'

He continued in silence up the hallway and Celeste had to painfully try and trot just to keep up with him.

'Sorry love, you are not my responsibility, you can do, or go wherever you want to.' He replied, stopping only to open the front door and continue his exit. 'Launceston is about twenty odd miles West of here, I'm sure you can find help there.' He said as he walked out of the house.

'How is it you're known as someone who helps? Someone who really cares about others, well it seems to me all you care about is yourself, in fact, you come across as a completely heartless bastard to me,' she shouted, 'and besides who would want to go there if they didn't have to?' she added.

It was late afternoon, the outside air was cooler now and the wind gently moved around them. On the pathway, Maitland stopped abruptly, he spun around and for the first time he saw her in daylight and clean.

She was about five feet four inches in height and her hair was dark brown, it flowed down her back where she had tied it. He saw her open eye, it was of the darkest, warmest brown colour: he'd not seen a colour like that for a long time.

His sudden stop made her run into him.

'Lady you got that so wrong. All you know about me is the myth, the rumours and nothing else. You see I don't even care about me,' he looked down at her, 'so I doubt that this little guilt trip you're trying is going to work.' He stood his ground, bearing down on her in an attempt to scare her away.

He judged by her stubborn stance that even with her small stature she could handle herself well enough, even after what happened.

To him, she seemed to have a strong enough mental resolve to get over this, eventually.

'Look I am sorry you've had to suffer in the way you have, but I can't stop to help.' He was calm and his voice was cold.

She looked into his hazel eyes trying to find something in them, but there was nothing, no humanity, not even a spark of life.

They looked as dead as the man upstairs.

Maitland turned, walking away in the direction of the barn and some minutes later, he shot out on the back of a horse and Celeste could only watch him ride into the evening, he did not look back and she began to violently shiver in the chilled wind against her wet hair.

Chapter Four

It had taken Robert Garforth nearly all day to travel the distance to Totnes from Launceston on horseback. It was just his luck to be given an old and unfit stead.

He was sore, he was tired and it was nightfall as he arrived at the start of the forest. Dismounting, he allowed the horse to run free within the confines of the fenced off field.

In an attempt to ease the pain in his seizing muscles, he stretched his aching body and as he rocked his head from side to side, relieving his neck, he looked around to get his bearings.

The Enforcer was looking for the entrance to the hidden pathway that would take him through the forest, leading him to the house.

There was a feeling of disappointment when Garforth spotted it and grudgingly he began his journey, knowing it wasn't only the additional mile still to walk, but it was a mile that would take him through the dense, pitch-dark trees before he arrived at the house.

He and Baker had come up through the ranks together and they had become firm friends, which was not easy when you live in an era where friendship meant nothing to most people. The two were possibly the best of friends, so he was happy to carry out Lattimer's order and bring Baker back.

On a count of three and with a lung full of air he began his journey, dodging the bushes and branches as he rushed.

As the darkness engulfed him, the voices and images of demons sprang to life ripping themselves from the darkest reaches of his imagination.

His heart pounded as his chest tightened.

He ignored their goading and laughing and moved as quickly as he could, but in the dead of night, normal everyday noises became amplified and they took advantage of this and encouraged his imagination to work even harder against him.

Halfway in, he had to slow his pace.

He could smell the musty, damp aroma of the forest and he could hear the sounds of nocturnal animals scurrying for food, or being scared away by his sudden appearance and the noise his squelching footsteps made on the forest's moist floor.

He stopped for a second.

Had he heard someone call out to him from the distance?

He listened to the wind as it blew through the trees, making the branches groan and creak and the leaves rustle against one another.

Feeling the trickle of sweat running down his face, he wiped it away, as the drum beat in his ears matched the thump of his heart in his chest.

Only the silence of the forest rang out in the night.

Garforth licked his dry lips and moved on in the direction of the house.

Soon the forest began to thin out, and with it his imagined demons reduced, as the shadows of his mind began to reach out, grabbing its naughty children and pulling them back inside.

He became frustrated, even though he knew they were all in his imagination, the darkness was the one place where he felt so completely vulnerable and out of control.

The darkness was the only place where his sweat inducing nightmares came to life, waiting for him to let them out of his subconscious domain.

He also knew that once they were allowed out to play, they would strike out at him, toying with his mind by bringing into existence his every fear.

Robert Garforth had visited the house many times before and no matter how fast he wanted to travel, it still took him fifteen minutes or so to complete the meandering and he changed direction several times, it was not 'as the crow flies.'

Finally, at the edge of the wood he stopped and being ever alert he fell into a crouching position, carefully peeking out from the undergrowth.

From his vantage point he secretly watched the house.

It sat in total darkness with only an inky black silhouette to give its presence away.

'Unexpected.' He thought.

He waited while gaining his breath back and trying to control his emotions.

Finally he moved on.

'Where are the cats?' He questioned on his slow, deliberate approach to the house. He watched the windows as he passed them.

Garforth had expected to see at least one light on, even a single candle with its flame flickering on a sideboard or something.

Nothing, but the darkness of the night remained in sight, that and the constant whispering sound of leaves chaffing as they swayed in the light breeze, was all he could hear behind him.

'Baker.' He called out, 'Baker are you in there?'

The chilled wind seemed to blow a little harder, adding to the eerie silence.

It made him shiver and he tentatively continued towards the house.

The rusting metal spring squeaked and squealed as he cautiously pushed open the weathered picket fence gate to enter the garden.

He looked down at it as he took two steps in and returned his glance back at the house and let the gate leave his hand.

Even though it was rusty, the spring still had enough tension in its old coil to quickly swing closed causing a loud enough bang for Garforth to be startled.

He spun around to see where the noise had come from and saw nothing but the gate and its residual movement.

He began to walk backwards up the pathway to the front door of the house.

'Baker, it's me Garforth, I'm coming in.' He called out but a little louder this time.

Stopping at the entrance to the house, he turned to face the door.

Garforth was not surprised to see it had been left slightly ajar in its splintered frame but the confirmation that something was wrong hit him hard.

The whole situation had gotten more than strange now, there was a real problem and he realised there was going to be no reply from anyone inside.

Whether it was his training, his natural instincts, or just the fear of the dark kicking in, Robert Garforth pulled out his gun.

Slowly he pushed the door open, allowing its old un-oiled hinges to scream out just as the gate did. This time, he didn't care about it. In fact he wanted to warn whoever might still be in there that someone was coming.

Slowly he crept into the darkened hallway and instantly caught the sweet, rubbery aroma associated with death hanging in the air.

So strong was the stench, the Enforcer had to place one hand over his mouth and nose trying to stop himself from inhaling the foul smell.

It failed miserably anyway and he started to automatically gag. The retching forced his stomach to spasm uncontrollably but by using his gun hand he felt his way inside and slowly managed to walk into the dark hallway. With his eyes blurry from moistness they adjusted to the darkness as he crept into the first room.

He found nothing except the old Cyclops mirror which was being entertained by the shadows of branches through the moonlit window as they tangoed and swayed in the wind.

Ignoring both the mirror and the shadows, he left the room to move into the kitchen and at least here, he found signs of recent activity.

He looked at the plates of partially eaten food that had remained on the table. 'Someone has definitely been here.' He confirmed in his mind.

He listened to the emptiness.

There was still nothing other than the sounds of the night and the humming of the fridge freezer which he noticed for the first time.

'Where in hell are you Baker? You're late, Lattimer is going absolutely mad. Will you just stop screwing around!' He shouted loudly from behind his hand.

With no reply and though he knew it was a waste of time, Garforth began to make his way up the stairway with whatever energy he could muster.

He blindly felt for the first stair with his booted covered foot.

Once he felt he was firmly secure on the step with his toes pressing on the riser he quickly leaned backward, allowing his spine to instantly cling to the wall. This was partly for guidance, but mostly for stability.

He pushed the whole weight of his body onto his leg and felt the muscles tremble under the strain but he began to climb them.

With every step his legs threatened to turn to jelly, but he kept his gaze up just to make sure if anyone was there, he'd be ready, should they charge at him from the darkness.

He noticed that the higher he climbed the more his legs felt like giving way from under him and that smell, it was getting stronger; 'must be nearing the source,' he thought as his trembling got worse and he would never get used to it.

As the leader of a team of Enforcement Officers, Garforth would normally have let someone else deal with the cause, but he was alone.

He had a duty to see what it was.

He took another step and whispered 'Baker,' then from nowhere tears started streaming from his eyes. There were tears because he knew he would find his friend dead and even alone he blamed them on the continuous gagging.

As he watched the darkness he noticed the darting shadows on the floor through his blurred vision, his racing mind conjured yet more demons.

'Fuck.' He shouted at himself, forcing his body to gain control again. He had to overcome these fears in order to continue to the top of the staircase.

When he called out again and still no answer came, a tiny spark of gratitude pinged at his soul.

It meant there was no one around to see him cry.

He ran out of stair treads eventually and stopped on the upper landing.

At the sight of the single glowing globe of yellow, sweat ran down his neck drenching his back and shirt. His breathing became erratic as his panic increased.

One-eyed Jack stood between him and the room; she arched her back and hissed at him on his approach.

'Not now Jack.' He said sternly to her.

The feral matriarch gave out a shrill cry and Garforth had to bend down to cover himself from the deluge of cats that ran from the room. He could do nothing about protecting his back from the needle like claws embedding into his skin, slashing at his jacket and cutting into his flesh.

74

He felt the last set of paws more painfully than the rest and slowly he unravelled his arms from his head.

He looked back down the stairs and watched the last tail leave the house.

His stomach involuntarily tightened again, he tried a cough in an attempt to stem the need to throw up.

He was shaking with fear, a fear that told him he needed to turn back down and follow the colony out, but his strong sense of duty made him continue on, even though he knew what he would find in the room.

He turned again to look into the darkness and felt the pain as one of Jack's claws tore into his face. She held on and stabbed at his forehead, trying to gouge out one of his eyes with her other paw.

Jack hated people far too much to leave them with what she had been denied. With a scream and a dragging of her claw down his face she let go of her foe and darted behind him, down the stairs to the bottom where she looked back at him and slowly walked away.

The pain was searing through his body, pain he could no longer take. He wiped the blood away from his face and checked his eye to see if Jack had damaged it.

Garforth opened his eyes.

It was dark but he knew it was fine and staggered on.

Garforth was afraid of death, only a lunatic wouldn't be, a lunatic like Lattimer, but he realised for the first time, his fear of the Elite Enforcer was stronger than the feeling of dread and panic that was now surging throughout his body.

Delicately, he followed the smell and entered the bedroom. His eyes focused on the pile lying on the floor and took no pleasure in being right about the discovery of the body.

It looked like the feral's had found the body to be a tasty meal and they did not seem to mind the aroma of dead human as they dined on a banquette of once living flesh.

He walked over to the cadaver and noticed various parts had been removed and were scattered about the room.

The body had been half eaten.

The corpse's hands and feet were missing, as was the head.

The animals had picked the flesh clean off the bones leaving the body completely unrecognisable.

Immediately, projectile vomit exploded from Garforth's mouth and nose when he emptied the contents of his stomach into the dank, empty room. He also emptied his bladder, though he thought he had prepared himself for seeing this, the worst-case scenario.

The shocking reality was it was just too much for him.

In sheer blind panic Robert Garforth threw himself out of the door and down the stairs, misjudging the last three treads as he neared the lower landing.

The stumble forced his right foot to slip from underneath and he came crashing down on himself. The impact forced his lungs to empty of oxygen, rendering him incapable of even crying out in pain when his arm cracked under the sudden pressure of his weight.

His hand let go of its grip on the gun and it spun away from him, hiding itself away.

The sudden scraping between his soft skin and the hard wooden flooring grazed his face, creating deep gouges in his cheek, but he was too scared to notice more pain and ignored the increasing amount of blood that was running down his face from the new cuts.

He picked himself up and ran from the house into the cold night.

The cold fresh air filled his empty lungs and he began to throw up again when he reached the end of the footpath.

He opened the creaking gate.

He took a moment to breathe and look back at the house. Nothing stirred from inside and nobody followed, but he ran into the forest all the same. Sweating profusely, he rushed back in the direction of the pathway, back to the company of his horse. He needed to get as far away from here as possible and in the quickest time.

*****

From the safety of the barn, Celeste watched the dark silhouette of someone running from the house and off into the forest. She knew it was only going to be a matter of time before Lattimer would send others to find out what was happening here.

She knew those others would be back.

Now was the time to move on.

This place was no longer safe.

Since being freed by the infamous and mythical Jon Maitland, Celeste did not have time to think about the predicament she was in.

It was not long for her to think about the options that were open to her and finally, with a decision made, Celeste slowly left the barn limping back to the door of the house and re-entered it.

She had found a wind up torch in the barn and used it to light her way into the house and back up the stairs.

Celeste packed what she needed for her journey, food and maps, just the essentials and while she packed she thought about her encounter with Maitland.

It made her wonder why he had turned up at Totnes in the first place.

More importantly where had he gone to?

His suggestion of her going to Launceston was not a practical one, but she knew perhaps it really was her only choice, especially considering what she had chosen to do.

One of the biggest problems for her in going back to the town was too many people knew her. However, it was going to be just as risky if she were to stay here.

Somehow, she needed to become invisible and on returning to the bathroom, Celeste looked at her reflection.

With the moonlight streaming through the window she could see the bruising was ripening nicely, her eye remained tightly closed and though her injuries were still hurting, the pain was less.

She looked at the vanity unit and saw the razor that Maitland had used, this made her consider shaving off all of her hair, but that together with her bruising would have made her more conspicuous.

For what she had in mind, she needed to be discreet.

Instead, Celeste pocketed the razor, just in case it was going to be needed and picking up the set of scissors she proceeded to chop at her hair.

She found the whole process more difficult than expected with only one eye functioning and her body aching.

Eventually she finished and looked at her reflection.

She saw it was not the best hairstyle she had ever donned, but it would be good enough.

Celeste looked down and ignoring the severed locks of hair that she was so proud of lying in the sink, she picked up a blue, denim peaked cap and placed it on her head.

At last she moved to the room where the part eaten corpse remained and shone the torch light on it for a last look.

She saw the whiskey bottle reflecting back at her from the torch beam.

She moved to it.

She crouched to pick it up and unscrewed the thin metal cap.

Celeste opened her mouth and raised the bottle to her lips so she took a large swig of the liquid. The rough spirit burnt her throat as she swallowed it, causing her to cough.

She then proceeded to spill the rest of the warming liquid over, what was left of, the body.

Taking one last look around the recent place of captivity, she watched as the lighter sparked into life after her thumb sharply turned the abrasive wheel across the hidden flint.

A flame instantly began to sway and flicker on the top of the lighter.

She crouched to allow the naked, dancing orange flame settle on the vaporous puddle by her feet and immediately a deep, loud whoosh of igniting alcohol vapours filled the room and as the flames grew, she left.

Limping down the stairs as quickly as she could, the feeling of control began to return to her and as she got to the bottom of the stairs, the torch revealed where the fleeing Robert Garforth's lost gun had settled. She promptly picked it up and continued, smiling a little as she finally left the burning house behind her.

For the first time in weeks, Celeste Baker now had a reason to smile.

***

By the time he arrived at the clearing, Robert Garforth was fighting for his breath and had to take a minute to recover. Before mounting his horse something had caught the corner of his eye. He glanced back to see flames from the burning farmhouse growing higher, illuminating the trees and becoming a beacon that gave away the secret location.

He suddenly realised, someone must have still been inside the house. Listening to him call out, watching him search the rooms.

They had been waiting in the darkness and he had probably just escaped with his own life.

Chapter Five

Launceston, an ancient town neatly nestled on the wrong side of the border of Devon and Kernow. Formally known as the gateway to old Cornwall, it was also once the capital of the county. It is a town that knows how to welcome you or repel you, depending on your intentions, of course, the people here were a proud community, proud of their heritage, proud of their history and they knew how to defend its honour when they needed to.

The architecture is a mishmash of styles reflecting the many eras that man had occupied this land and the houses stood just as proud as the people having survived invasions and wars over many years and more recently, civil unrest.

It had turned out to be such a gloriously sunny day and Russell Lattimer decided he would take the afternoon off. There was a slight spring in his step as he made his way for some well-earned rest and relaxation at Launceston Castle.

The stone built circular structure, constructed by long since forgotten artisans, was situated on top of a natural hill.

It was a strategic placement on their part, enabling not only a great view of the town, but having the added advantage of observing all points of the compass for signs of trouble, like invading armies.

Lattimer had laid claim to the castle at the same time he had taken the role of Elite Enforcer. He had it renovated to a high degree of lavishness and made it his personal residence, thus bringing the old relic to life once more. Though to him it was a thing, just another possession to own and boost his ever fragile ego and like the penthouse that lay in the shadow of the castle, it was decorated completely in white.

The castle was where he enjoyed the finer things that came into his possession. Items, such as Art and Furniture that had been traded or plundered from wherever he could get it, along with fine food and wine that were confiscated from others.

It was as if anything he wanted appeared, anything materialistic, that is.

Inside the Castle he made his way into the bedroom where he stripped naked and on the intricately carved, ornate wooden four-poster bed that was reputed to have been owned by Henry the Eighth, the Elite Enforcer laid down.

His irritated skin cooled as it made contact with the soft, white cotton sheets and covered his genitals in the cool wet towel.

He was on his back when the woman he had chosen as his new nurse had joined him. She was kneeling next to him, reluctantly rubbing the herbal cream into his rough skin.

Clare Adams was maybe in her late twenties he guessed, as he had never asked her about such details, but he could see for himself that she was an extremely attractive woman with deep blue eyes.

She was a sexy creature by anyone's standard, especially with her long blonde hair teeming over her shoulders, like liquid honey flowing down her back. Then there were her even longer legs that seemed to stretch forever from the floor.

Looking at her well-trimmed, firm figure it was hard for him to believe she had given birth to two children.

Lattimer chose only the most attractive women he could find to be yet another possession at his disposal. They were just one more signal to the world that he could have anything, or anyone, he chose.

Clare was visibly repulsed by him as he sweated and moaned under her gentle touch. He looked 'just like a pig' she thought while spreading the cream over his bright red sores. The feeling of his flaking skin building up under the gentle touch of her cream covered hands was so very nauseating. Instinctively her body wanted to pull away from him, yet she had no choice but to pamper to his vile whims.

'You know my dear,' Lattimer said to her as he twisted his head, sneering at her, 'it really was a good day when we found you in that barn.' He lay his head back down and smiled as he continued, 'I wonder now, what is it that I'd like you to do for me. Can you guess?'

Her eyes widened allowing her face to show the disdain and shock she was feeling.

Lattimer laughed as he removed the towel from around his waist to reveal his excitement in all its sore covered glory.

She didn't try to stop her automatic reaction this time, but the fierce grip he had on her tiny wrist arrested that movement of running away.

'Don't worry my dear, you'll soon get used to me I promise, besides, it never lasts very long to be totally honest,' the little pep talk did little to ease her horror. 'Come on Clare, you know it will be worth it, don't you!'

Finally, knowing she had no choice, she gave in to him. He had her two children and had placed them in the reformation centre. This twisted manipulative bastard had promised to look after them, but only in exchange for her services and that meant any service he demanded.

Unwillingly she relented.

Clare Adams was thinking only of her children and her dead husband as she began to undress quickly and shyly.

'No, no, no, my dear. Slowly, slowly, I want to watch. I want to enjoy a dance perhaps,' he softly said to her.

She knew it was an order rather than an option and with tears rolling down her face she nodded.

These were the tears of the abused that would fall from her eyes in secret and only Lattimer would ever witness the flowing of this river because he was the source.

Clare Adams started her hedonistic gyrations and under the circumstances she was trying to be as sexy as she possibly could.

Clare could not bring herself to look at the smiling pervert as he lay on the bed watching her.

But she caught a glimpse of him pleasuring himself.

All she could do was to close her eyes and try to conjure up a mental image of her loving, but recently deceased husband. How she longed for his strong, safe arms to be wrapped around her, to hear his voice tell her that everything was going to be ok and his lips tenderly nuzzling into her.

At the thought of this, her skin visibly rippled with tingling goose bumps appearing in waves that ran up her spine. She continued to remember how he would whisper his undying love for her when they both danced, naked and slow. She thought of her skin hotly sticking to his, arousing one another's bodies as they caressed every inch. Both warm and silky smooth to the touch, gently probing every crease, bump and fold with fingers, hands and tongues.

'Good Clare, good, now open your eyes my dear, I want you to look at me.'

Her heart sank as Lattimer interrupted her dreaming with his vile order, but she obeyed and opening her eyes she tried to look beyond him and stared into space as she slowly waltzed around.

Lattimer watched this angel who was floating in front of him, removing her clothing just for his enjoyment.

'She's so fucking perfect,' he thought to himself as he lay wide eyed, with some drool escaping from the side of his mouth as if he was a starving man watching his dinner being served.

He wiped away the moistness on his lips with the back of his free hand and tasted the salty sweat that had formed on his skin and it made him smack his lips together.

She caught glimpses of the sad, lonely bully who continued to repulsively toy himself after he had wiped away the spit from his mouth. He had worked himself up into total excitement until she heard another of his sickening orders.

'Now come to me my dear, I'm ready for you.'

Clare Adams stopped and looked directly at him.

He was still licking his lips.

Her tears continued to fall, just as the last of her clothing, to the floor and finally she was naked.

She slowly moved to him.

'That's it my dear, that's the idea.'

She mounted the bed, still trying so desperately to keep the picture of her husband in her mind.

Inevitably she straddled Lattimer and allowed herself to be molested, abused and invaded.

Automatically the Elite Enforcers rough hands carelessly groped at her perfectly shaped breasts.

'Ah, oh yes' he moaned as he violated her and not even her crying put him off as she began to impale herself on his disgustingly mutilated shaft. Lattimer had complete control of her body as she rose and fell on his erection, working her way into a quickening rhythm.

There was a sudden banging at the bedroom door, it interrupted her stride and she spun her head round to see Robert Garforth rushing in.

An instantly enraged and disappointed Lattimer disengaged himself from the not so ungrateful woman and pushed her to the side, discarding her as he would an unwanted piece of meat on a dinner plate.

Lattimer stood up from the bed unintentionally leaving the towel behind him. Clare grasped it and used it to hide her nudity and indiscretion.

'What the hell do you mean by barging in here like this?' Lattimer shouted, his face reddened and contorted, his erection quickly deflated as he moved away from the bed towards the terrified and panting Garforth.

A bloodied Garforth flinched and squirmed, lifting his hand as if to try to slow down the on-coming madman.

'Forgive me Elite Enforcer, but I have just returned from Totnes. It's Baker Sir, she's dead, murdered!'

On hearing the news Lattimer suddenly stopped, he physically recoiled as his ever-changing mental disposition hit him right between the eyes, sending him reeling into a maniacal state with a rushing storm of uncontrollable anger building within him.

Lattimer then continued to rush forward, headlong towards the flustered, cringing Garforth.

Unnoticed the maniac palmed a small knife from the sideboard.

'What about my merchandise you idiot, do you have it? Is it safe? Is it fucking safe?' Lattimer was shouting at the top of his voice, even as he stopped walking just inches from Robert Garforth who had dropped his head.

'No Sir, the house was set on fire as I left. I only just got away with my own life.'

Lattimer was panting heavily, so heavily in fact, his sinuses forced mucus from his nose and he ended up snorting like a raging bull as he unnervingly stared at Garforth in complete disbelief at what he was hearing from his loyal subordinate.

'What on this earth makes you think that your life is more important than my merchandise?' and without any type of warning, without a second thought the naked man lunged, screaming at his student.

In his uncontrollable, maddened state, Lattimer plunged the razor sharp blade easily and cleanly into Garforth's unprotected neck.

For a moment everything stopped.

It gave Lattimer time to think of how using a knife on a man, felt no different to taking a piece of beef off the bone while preparing a meal and so the 'butcher of Launceston' once again proved the truth behind this most horrible of reputations.

Time restarted and at first a look of confusion stretched across Garforth's face then as he reeled back, shock overtook the confusion and won the race to reach his brain first.

A dying Garforth had raised his hands to his neck.

He began coughing and choking while trying to locate the implement he knew had entered his body. He wanted to pull it out, wanted the pain to stop.

Clare Adams was shrieking at the terrible, blood soaked, scene she had to witness.

Lattimer managed to ignore her and calmly move toward his dying victim where he proceeded to remove the deadly instrument protruding from the neck of his best student.

Robert Garforth tried to stem the spurting blood from the now open wound, as the Elite Enforcer watched in silence.

His face remained screwed up in anger as Garforth began to writhe about and shake the very life out of himself.

Russell Lattimer's eyes followed Garforth down to the floor as he looked at his own hands with incredulity. Somehow he didn't believe the blood on them was from his actions. Lattimer actually doubted it was he who had carried out the horrendous murder of such a loyal and promising young man.

At this thought Lattimer suddenly began to wail like a bereaved parent and he fell to his knees and started to cradle the dying man.

'I'm sorry Robert, so very sorry.' Real tears ran from the leaders eyes and they mixed with the blood of his fallen protégée. Wiping the moistness from his own cheeks, Lattimer painted his face in flowing streaks of claret marbling.

'Robert, please forgive me,' he begged, sobbing as he returned his victim to the place where he had fallen.

As suddenly as his apparent break down, Lattimer regained his composure.

He stood and coldly left Garforth on the floor to die.

Most of the maniac's naked body was now spattered in red and pink, with the young man's blood.

It covered him like a red blanket.

The leader walked bare foot toward the door, leaving a trail of crimson footprints behind as he walked through the bloody pool.

Opening the door with his red, sticky hand he calmly called out to the guards who were waiting down the hall.

Immediately they rushed to follow him inside.

'Clean this mess up now, and you stop that fucking screaming you're giving me a damned headache!' Lattimer pointed the blood stained knife as he shouted at the woman.

Somehow, she stopped immediately.

Garforth was making the final sounds of death when the stunned guards hurriedly grabbed him by the feet. Carelessly they dragged him away to be disposed of, just like a worthless piece of rubbish.

The final thought of Robert Garforth was, if there is such a thing as an afterlife; then he hoped there would be no darkness to fear and with a final shudder, his existence ended.

Lattimer slowly reclined on an antique armchair that would not have looked out of place in a French Palace two or three hundred years ago. He held onto the knife, the tool of Garforth's destruction and began to toy with it as he stared, looking at nothing in particular.

A stray thought of another lost love entered his head. 'Sonya Groves.' Clare Adams watched as a confused looked appeared on his face.

'Where the hell did that name come from?' He thought to himself.

By this time Clare Adams had covered herself with the bedclothes and she remained there, shaking, trying to stay as quiet as she possibly could, that was until an uncontrollable sob leapt from her heaving chest. She buried her mouth in the material to stop the noise.

Too late, the sound made Lattimer return from his trance.

He turned toward her and he glared.

'Ah yes, well you had better go now my dear,' he said through gritted teeth, 'we will have to finish this some other time.'

Clare Adams did not need to be told twice, she jumped off the bed, picked up some of the clothes she had discarded from the floor, before running naked out of the room.

Russell Lattimer had a lot to think about, Celeste Baker and Robert Garforth were both dead, his merchandise was gone, maybe even destroyed.

He knew that his contacts in Kernow would not be happy with this situation, but never mind the Kernow people, he was not happy and he was not one to take disappointment at all well.

Except for the drying blood covering his body, Lattimer had remained naked for hours in the cold room just staring into space.

He suddenly got up from his seat and made his way to the window. He watched through the thick filth on the glass. The film of dirt helped the dusk eat away the daylight as it drew the black cloak of night over Launceston, matching his mood as he looked over the town.

Lattimer watched the extinguishing of glowing pinheads of light that danced in the windows of the houses below. The business of the day had ended hours ago and the curfews were now falling into place. No one should be on the streets, although he could still hear the faint sounds of dogs barking and Enforcers calling the blackout.

He liked the shutters closed over windows, keeping the people inside their dwellings. More maniacal thoughts rushed around his mind. He was pondering the situation, looking for an answer to the mounting problems that were emerging.

Finally Lattimer concluded that the world had once again conspired against him. He closed his eyes, imagining a list of names, which now appeared in his mind's eye.

He read the names that topped the list.

Celeste Baker was followed by Robert Garforth.

The two erased names at the top of the list were certainly not there before today, nor will they be there-after.

He raised a finger in the air and drew an imaginary line of flame, it slowly materialised, burning through each of the letters, eliminating them from the long list of other names in a cleansing burning.

A knock on the door coincided with him opening his eyes and returning his gaze to the vista before him. Lattimer spun his head around and called 'enter'. He quietly watched the reaction of the young girl and a middle-aged woman as they entered the room. They were both more startled then embarrassed by his nudity, but mainly shocked when they saw the floor was covered in blood.

'We're here to clean up some mess sir and turn the bed down.' The old woman added to the young girl's introduction. Silently he nodded his approval and returned his gaze to the window leaving the women to work quickly and silently.

There he remained with no thought to the embarrassment he was causing the cleaners by his immodesty.

The Launceston streets were empty and quiet now, there was no one around to concern himself with and he allowed his mind to return to thoughts of Celeste Baker.

She had become the best of his students, the most promising of her peers. She was honest, reliable and fearless. This young woman had a bright future ahead of her. Lattimer had considered her to be possibly his greatest success, after all had he not embraced her anger for him? Did he not manage to turn her feelings of hatred into respect for him?

As time went by she finally became more obedient and she, like so many others, began almost to revere him. The thoughts of Celeste warmed him and he gave himself a little smile.

She was certainly a good soldier, someone he could rely on always to follow his orders. Oh yes, she was an exceptionally good soldier indeed. That was until recently and no matter whom it was, he would not tolerate insolence or complete disregard for orders.

Lattimer caught his reflection in the window pane, it was grimacing back at him, his smile had gone and anger and frustration again started to rise in him as he recalled the recent change in her. Why had her compassion for others started to get stronger, how dare she let people off with a simple warning or caution. He banged his hand against the glass panel, making the cleaner jump.

That is why she needed to be punished, but he certainly did not want her dead, far from it. No, not her, he only wanted her taught a lesson. In reality, he could not easily turn a blind eye, even if he wanted to and where Celeste Baker was concerned, he certainly wanted to.

On this occasion, it appeared as though the punisher had gone too far and although it was not the first time an over enthusiastic beating had happened it was the first time one of his Enforcers was the target.

The Elite Enforcer thought about what had happened to his property; property that affected his plans. Then his thoughts moved to the Punisher and tomorrow he will find that Punisher and have him taught a severe lesson. Lattimer determined he would not get away with this.

Lattimer despised the thought of himself being perceived by others as a weak leader, just as he did with the last Elite Enforcer. He had to show the people he was strong enough to make all necessary decisions, even if it meant causing pain or making personal sacrifices.

The women had finished the cleaning and hurriedly left the room in complete silence. As he heard the door click into place, Lattimer made for the shower, he needed to scrub off the real blood, sweat and tears of the day.

As the water sprayed his body clean, the walls and floor turned pink. It was as if the water blushed, embarrassed for unwittingly removing the evidence of the terrible crime he had committed.

He was finally clean and he left, dried himself on the clean towel, after which he walked to his bed and lay down.

Breathing deeply he continued his reflection on recent events. This had not been a good week at all for him. Two of his star pupils dead, his merchandise gone, maybe destroyed. Someone was responsible for all of this and that someone was going to have to pay.

Tomorrow is a new day and accountability will be the topic.

Lattimer stretched out his sore covered hand and with his fingers he extinguished the candle on his bedside cabinet.

He dropped his head onto the pillow and closed his eyes.

The night always brought the irritation to the fore of his consciousness and the non-stop itching began, just as it did every night for as long as he could remember.

Nevertheless, he soon drifted off, ignoring the solitary tear that rolled down his cheek.

Chapter Six

Casually sitting on the horse that he had taken from the barn, Jon Maitland recalled how, over the years, he had developed the knack of befriending many creatures, from cats, right through to the horse under him right now.

Man and beast slowly made their way along the old road and he realised just how grateful he was for this gift as he patted the muscle filled neck of his mount.

Maitland felt hot as transparent beads of sweat rolled down his hair onto his bare back, acting like tiny magnifying glasses in the sun, heating skin and making him glisten and itch.

He had travelled all night and as he pulled his arm across his face to wipe the moistness of sweat away, he could already smell his own body odour emanating from under his armpits. He also noticed bristles were reappearing on his chin when he rubbed his face.

'So much for that shower and shave,' he said to the horse for the sake of hearing a human voice, even if it was his own.

With no plan other than to get to Launceston, man and beast ambled along the Old Graystone Road, they crossed the bridge over the river and headed past the old quarry and though the sun warmed him through, it did absolutely nothing to lift his spirits.

His thoughts returned to the house and the death of the anonymous Enforcer, his mind moved to the past; making him recall some of the things he had to do in order to survive.

Yet when he searched his feelings that came with the forgotten images he found he had no guilt about taking yet another human life.

There was perhaps a pang of regret; perhaps he should have some guilt, if only to show that a glimmer of humanity still remained.

Killing was just something else he had gotten used to in this new era and no, he had no regrets whatsoever about yesterday or anything else he had done since he embarked on this path. After all, he only killed those who, in his opinion, deserved not to live.

He stopped wasting his time searching his feelings and remained more than just a little curious about the discovery of the house; why had it been hidden in the woods?

The girl was obviously being punished for something, the reason he didn't really care about, but the contraband packed ready for shipping; now what was all that about?

None of it fitted with what he had seen in other parts of the country, but his main niggle was who could be behind it all?

The whole thing stank of corruption at the highest level, sure there were people out there who are always on the fiddle but Jon Maitland was not one of them.

He was and always had been, an honest and just man, a man who tried to hold on to his standards while others had all too willingly abandoned theirs. Nowadays though, in all this turmoil he only wanted a quiet life in search of death, but something felt strange about this situation.

Of course, he had been in trouble before but somehow this was different, there was a certain familiarity about it, not just because he had been here before.

It felt like he was supposed to be here.

The boxes of contraband were for or from somebody especially well connected to the Celts and being this close to the border of Kernow he could only assume that it was from Launceston.

Maybe that is where he would find an answer.

Jon Maitland had a lot to think about, not least his unplanned and reluctant return to this part of the God-forsaken country.

During his journey around England, Maitland had become unintentionally famous, if not infamous, for his fight for the common man. He was known as a fighter against oppression and aggression, but this notoriety was not what he wanted. Fame had somehow found him.

History is filled with such stories. Myths and legends sprinkled with elements of truth, turning into folklore. But the folklore of Maitland, the myth of 'The Reaper', was the stuff made up from a series of coincidences.

He did not want to be anything other than he was.

Just a man.

As he rode on, getting ever closer to Launceston, his mind squeezed out more recollections and memories of how, for him, it all started.

Eighteen years had passed yet the images in his head were still too painful for him look at. It remained still far too fresh in his mind and as usual he pushed the mental pictures back into the shadows that sat in the back of his memory.

Passing a small copse he involuntarily stretched his aching arms, tiredness was catching up with him and he looked down to stroke and pat the mane and neck of the horse.

He thought the stead also was due a rest and some food if nothing else.

Deciding the thicket of maple trees and shrubs was a good place to stop, he guided the majestic beast beneath him and on entering the shaded area he found the river ran through it.

He got halfway in and stopped the horse.

He jumped down from the six foot drop and being ever alert, he studied the shadows made by the leaf-covered branches of the trees. He wanted to make sure he was alone, that nobody else was here hiding in the bushes.

He watched the horse as it moved to the bank.

It lowered its head into the river and began drinking from the fast flowing, cold water.

Maitland studied the beast a little while longer for any signs of apprehension or fear and it was only when the animal had settled, did he feel it was safe for him to settle too.

He moved to a tree and sat on the damp, dewy grass. It helped in cooling him down as he rested his back against the gnarled and knotted trunk of an elderly maple tree.

The Reaper kept watching the horse as it walked freely about, enjoying the lush green grass that nature had provided.

The copse gave excellent cover from the road and at least for a short time he reassured himself that it would be safe enough for him to fall into his usual light, disturbed sleep.

After what felt like the blink of an eye Jon Maitland suddenly woke, startled by the sound of a woman screaming. His abrupt movement frightened the horse and it backed away from him quickly.

It took only a second or two for him to be fully awake and Maitland realised that he had, once again, only imagined the screaming. The shrill cry was now gone, quickly replaced by the sound of a helicopter flying in the distance.

It was either going to or coming from Kernow.

He looked up to see if he could see it defying gravity in the bits of sky the maple leaves allowed to be visible.

There was a feeling of disappointed when he saw nothing except the falling of maple seeds, emulating the spinning of rota blades.

He held out an open palm and caught one.

The tiny brown wing that held a seed at the end of its spine sat in his hand and the distant heavy shuddering of the whirring aircraft reminded him that many years ago he was supposed to be on one of those damned machines. Anger again rose in him and the seed was easily crushed in his tightly closed fist. He emptied his hand of the damaged seed and wiped his palm on his jeans.

His nightmares continued to plague him and the closer he got to Launceston, the worse they appeared to be getting.

Though it seemed like only seconds to him, he had actually slept for the best part of the morning. He stood in the hot, mid morning sun as it travelled the sky to reach its apex.

Yawning loudly, he stretched out his body.

He looked around at the sun-mottled clearing to see if anything was amiss, but all he saw was the horse settling again. He closed his eyes and listened to the sound of the trees whispering in the breeze and the river splashing an irresistible invitation nearby.

The river was calling to him.

It was far too tempting an invitation to ignore, so he stripped naked and walked over to the edge of the bank only to plunge himself into the ice cold liquid.

In that heart stopping moment, when the intensely cold water hit his hot skin and surrounded him, embracing his body in its cold caress, he found the feeling and muffled bubbling sound in his ears comforting and strangely calming.

A small glimpse of a distant dream of being back in his mother's womb tried to break out of its deep hiding place. But the spark was too weak to form a full-blown memory and instead it gave him a mild, yet comforting feeling of déjà vu.

Maitland wanted to stay just like this, hidden and safe from the world, under the fast flowing river. However, the shock of suddenly being submerged into freezing liquid had emptied his lungs of air. His body instinctively begged for the breath of life to resume, his lungs cried out for the oxygen supply to be restarted.

For many years he had wandered around alone, with no reason to live. He had lost count of the number of attempts he had made at ending it all, but his overwhelming natural instinct for survival made this particular urge impossible to satisfy. So here he was, wanting to die, needing to be no longer alive, yet still driven to survive for no reason he could see other than being forever tormented.

Maitland broke through the surface fist first and gasping at the air. He yelled out and coughed, clearing the water that had entered his lungs.

He settled down, floating on the surface and brought his breathing under control. He tried to relax as his thoughts came back to recent events once more.

He again searched for regret and remorse, but for Maitland no matter how he looked at it, he was still justified in his actions.

He wanted justice, he wanted law and he killed only those he judged to cause pain and hurt in others, didn't he? He only hurt the people who made victims of the weak and innocent and that does not make him any type of monster, does it?

He recalled he had once been a victim and he vowed never to be one again. Instead he had become merciless in what he called his 'civic duty'. It is what he believed was the right thing to do, but always with the hope someone, someday would end this torture for him.

After a while his belly decided he was little hungry and he swam back to land. His naked body chilled as he pulled himself onto the bank and a cold breeze caught him.

He walked across the grass and found it soft and springy under foot. Stopping at the horse, he steadied him to take some of the provisions he had stashed in the saddlebag. The horse took little notice of him and continued to chomp at the wonderful green blades at his hoofs.

'Good Boy.' Maitland told him as he patted his side.

The stillness of the copse was disturbed occasionally with the song of birds somewhere out of sight, this coupled with the now warming air fluting over his naked body gave him the unusual feeling of security, which, strange as it seems, was a feeling that actually unsettled him.

He sat back on the tree, allowing the balmy air to dry his skin as he prepared what little he had to eat.

'Do you want some?' He called out in a loud voice.

There was no reply.

'It's OK; I promise I won't hurt you, as you can see I don't have any places to hide a weapon.' He stood and turned around proving his nudity to the trees and as he completed his twirl, he noticed there was a small movement in some bushes, he also heard what he thought was a giggle from the bush in front of him.

He looked in the opposite direction, now playing a game of hide and seek.

It made him smile.

'Suit yourself.' Maitland shrugged as he returned to the tree and sat to continue to eat.

'Put some clothes on first, I don't want to see you like that.' A young, but firm female voice came from the bushes.

He knew at least one person had observed him.

He noticed someone skulking about when he emerged from the water, but he did as he was 'instructed' and found his clothes and dressed.

'Now will you come out?'

Two ragged and filth ridden children hesitantly left the relative safety of the bush and moved carefully to where he was standing.

In front of him, at arm's length, stood a young girl.

He surmised she was around the age of twelve or thirteen and a small boy who Maitland judged to be about nine or so.

'Like I said, I won't hurt you.' His voice was calm and he suddenly found the ability to sound caring.

The children nervously sat a little away from him, but they accepted the food he offered.

The boy snatched the food urgently from Maitland's hand, almost eating the portion of bread in one go.

'Now what are you two doing out here, are you alone?' Maitland asked keeping a low, gentle voice.

'John, don't eat like that, you'll be sick again.'

The boy shot a glare at his elder sibling and he started to chew a little slower. She turned back to Maitland and gently took the food he offered to her.

She tried to be a little more polite.

While studying her face Maitland could see that she too was starving and making sure she thanked Maitland, she smiled then ate, slowly at first. But despite this act, her hunger took control of her etiquette filters and switched them off.

She too finished hers by scoffing it down.

Maitland giggled a little as he passed the water bottle around for them to wash the dry bread down. He then waited and watched until the children settled. He managed yet another smile as it migrated across his lips.

The children finished and again she thanked Maitland for his kindness with a return smile.

'I'm Maria Adams,' she proudly announced 'and this is my greedy pig of a brother, John, we came from Launceston.'

Maitland nodded and looked down at the boy.

'John? that's a good name to have young man, that's my name too,' the youngster looked up and smiled as he shyly cuddled into his sister, 'so why are you two out here, where is your family?'

He watched as a deep sadness washed over Maria.

She looked down.

'Daddy died about two months ago, the Enforcers killed him. Mum said it was because we wouldn't pay Lattimer what he wanted, so we had to go away. She said that if we did not, we would be taken away by Lattimer and he would put me to work and stuff.'

Maitland listened as she continued her story.

'I told mummy I didn't mind helping, but she said no when I asked her, she wouldn't tell me what work I would have to do. All she said was it would be safer for the three of us to leave Launceston and move to another town.'

As she talked of her parents, the little boy started to cry.

'Where is your mother now?' Maitland asked.

Maria cradled the youngster tightly in her arms.

'We don't know, we were all hiding in a barn when an Enforcer came in. He was searching for something or someone. He looked behind some boxes and nearly found me and John, that's when Mummy stepped out, she gave herself up to save us. We haven't seen her since,' her voice became filled with sadness as she continued, 'he must have taken her somewhere.' She lowered her head to shield her moist eyes from him.

'Mummy told us if we ever got split up, we had to stay quiet and wait, until she came back.'

She did not have the strength to hold back the tears any longer and cried.

'After two days we got hungry, that's when I knew she would not come back, so me and John continued on just like mummy told us.' She wiped her eyes dry.

Maitland sat listening.

'I think she's dead' Maria said flatly, looking directly into Maitland's eyes, she wanted to join her brother in sobbing her heart out, but from somewhere she found the extra strength inside and Maitland realised here was yet another innocent who had to grow up overnight.

He could not help but admire her resolve in taking care of her brother.

'So Maria, tell me why you came out to me? I could have been a bad man.'

'You like horses, I can tell by the way he trusts you. Horses can tell between good and bad people you know and I can tell he likes you.'

A healthy, hearty smile appeared on her face when she spoke about the horse and having a surprisingly incisive answer from a child impressed Maitland.

'Well Maria thank you for your trust, but what are you going to do now?'

'I'm not sure, we have to go I think, move on like Mummy told us to.' She replied.

'OK, but before you go what can you tell me about Lattimer? Who is he?'

The boy rested his head on his sister's lap and she began to stroke at his filth encrusted blonde hair. Maitland imagined she had watched her mother do the same to him and she was now copying her parent, training her own maternal skills for when she has her own children.

'Lattimer? Oh he's the boss of Launceston and Daddy didn't like him much because for us to stay in the town, we had to give Lattimer a lot of our food. Daddy was a farmer and everything he grew had to be sent to the town hall for processing, I think they call it. Lattimer would only give a little bit back to us and that wasn't enough, so Daddy used to say Lattimer was a bastard and he wanted him dead.'

Maitland sensed the girl was repeating the words of her parents, parrot fashion including the whispered 'bastard'. Her face reddened as she cursed, but she seemed to know the system well enough for Maitland to get the picture.

'Mummy always worried that someone would hear daddy say that and tell Lattimer and daddy would get into trouble.' She suddenly stopped, her voice cracking again.

'It's OK Maria, look your brother is asleep; why don't you do the same?' Maitland gently suggested to her. The girl nodded and slowly lay down, placing an arm around her brother as she snuggled into him for warmth and comfort.

Jon Maitland leaned over and whispered in her ear.

'I'll leave the horse for you and when you wake up you get yourselves as far as possible away from here.'

Maria smiled and nodded as she closed her eyes and began to drift off. Maitland left them enough food to see them through for a few days as long as they ate sensibly. Finally he left one of the guns and some ammunition from the bag, hoping that being a farmer's daughter she would know how to handle the small weapon.

He quietly exited the copse to continue his journey to town on foot to get there before night fall.

Chapter Seven

An exhausted Celeste Baker arrived on the outskirts of Launceston with her agonised body screaming out for her to rest and take in some food.

Though beaten and bruised she had, one way or another, managed to find the strength she needed to hobble the forty or so miles from Totnes across Dartmoor to Launceston and through the night.

She made her way down Tavistock Road.

The street was awash with litter, burnt out skeletons of old cars and vans and there was debris everywhere. She passed the empty, burnt out shells of houses that had been left behind on the street and she somehow imagined she felt the same as they looked.

Abandoned, damaged and in disrepair.

Celeste Baker continued to shuffle about in the early morning sun, thinking differently about the dilapidated shells lining the lonely thoroughfare.

The dwellings took on a new meaning for her as she thought the boxes of bricks and mortar were not just property for someone to own, or a house that someone once rented only to make some greedy property owner richer. No, today she realised that they were once homes, places where people lived out their real lives, playing their real games and sometimes dying their real deaths.

They were the roots of family life, roots she never had in hers. This morning the empty dwellings seemed to be haunted with ghostly memories, playing with the dark and dusty shadows. The memories were waiting for just the right person to appear at the right moment in time.

That would be when the forgotten memories were ready to jump into a mind, allowing people to recall a pleasure, or the pain of a bygone recollection.

Since the last uprising in the town, the people of this quarter were ordered to move behind the barricaded part that lay closer to the castle. It was said to have been safer there, in case of an attack from another encampment.

It was an assumed attack that, so far, never happened.

'Why was that?' she questioned herself.

'Why?' came her own reply, 'because Lattimer was always expanding his grasp, it was him invading and attacking other towns, it was him waging war in the area and it was he and he alone who wanted to control everything.'

Celeste couldn't walk anymore and was so very tired of fighting, so sick of Enforcement and at the end of her tether with the unreasonable, whimsical orders that came daily from Lattimer.

She stopped outside a grand town house, with its dirty, white paint peeling from the walls to reveal it was built of red brick.

Its large panelled green painted door broken from the three steel hinges and the filthy glass in the once white sash windows were smashed.

Fatigue forced her to enter the house and as she began to walk along that path, she took no notice that the black painted iron fencing had been removed.

Under normal circumstances Celeste would have taken her time on her approach to the house. She would have had the time to develop a strategy for entering an unknown environment with her team and only after having sent one or two members in to ensure it was safe, would she have entered herself.

Except these circumstances were anything but normal!

In fact she did not know what normal was, she was only used to her normal and today she was just a team of one.

She was barely able to walk, with only her own inertia of exhaustion driving her on, but she somehow managed to stagger into what could have been a living room and immediately her legs imploded, making her collapse in on herself and drop heavily to the floor, throwing up dust and debris caused by the impact, imitating the body of her dead punisher.

Fortunately for Celeste she was already asleep before she hit the floor and without any of the pain she felt registering in her brain, she slept.

Images of what may have been her childhood crept out from the dark recesses of her mind, to find refuge in her sub consciousness. Long forgotten, suppressed memories leapt into her sleeping memory, transporting her back to the first time she was forced to come to this town.

She was back, on that sorry day where for the first time she saw what they called the 'compound'.

The new regime in Launceston had turned the old college campus into a maze of buildings, all of which had been designated different uses that were supposedly for the good of the town.

One of the buildings was utilised to train people in all aspects of farming, another for building and construction. They used one as a hospital wing and next to that, the detention centre.

They even set a barrack up to train soldiers to feed the wars and battles with fresh, new blood to replace the injured and dead quickly.

Finally, the Reformation Centre!

Its sole purpose is to turn people into 'useful members' of this new society, but that depends on how you define useful.

The Reformation Centre is not a pleasant place to be, it is a place where no-one ever wanted to be, either by choice or by force, no matter what age you were.

If you found you were placed in here as a child, then either one or both of your parents were dead, possibly killed by the same people who were about to transform you, and from day one and regardless of age or gender the regime was harsh and abusive and the discipline brutal.

They called them recruits, but the reality was they were inmates. Prisoners who were constantly told their reformation was for the greater good of Launceston.

The change would give them a sense of purpose, a new direction in becoming a better person. It was explained to them that pain and suffering would make them productive citizens, and that it would be so much easier for them if only they would simply comply.

That was yet another lie.

Celeste was so very young, just a child who had literally been ripped from the bosom of her loving family and now she was standing in the dark. She was freezing with only a white, thin smock to wear in the cold room.

But it wasn't only the chill making her shiver, it was the fear and confusion she was feeling. Feelings that were completely alien to her, never had she been so afraid before, she always had the secure knowledge that her mum and dad would protect her from everything.

But they were gone and she was alone.

She wanted to cry, but the child was stubborn and she refused to allow herself to shed one single tear here.

They goaded her, telling her that her parents had agreed to leave her there. They told her that mummy and daddy hated her and wanted her to go away forever. They told her that her parents had arranged for this to happen.

But the youngster knew better than that, she was sure her that her parents love was real and strong.

In the beginning she was aware they were lying to her, none the less the system was relentless and slowly they began to break her down.

She was no more than a baby who was made by what they called 'retraining', to forget her past. For the child her parents simply did not exist, she was essentially an unwanted orphan.

Her home had been destroyed and she had nowhere else to go.

This was going to be her home now.

At such a young age she showed how much of a fighter she was and her instinct made her fight them every step of the way, and in any way she could think of.

She wanted to make it hard for them, wanted it to take longer for her to be reformed.

She refused to become compliant and her deep rooted pride and uncompromising self-respect, made each process in her retraining as hard for them as possible.

This child struggled for a long time against any and all of the punishments used on her. Despite her best efforts in fighting them, she was only human and in the end, she was made to forget even herself.

In the end the system always wins and she was left with nothing.

She was nothing.

An empty shell with no past and possibly no future.

She had no family.

No identity.

She was empty and alone.

Beaten and tormented.

She had no tears left to cry.

To complete the process of change, each child was given a new birthday, along with a new name.

They held a 'party' for her and the others who had 'passed' their training. It was the first time they were allowed to show any type of happiness without being in trouble for it.

The next day Celeste Baker started her new life.

Initially she had been assigned to a role in servitude and found herself cleaning, fetching and carrying. Doing other domestic duties for her masters, yet through it all she still managed to maintain a certain grace and dignity.

This aloofness gave others the impression she had an air of superiority about her. As she settled into her new life, this attitude of hers made her a target with some of her peers and all too frequently she found herself in conflict. They may have changed her, but she still had her spirit and she always stood her ground with the inevitable fight breaking out somewhere on the compound.

The others wanted to show her that no matter how good she thought she was, it meant nothing whatsoever when your head is down a toilet bowl, cleaning it after it had been used by twenty or so people, hell bent on proving a point.

On her fourteenth birthday and quite without explanation she was taken, along with another girl Marta Brunning, to the Penthouse for the very first time.

They had both reached the 'age of option' and it was time to meet with the Elite Enforcer. They need to decide on their future within the community.

Celeste had seen this happen to other girls before, only for some of them never to return to the servant's quarters. She was never able to find out what happened to them and in the end she learnt, the hard way, not to care either.

The two girls nervously walked along the deep piled, clean red carpeted corridor. Its walls were filled with colourful paintings in huge gold frames from long ago. She was amazed at the beauty in these pictures; she had never seen anything like them before. The duo moved quickly and quietly towards the large brown double doors. When they eventually got there

Celeste banged her hand as hard as she could to announce their presence outside on the solid wood surface.

After a moment they heard the muffled response.

'Come.'

The girls looked at one another to see if the other was ready and with both hands Celeste pushed down on the brass, flat door handle. The shining, yellowish lever fogged up as her warm hand held on to the cold metal.

It capitulated under her touch; unlocking and she pushed open the heavy door, allowing the two girls to enter.

Their nerves turned to fear as they were directed to stand in front of what looked like a large gold throne, with blood red padding.

Sitting on it was an elderly man who looked stick thin as he talked quietly to the rather large woman with her giant rosy cheeks. Celeste recognised her voice as the one who directed her from when they entered the room.

When the girls got closer, he turned to face them.

Here was the Elite Enforcer, a man you should stay away from, if you had any sense that is. He was feared by everyone simply because, he needed to be.

He watched closely as the two teenage girls approached and a sickly black toothed grin appeared on his wrinkled face as the teens came into his focus.

Celeste noticed the way he was looking at them; it was a look that made her feel dirty and it took all her courage to stand there, as she wanted to hide away.

His stare made her uncomfortable and caused a shudder to run down her spine and radiate through the rest of her.

'Now,' he said after licking his hand several times and smoothing what was left of his, greasy hair, 'who do we have here?' He wheezed as he spoke and his tone was as rough as his face while still attempting to look friendly.

'Elite Enforcer these girls have reached the 'age of option', they are now ready to be allocated a new life role.'

The large woman spoke with a loud shrill voice which Celeste found irritating and as the sound of the matron's voice entered her ears it sounded like fingernails being slowly pulled down a blackboard.

Celeste still didn't quite understand what was happening to her, as no-one had said anything or instructed her about options, but the unprepared Celeste continued to listen.

'Ah I see,' the old man said, 'now what are we going to do with you two?' The woman bent over and whispered something into his hair infested left ear.

The man wangled his bony hands together.

Celeste carefully watched his face as he lifted his hedge like eyebrow's, a sign that what he had heard was of great interest, then the horrible smile on his stupid, wrinkled face got creepier as he addressed the girls.

'OK, so I understand from Matron here, you two like to fight! Is that correct ladies?'

Celeste and Marta looked at one another, their cheeks reddened and they turned to face him again and nodded in unison.

It wasn't so much that she liked to fight, it was more of a case of her not liking being bullied and if it ever happened she would defend herself, but at this point Celeste knew better than to talk back or try to defend herself.

It was always the opinion of the old man that silence was compliance, so he continued.

'OK then,' he clapped his hands together, 'how would you two like to work for me in Enforcement? You see I would like the two of you to help out in ensuring Launceston remains safe for us all.'

Suddenly realising that with this, so called 'age of option' thing, they really had no option and with the same amount of enthusiasm as going to see a dentist, both of the girls meekly nodded in agreement.

'Lattimer.' The old man called out as he reclined in his chair and from behind a closed door of an adjoining room came a tall man, in the black uniform of a high-ranking Enforcement Officer.

'Sir.' Barked the immaculately dressed Enforcer as he entered the room and sharply stopped between the terrified youngsters. His abruptness had startled the girls and Celeste dared to look up at the towering figure.

Looking up at him Celeste noticed there was something wrong with his skin. It seemed to be flaking from his body, leaving a fine white dust sprinkled over his freshly pressed dark uniform.

She had heard the name Lattimer before of course, but she had never met him until now and the sight of him made her nerves jingle, just as they did on the night she had been brought to the compound.

'It would seem that I have two new recruits for you Russell, tell me, what do you think of them?'

Lattimer turned to face the increasingly terrified youngsters and as he looked down at them, Celeste could not help but shudder again. A shiver of vague recognition reverberated throughout her body, but she couldn't quite recall where she had met him before.

'Maybe it was in my role as a servant' she thought.

'Sir, I believe we can do something with these two pieces of weak rubbish, but don't ask me to give them any special treatment just because they're girls.'

The old man giggled. 'Oh just take them away and deal with them would you Russell, there's a good chap!'

With a click of heels from his highly polished boots, Lattimer retreated from the room with Celeste and Marta following in silent pursuit.

They almost had to trot in order to keep up with him and his long gait.

The three of them left the Penthouse for a long, silent walk back to the Reformation Centre. They were approaching the building when Lattimer suddenly diverted from the route the two girls would normally have taken to the servant quarters. They had to turn quickly as they followed him through an entrance that was normally forbidden for them to use.

On entering, they found themselves in some sort of reception area. It had, what appeared to be, a shop counter and standing behind it was the obligatory miserable, bored looking man waiting to serve someone.

Their presence did not seem to cheer him in the slightest and he silently gave them the dark green uniform of a novice Enforcer.

Celeste gently stroked at the material and felt how rough it was to the touch. Just by looking at it she could tell it was maybe two or three sizes too big and with a smell of other people's body odour humming from it.

She looked up at Lattimer as if to ask if he was joking, but decided she was not stupid enough to actually ask.

Ignoring her look of disgust, Lattimer spoke for the first time to them.

'You are expected to look after this and any other equipment that will be issued to you. That means you keep it clean, always at hand and as you won't have any spare time to socialise, this uniform will be the only clothing you are going to need for a while. Is that clear?'

The girls nodded as he dismissed them when they were both taken by another Enforcer to their new room.

It was situated within the girl's domicile and that was well away from where the boys congregated. The two teens entered the room and moved to the single bunks they had silently chosen and sat on them as if to claim them as their own.

The beds were made of wooden boxes that were smooth to the touch with the corners rounded off. While they resembled a home-made divan of sorts Celeste thought they were more akin to coffins.

On top of the box was a large stuffed pad stretching from one end to the other. It was something like a giant version of the pillow that rested at one end.

So this was to be her mattress, it was covered in some sort of grey material. Celeste guessed it used to be white when, however many years ago, it was new. Not exactly luxury, but in her life she didn't even know what luxury was.

The door closed and the two waited to hear the usual 'click' as the lock slid into place. Instead all they heard were the footsteps of the Enforcer walking away.

They waited in silence just looking at one another, until Celeste plucked up the courage and stood up. Marta Brunning made a quiet protest and tried to stop her, but Celeste ignored Marta's pleas and she slowly walked to the door.

Calming her breathing she listened, but couldn't hear a sound from the other side, instinctively or through stupidity, she placed her hand on the cold metal doorknob.

She held the dented, uneven globe of the door knob with its chipped white paint and firmly turned it.

The door became free from its catch and the warp in the wood released its tension, causing it to spring towards her. She stopped it before the square edge banged into her head. Celeste steadied herself, fully expecting to be barked at by whoever was on the other side, standing guard.

She looked through the small gap and at the sight of a girl passing nearby, her heart accelerated when she looked in Celeste's direction and stopped in her tracks.

Changing direction she began to walk toward the room and before Celeste could manage to close the door, it was pushed open from the other side.

In a panic Celeste backed away and stood with her head lowered, waiting for whatever punishment was due to her for making such a mistake.

'Hello you two, they call me Amber, welcome to paradise.' The girl sarcastically said with a giggle and a tease of her red hair.

A very surprised Celeste snapped her head up at the open friendliness the girl was showing them, but why had she left the door open? Celeste looked at the open door and then turned her gaze back to Amber.

She guessed the girl was about seventeen or eighteen years old. Her jade green eyes which glowed from the pale skin of her face were in stark contrast to the fantastic mop of tight red curly hair.

Amber's eyes were wide open and sparkled, looking as excited as she sounded when she spoke. However, she spoke at such a speed that made it difficult for Celeste to take in all of the information that was being passed on.

Despite this distraction Celeste stood with one eye firmly on the door, worrying that their talking would be heard by others outside of the room who would report them.

'It's OK, you're Enforcers now and we Enforcers have different rules to the others. We have freedom, well sort of. When I say freedom, what I mean is freedom in as much as we can walk about the dorm, but not out. Well not yet. We can talk, sing and laugh; in your own room at least. It is OK I promise you.'

It seemed to Celeste that Amber's arms and hands were somehow directly connected to her mouth, because with each word that Amber uttered, these limbs would move about in complete synchronisation. It was as if Amber was trying to paint a picture in the air of what she was saying.

Just then a section leader came walking past the open door. The talkative Amber stood still and silent. She threw a sort of salute at the passing man, just as Lattimer had done in the penthouse.

The section leader walked away without replying or paying them the slightest bit of attention.

'See, I told you, it's alright like I said. He didn't say anything because you're both novices. Don't worry though, you'll soon get used to it here.'

Finally, Amber stopped talking and gave the girls a reassuring smile.

She then took Celeste's hand.

'Listen I have to go, but I'll come back later to get you two for supper.' And with an exaggerated wave and another beaming smile, Amber departed leaving a stunned Celeste and Marta, who had remained seated on her bed, completely dumbfounded.

Celeste moved back to her bed and sat down, she smiled at Marta and for the first time in her short life Celeste started to feel she was no longer just a skivvy. She was now someone with proper responsibility, she now had a real part to play and it excited her.

Reclining her head on the pillow, Celeste stretched her legs out on the bed; at last she had found a sense of belonging. She held out her hand in front of her. She was sure she could still feel the soft touch of Amber on her skin. This was unexpected; she began to feel an attraction toward Amber.

The thought of the flame haired, bubbly young woman started to excite her in a way that never happened before. She was happier today than she could ever remember, but inside she remained an extremely angry teenager.

As Celeste relaxed on her new bed, in her new room, with her new friend she smiled to herself before dozing off.

***

Darker images then began to emerge from the deeper depths of Celeste's sleeping recollection, stirring in her mind, taking her even further back in time.

She had been so very young when she was taken from her family. She had no memories of her parents, just some vague shadows in dreams.

A battered Celeste dreamt she was that young girl again, standing alone in a darkened room and all around her hundreds of dismembered hands were flying about, trying to grab at her. Pulling at her limbs and clothes, there were hands covering her mouth, trying to stop her from screaming out as she watched, wide eyed and terrified when a faceless woman came into view.

She too was struggling against being dragged away by yet more of the unattached hands.

To stop her from seeing what was happening, the hands placed a smelly cloth hood over her head and in the darkness the frightened child could hear someone laughing.

It was a deep laugh, the laugh of a man and all the while she could hear the woman's screams growing louder.

It was the sledgehammer of recollection that smashed through the walnut shell of her dream and Celeste woke screaming for help.

Screaming for her mother.

Beads of cold sweat rolled from her forehead and down her face. Breathless and dazed, Celeste had to ask herself if she was still sleeping or not.

The shadows dancing around the floor of the living room played cruel tricks with her startled mind, as she watched the shadows form the shape of hands coming into the derelict house. The sound of a bird singing through the window made her realise she was awake.

Thankfully it was only a shadow as they darted about the floor and walls of the moonlit room and through the window; she saw the black cloak of night had surrounded the house.

Celeste had slept through the entire day and was shivering with cold rather than fear. Then her belly loudly rumbled.

Carefully she attempted to get up from where she had lain, but her aching body submitted to the pain and Celeste gave up. She was too sore to move right now, but managed to sit up next to her bag and rummage around in it.

With great relief she found some food and as she ate, she thought about her dream.

Lattimer! It was him who had taken her away from the family she so desperately loved and who had loved her unconditionally in return.

That bastard and his friends were the reason for her being in Launceston, working like a slave, maiming and killing people.

Her thoughts turned to that first encounter with him in the Penthouse and she realised when he looked at her, there was absolutely no sign of recognition on his face.

'I could have been anyone,' she said aloud.

It made Celeste's anger increase.

Something so traumatic had happened to her and at such a young age, by his hand and he didn't even have the common courtesy of recognising her.

But it had happened so long ago and no matter how hard Celeste battled with her memory, she could not fully recall the details.

She knew that he was somehow involved.

It was his fault she was lonely and angry.

Celeste now remembered how, as time went by, the training and indoctrination she had received managed that anger, they steered it in way that was positive for them and by the time she had blossomed into an adult she had completely forgotten her former childhood and resigned herself to this new life.

She also remembered that since taking on the role of an Enforcement Officer she had become the star of her unit. It was a job that gave her some pride and surprisingly she found she really enjoyed it, for the most part. Then there was the unexpected development of the firm belief in Lattimer, what he stood for and especially in the building of the community.

'Where did that come from?' She asked herself.

Celeste worked hard, learnt quickly and slowly she forgot to question the motives or the reasons for some of the assignments she had been given.

That was until recently.

Her outlook began to change and her beliefs and ideals began to differ from those of the hierarchy.

She started to question procedures and orders, after all, it was one thing punishing law breakers, but quite another brow beating innocent people into complying with some new, unaffordable edict that increased taxes or donations for the 'greater good' of the community.

Celeste Baker had the unforgiving curse of allowing her conscience to rule her head at times. She must have been born with it or something; this is how she justified it to herself because during her retraining, she was in trouble far too many times because of it.

In the end she learnt to hide it and always the hard way. In this world, a conscience was a trait that was seen as a sign of weakness, especially in an Enforcement Officer.

For Celeste though, the final straw came two months ago. She and her team were ordered to attend a farmer; the man had decided he would not fulfil his quota of Lattimer's latest demand, not without his young family suffering anyway.

Lattimer did not care about such things and had given the order for him to be punished. It was to be Celeste's unit who was responsible for carrying out his orders.

Reluctantly she complied, but to her shock and disgust the team were overzealous in their duty and the man was beaten to death.

Lattimer was informed and the next day he ordered the wife and female child be taken into service, while the young boy was to be 'enrolled' into Enforcement training.

Celeste was dismayed that not one person from her team had been made accountable for this unnecessary death of a good man, a man who was only looking out for his family.

That day, for the first time in her life, Celeste dared to fully think for herself. She no longer knew how she fitted within the regime of Launceston.

She thought about how her relationship with Lattimer had developed over the years and in the end she decided the system was fundamentally wrong. This action was not justifiable and she was not going to let these people suffer any longer.

Before the rest of the family could be 'rounded up' Celeste had made her way to the house and given the woman and her children time to escape.

It was a decision and an action that gave Lattimer the reason to send the punisher to her. The punishment was a message from him, telling her how disappointed he was in her actions against him.

But thanks to Maitland, she was lucky to be alive.

Chapter Eight

Maitland arrived at the Westgate Street entrance of the barricade and was instantly impressed with how one of the sleeping guards reacted quickly to seeing his partner being killed.

The man went from dozing to fighting in less than two seconds, this was admirable for anyone and when Maitland squared up to the big fella he guessed he was ex-army or something.

His was a bigger build than that of Maitland and his punch felt akin to being hit by a solid metal pole, but it was of no consequence when he too found out that when 'The Reaper' comes calling no one is safe, no matter how big they were.

The body fell and remained motionless on the floor and Maitland paused.

Then relaxing his defensive stance he left the cabin and after an absence of eighteen years, Jon Maitland walked back into Launceston not knowing what to feel or expect.

His return meant his life had now come full circle, bringing him back to where it all started as he walked along Westgate Street.

It was a long walk.

He was hampered by reluctantly allowing the memories he had worked hard to suppress over the years to now emerge from their neurological graveyard. He passed Dunheved Road on his right and tiny flashes of recollections sparkled in his head.

Brazenly and unflinchingly he ambled through the dark, passing the strangely named turning of Dockey. He followed the road as it took him left to continue up Westgate Street.

Here the street used to be filled with restaurants, pubs, jewellers, but they had all gone leaving the area deserted.

At the junction of Western Road he continued walking along Launceston's filth laden High Street, where shops too were closed and deserted with their windows that once proudly publicised the shops wares, now broken with the contents looted no doubt.

The stench of rotting, discarded vegetables somewhere in the street was attracting rats and other vermin. The smell hung in the night air, but seeing that the memorial to the two world wars had remained standing was a welcome sight for his sore eyes.

We have forgotten haven't we, he thought as he passed it and turned right into Broad Street which was also lined with the fronts of old shops.

It was when he entered into Market Street that he found the empty wooden stalls hanging about the pavements waiting for the morning trading to begin.

Here again, no one bothered to clean up from the previous day's trade.

Oh yes, Launceston had changed.

This once picturesque town had become a ghetto, a slum. The people living here no longer had any respect for the place. But then most of the original inhabitants had been lucky enough to move into Kernow and those who stayed behind had fallen into the ways of the new residents.

A shop sign had caught his eye; it was the butchers.

The image of a pig dressed in a blue striped apron and holding a meat cleaver in its cartoon hand while a straw hat sat on its head had remained mostly intact, the colours had faded and there was no longer a name above the doorway.

He didn't stop when he looked at the window; he knew there was always a memory lurking in these shadows. But after waiting all this time for this man to arrive Maitland had no choice but to allow the memory to come to the fore.

It jumped so hard into his unwilling mind that it made Maitland sway a little.

Around him the deserted night dissolved into hustle and bustle as the bright market day got under way. He recalled how he and Laura would come here, to this very street, to buy meat or fruit.

Maitland also remembered that in this chaotic new world they lived in, it was dangerous for them to mix with the locals. Kidnapping and hostage taking was rife in this desperate part of England, but a family shopping trip was one of the things that gave Jon and Laura a sense of normality. Even if it did mean they had to wear heavy coats with the hoods pulled over their purposely dirtied faces in order to blend in with the locals.

Laura loved to shop, all women did in his opinion, especially before the old one two. One thing Laura loved was to haggle and in the free economy where barter was currency, she was expert with the pies and cakes she lovingly made, they were always good for swapping in return for any supplies they needed.

Maitland recognised the woman's giggle that came from behind him. But when he turned to see who it was, the darkness instantly returned and with it, his consciousness came back to the present.

His mind was back in the same dark street as his body, with the wind of the night gently blowing around him, taking the sound of the sweet giggle with it. He managed a tiny smile as he listened and heard the buildings making creaking noises as they cooled from the hot day. It reminded him of an elderly person as they rested for the evening.

He continued walking and despite the pleasant interlude, his mood remained confrontational and it didn't matter what situation or town he found himself in, his mood never really changed. However, tonight his mood was exactly how he wanted it to be, just as dark as the night.

Of all the places he had been to, surely it would be here in Launceston he was going to find the release in death that he so very much craved.

He looked around at the darkness.

He sniffed the air mimicking a wolf when trying to find his prey. The smells and the sights all reminded him that he was home, but under the cover of night he could not see too clearly.

Maitland looked up, trying to find the dark outline of the castle, but the buildings were in the way and he did not see a lone light go out in the castle window.

He lowered his head and walked some more and began to deliberate whether he should go to the site of the old house or not.

He argued aloud with himself as he walked; stopping and re-starting his journey every time he changed his mind. Eventually he reasoned it would be a pointless exercise, he knew he had destroyed it that night and besides, what value is there when all he would find is the scorch mark reminder of his actions.

Looking around the street he saw nothing, no animals and no life but in the distance, he could just make out faint raised voices of Enforcers, chasing a curfew breaker maybe.

'No matter where I end up it's always the damn same,' he thought to himself, 'the weak oppressed by the strong.' Shaking his head he turned back to walk along Broad Street.

He was not trying to find anything or anyone in particular, no, for Maitland this was purely reconnaissance.

Tonight, he only wanted to become reacquainted with the town he promised he would never again see. For now, he was content enough just to walk around until he could find something of interest.

In the complete darkness he could not see how, if at all, the rest of the town had changed in the intervening years and it was hard for him to remember everything as he wandered around in the moonlight.

About half way down Broad Street, from what used to be a bank, he caught sight of something flickering in the corner of his eye.

Something or someone was in the shadows of a side street and they seemed to be trying to get his attention.

They had succeeded.

Maitland stopped and quickly crouched low as he began to stare in the direction of the perceived movement.

He stayed like that for a moment, stalking his prey and waiting for his eyes to adjust to the different light levels around him.

He concentrated hard, trying to will the shadows into revealing the secrets they held within their dark hiding places. His eyes were starting to strain and his head began to hurt, but nothing stirred again.

The wind continued to blow gently in his ears and his heart beat slightly faster than normal as he thought for a moment.

He stood, deciding it was a trap and such an obvious ploy to lure him.

Another small smile appeared on his face as he rubbed his bristly chin. He shook his head in disbelief at his next decision.

He was going to spring the trap, after all a fight was the reason he had come here, wasn't it?

On approaching the side street entrance he heard a shuffle of feet, and when he entered it he received a loud and extremely painful bang to the back of his head.

It would seem Maitland may have made the right decision to come back after all.

He fell to the ground.

His brain seemed to spin and just before he blacked out, he figured he found the fight he wanted.

***

Launceston is a town built on the side of a large hill with a medieval castle standing guard, sentinel like at its peak.

Celeste Baker looked at the ancient monument from the derelict house to see a light flickering in the window.

Lattimer was in there and she needed to be in there too.

He was the one needing punishment now, but a healthy person would need help in getting to him, and in her beaten, bruised condition she knew she wouldn't be able to do it alone.

The help she needed could only come from a friend and there was only one person she could trust right now.

After an hour or so of eating, resting and gathering her thoughts, Celeste's strength improved and she began to feel a hell of a lot better than she had. Carefully she stood on her unsteady legs, slowly regaining her balance. After a few minutes of hobbling around the room she left the house.

Each step she took brought a new ache for her as muscles she never knew existed painfully announced their unwillingness to assist with any type of forward propulsion.

Only through her sheer stubbornness did she manage to scrape one foot in front of the other, forcing her body to respond and eventually make her way out onto the deserted lonely street.

She headed south-east, down Tavistock Road and then turned into Bush Road. The overgrowth from unkempt gardens and allotments had created some good cover for her until she arrived at the junction with Race Hill.

The street was split down the middle by the barrier, with one-half lined with more empty houses, abandoned and wrecked, while the houses behind the barricade had their windows intact and fitted with wooden shutters, keeping any of the occupants inside during curfew hours.

Celeste stayed low to the ground while looking both ways onto Race Hill. As far as her impaired vision told her, the way was clear. She stood, then darted, as best her body would allow, along the street.

The night breeze cooled the sweat as it streamed from her pores over her body and though her pace was slow, she made her good progress through the dark with complete determination to finish the job. She befriended the shadows cast by the ageing Georgian buildings that slept in the moonlight.

The dark caches obliged by hiding her whenever she heard a sound, or when she thought someone was nearby and before long, a much relieved Celeste saw the barricade looming on the horizon and with an extra burst of energy, she dashed over to the fence.

Her heavy breathing coupled with her grunts and groans disturbed the ghostly silence and she slowly picked her way along the barricade.

The lack of even a rudimentary design had made the barrier seem impenetrable, almost impossible for anyone to proceed any further, unless they went through one of the four or five manned guardhouses dotted around the perimeter and there have been those who had tried.

The injured ex-Enforcer stood at the base of the barricade and examined the mountain of a problem. The layout of corrugated metal sheeting, that were once roofs of sheds sitting in the gardens or allotments of Launceston, now showed signs of being eaten away by the onset of rust from the nails that held it together. In other places, old doors with their paint stripped off by the weather, showing the wood rotting beneath or wooden sheets interspersed the pattern.

The barricade was finally topped off with curling loops of sharp razor wire.

Celeste looked at the patchwork quilt of bare wood and rusting metal, not really interested so much in its history, more so the history it could be helping to make today by allowing her a quiet, safe passage through to the other side.

She was careful not to alert the security guards as she began her inspection along the perimeter, holding out her arm while allowing her fingertips to stroke softly the mismatched textures of rough and smooth panels, just as a blind person would read some Braille text.

Her experienced touch searched for one particular panel. This one single piece of rusting metal may, or may not, present her with yet another problem.

Hobbling along, Celeste tried to remember all of the weaknesses the barricade had and kept secret with only a few people being trusted with the knowledge. She found the one and now it would be as if the barrier might not even have been in place for her.

She stopped with a wry smile and as she turned to face the challenge, her fingers slowly stroked the surface of the metal panel again. Ah yes, this was definitely the one she was looking for.

Each of her digits seemingly worked individually as Celeste began feeling around the edge searching for the hole that she needed, that she knew was there.

She tenderly stroked the panel, trying to seduce it into submission as she closed her eye while whispering sweetly to it. Then she began to pray the metal would fall to her charms.

The panel remained stuck.

It hasn't been moved in such a long time and is fixed in place by the build up of grime. Celeste pulled harder and it started to give. She let go and tensed up, 'please let me in.' she whispered while looking to the sky and with a final sharp tug, the panel moved and it remained quiet as she gently shifted it against another. Just like an old lover, the panel had relented, obeying her guiding hands, opening up just enough for her to penetrate the small opening.

Thankfully, it was still curfew on the other side and she was sure no one witnessed her emergence. Celeste knew that from here on in, the risk of her being caught by Enforcers was real. Thankfully she didn't pass anyone along her route and this made her feel a little more relaxed about her actions, if not her intentions.

With the adrenaline rushing through her body, it eased her pain and sharpened her focus, helping her to keep the distractions of her recent ordeal from her alert mind.

'This is the opportunity I've been waiting for,' she thought as she continued to skulk about the streets and in her new frame of mind even this part of the town somehow looked different to her.

It seemed the soul of Launceston was something more than just a place where the unwanted had gathered. Through following the misguided directions of a mad man, they had unwittingly built a community.

This town was definitely worth saving, especially from the lunatic in control and besides, this place was her home.

As quietly as she could Celeste headed across the green for the compound and then on to the Reformation Centre. She made her way through the make-shift pens housing the town's livestock.

Some of the more skittish creatures livened up at her disturbance and eventually Celeste was out and in complete darkness. The centre looked just as impressive as it did in the light of day, especially to anyone being introduced to it for the first time.

From the outside, the tall black painted walls of the compound bore down oppressively on her from their great height. They implied on her this is a building of some importance within the compound. You only had to look at it to be able to tell that this foreboding structure emanated control, discipline and repression.

The building had been constructed in such a way that it was impossible for anyone crazy enough to attempt to break out, would it be the same for anyone insane enough to break in?

However, Celeste Baker wasn't just anybody, she was not crazy, or insane as far as she was aware, but she was just desperate and it wasn't just her life that depended on her gaining entry.

Standing silently in the shadows of the buildings, she watched the street, making sure no one was about to witness her arrival and entrance.

If someone had told her a year ago, that this would be happening to her, that she would be hiding in the shadows of Launceston, evading the authorities like one of the criminals she had been trained to chase, hunt and capture, she would have had them locked up for lunacy.

Celeste couldn't help letting a slight giggle of irony erupt, but told herself now is not the time to analyse the situation.

'It is what it is.' She thought.

It is what she wanted, she realised as she looked up in the direction of the penthouse and watched the light in Lattimer's room being extinguished.

'It's time that bastard was taught a lesson.' She thought.

It was going to be up to her to give it to him, the only question was how?

All that stood in the way of getting into the compound was a hidden hatch. A doorway that was not a secret among the trainees, it was somehow ignored by the Enforcers. They seemed to have ignored the nocturnal comings and goings of the youngsters, allowing them a small victory.

She approached the wall and placing her hand behind a piece of downpipe, she felt for a concealed latch. Baker hoped it had remained in working order as her fingers pressed down on it hard. She hadn't used it since passing out as a fully-fledged Enforcement Officer some years back.

There was a slight but gratifying click, followed by the release of the small square hatch.

Celeste puffed as she squeezed herself through the tiny opening that was only really big enough for a child and a fit one at that.

She agonisingly pushed and pulled her body through the opening. Once inside, for her it was now a simple case of avoiding the few hundred Enforcement Officers that were beyond the wall and trying to remember the route to take along the passages and corridors.

At last she found herself looking at the closed door of the room that had been assigned to Robert Garforth and carefully turning the knob she blinked at the sudden release of the latch.

She firmly took hold of the door, slowly pushing it open hoping the hinges didn't make any sound as she remembered they usually did and when it was open enough Celeste slipped inside and closed it behind her.

After a moment with her back against the panelled slab of wood, she reopened it slightly and peeked through the gap making sure no one had seen her.

Closing the door firmly shut she turned and her heart sank to her stomach while her stomach jumped into her throat.

She was shocked to see the empty room and instantly Celeste felt the thump of realisation hitting her from inside her head, the empty room only meant one thing.

Robert Garforth was dead.

She guessed, without knowing the details, that Lattimer was again responsible for this as well as her other losses.

The score was starting to increase in his favour; he was winning in the body count stakes.

Crouching low, Celeste painfully moved to the window and sat on the floor while cradling her knees. She looked through a tear-filled eye at the bare bed and felt the tickle of tears on her cheek as they travelled down her face.

She turned her head and looked at the open but empty wardrobe. Her eyes fell to the floor of the cupboard and stared at Garforth's D.I.A.L.

All Enforcers have a 'Died in Action Locker', it was a type of safe where they kept personal possessions and letters to be passed onto whoever they wished, but only in the event of their demise.

Celeste crawled on all fours over to it and stretching out her hand, she slowly and tenderly touched it. The sensation of the cold metal was too much for her emotions and she finally gave in, breaking down and quietly sobbing uncontrollably, contorting her face and silently lashing out at thin air to release the anger and frustration she felt.

Pure anger flowed through her, not only for the loss of possibly the only real friend in the world, but she also realised now that it was Garforth who had been at the house.

If only she had called out to him from the barn, to warn him of what was going on, then maybe, just maybe, he would still have been alive today.

But her life has never been that well organised and it was not as though she planned any of this. It appears her life now had a different purpose and it would seem fate is going to reveal what that purpose is, in its own good time.

It was several minutes before Celeste was calm enough to open the box. She knew how, just as Garforth knew how to open hers and once opened she found an envelope.

It simply read, 'No 13'.

A pun on her name, a reference to a baker's dozen, it was also the date they had met and coincidently the room number where they had spent most of their training. Garforth had once said to her that for him, since meeting her, the number thirteen would be a lucky number.

Celeste tried to smile through the tears as she opened the white paper envelope and took out the note. She looked at the hand writing of black ink; it was neat and tidy just as Robert was.

'Celeste, if you're reading this letter then either I must be dead or you're being too damn nosey again. Seriously though, I have been ordered to the house to bring you to Lattimer. Now I don't know what's going on or if anything is wrong, but all I can think of is that the punisher sent to you has gone too far.

So I am on a hunt or a rescue, not that I want to be on either where you're concerned, but Lattimer is really pissed at you. He needs the stuff here as quickly as possible and sees your delay in getting it to him as a personal swipe. You know how he is, mentally I mean. Look I have a duty to do and if it all goes wrong, I want you to know, it's not your fault. If you are on the run then you need to be out of here as soon as you can, take the pouch. I've placed an ingot inside, I took it from a resistance member and when you show it to the right people, it will allow you access to the resistance. Use them to get away from Lattimer, but make sure you do it soon or you're going to face the same fate as me. You will always be my friend. Rob!'

Celeste picked up the small, black velvet pouch and held it to her face, imagining she could smell Robert close to her. She closed her eyes and cowered into the corner of the wardrobe and while crying quietly, she drifted off to sleep.

***

Maitland became vaguely aware of the feeling of pain as he started to regain consciousness. The massive headache, the vomit down his front and the room spinning out of control, he knew were classic symptoms of a concussion.

He lifted his hand to rub the egg-sized lump now protruding from the back of his head, but the lack of movement in his arm made him he realise he was tied to a chair. Slowly he opened his eyes, grimacing at the bright lights, remained bowed and all he could see were a pair of shiny, black leather boots standing in front of him.

He finally concluded he was in the deepest of deep trouble, possibly deeper than ever before and that pleased him.

He tried to raise his head, wanting to see the rest of whoever was using him as a punch bag, but the room span faster and the throbbing increased to what seemed a thousand fold.

He vomited again with his torso moving forward, he saw the pair of boots jump away from him, getting out of the firing line of Maitland's spew.

It was hard to ignore a clenched fist, the size and weight of a small club hammer, as it smashed into the side of his face. Maitland had the surreal feeling of being half awake and half asleep, while receiving the punch squarely to the jaw.

This was not the best of alarm calls, but it made him smile again as he recovered from his head being suddenly forced to one side by a well-placed punch from a leather-gloved hand.

Blood filled saliva erupted from Maitland's mouth, mixing with the vomit on his chest and floor, as any hope that this would be the fight which would kill him off, increased.

The trussed up Maitland recoiled, waiting for the next punch.

He didn't have to wait too long.

'Is that it? That's all you've got?' he spluttered, choking on the blood-filled spittle filling his mouth.

He then laughed.

The heavy set Enforcers were completely taken aback by his reaction, they weren't used to being laughed at, especially in the middle of an 'induction'. The prisoner was supposed to take this seriously, he was meant to play the game.

However, Maitland was in no mood for games.

He was without fear and there was no leverage for them to use against him. The Reaper was immune to their constant beatings and a new tack was needed by the Enforcers.

Unsure of how long he had been in the company of these wolves, Maitland continued to be 'inducted' for what seemed like hours. It was only when the door opened so that he could just make out through a small window in the corridor, dawn was somewhere on the horizon.

Another man, also dressed in black, entered the room and walked into Maitland's view. The others saluted him and Maitland struggled to keep his head raised and his vision from blurring.

He felt someone grab his hair from behind and become steady. Another hand appeared from the front, the fingers of this one gripped hard around Maitland's throat.

Today it was Maitland who was having the life crushed from him.

He mentally egged his captor on, wanting this new man to crush the windpipe even harder and it got to the point where Maitland tried to relax his neck muscles, in order to make it easier for them both to achieve their mutual goal of his death.

'Well now, tell me who you are and what the hell you're doing in Launceston?' The firm grip somehow contradicted the soft voice coming through slightly gritted teeth. This guy almost sounded warm, friendly even. Well friendly enough to give a frightened prisoner a false sense of security, had it not been for the fact he was trying to choke his prisoner to death that is.

Maitland managed another smile and showed his blood covered teeth as he opened his swollen lips.

'Fuck you!' He gasped, spluttering sticky thick, bloody saliva over his captor's jacket.

The man in black bent over to bring his face to the same level as Maitland and returned the smile.

'Tut, tut, bad language is a sign of ignorance. It belongs to the uneducated,' he let go of Maitland's throat and continued as the tethered man coughed some more, 'and I know you are not uneducated,' he moved his face to the ear of the trussed up prisoner, to make sure he could get close to whisper, 'in fact Mister Maitland, I know you are an awfully well educated and well travelled man, are you not?'

Maitland stopped smiling and tried to fix his eyes onto the face of the man in black, attempting to recognise his captor, as it clearly seemed he knew who Maitland was.

The dark shadow pulled back out of the focal range of Maitland's blurred vision.

'You see, your reputation precedes you Maitland,' he had the prisoner's complete attention, 'for instance, I know you are the famous Jon Maitland and that you are responsible for many, many deaths around the country, hence the reputation of 'The Reaper', but what I don't know is, why you are here?'

There was no reply from a breathless and bloodied Maitland.

'I take it you are responsible for the death of the Enforcer and the woman at Totnes, as well as the burning down the house with our property still inside.'

Maitland remained silent, trying to get the words to make some kind on sense in his jumbled head. He shifted his stare, trying to focus and make eye contact with his inquisitor, who suddenly became uneasy.

Daniel Archer decided to move further away from the prisoner.

Maitland moved forward in the chair and the tethers tightened against Maitland's straining muscles. Veins began to protrude in his arms and neck and his breathing remained heavy, this time to fuel his body as his hands clenched over the chair rests so tightly, his knuckles turned white.

'No answer eh? Yet another sign of ignorance, but not to worry Mister Maitland,' he said, being reassured that the prisoner remained tightly tethered.

Archer then became braver and once more he leaned into Maitland's face to continue in his arrogant tone, 'you will soon pay for your mistakes my friend. You see, we are so near to completing our goal that you being here cannot be a coincidence, but be sure of this Mister Maitland, we will not let you or anyone else stop us; do I make myself clear?'

Maitland began to shake and fight his restraints, trying to release himself. The man finally and sharply pulled away and headed for the door as he gave an instruction.

'Use the chilli powder on him; that will loosen his tongue.'

One of the guards nodded and from a shelf on the wall, he pulled a plastic tub containing a powdered red chilli mix.

The guard kept his gloves on as he gently peeled away the lid. The strong smell of hot spice instantly filled the room. He took a pinch between his thumb and finger and with Maitland's head still held tight he rubbed the powder hard into the helpless prisoner's eyes.

The other man began to close the door and a satisfying smile crept across his face at hearing the screaming prisoner.

The guard proceeded to dust his gloves in the powder.

'Don't kill him boys, I need that piece of shit alive. Lattimer will want to talk to him.' And with a wave of a stump where his hand used to be, the man in black finally left.

Chapter Nine

As Lattimer drifted off to sleep he felt himself falling, the room was spinning until his mind stopped at a point in time from his distant past. An adult Russell Lattimer watched the spectre of himself as a fourteen-year-old child. The boy was sitting on a sofa and was covering his face with his hands, shrouding the tears that were streaming from his eyes and not for the first time.

The invisible witness and the child reacted in the same way of gulping in fear when they heard the voice of a man shouting, coming from another room.

'What do you mean he's being bullied? Bullied for what and by whom?' Lattimer heard his father shout.

'I don't know Phil. I had a call from the school today; they said he was caught fighting with another pupil. We have to go tomorrow and sort it out.'

Russell Lattimer watched the child's reaction helplessly as the footsteps approach the living room and his angry father entered.

The boy seemed to know to keep his head down, even as an adult Russell felt he had to fight the need to do the same as he observed the events.

'What the hell have you been up to boy? Eh?'

The sad child didn't have a chance to answer as the angry parent walked out to once again shout at his wife.

'Well I'm not going. You'll have to deal with it. I am not going to apologise to anyone for anyone, especially for him. It's about time he took some responsibility for himself.'

The boy lifted his head and looked at the wall.

He imagined his father was now towering menacingly over his mother and always with a finger digging into her chest, ramming home every word he uttered, as was his way.

The boy laid himself out and placed one of the green scatter cushions over his ears.

It was fifteen minutes before the back door slammed shut and he heard his mother come in.

'It's OK love, he's gone.'

He pushed himself to a seated position and allowed the cushion to fall to the floor.

His mother huffed, picked it up and replaced it on the sofa, smoothing out the creases.

'Come on lad; don't do that, you know he'll go mad again if this room is untidy when he gets back.'

After releasing the soft padded parcel, she sat next to him and dusted off the arm of the sofa, where his head had lain.

The lonely child smiled a little, as he put his arms around her and held her tightly. He could hear her heart beating in her chest.

Apart from his own, hers was the only other heartbeat he had ever heard.

After a minute, she gently pushed him away.

'Look love, are you going to tell me what happened?'

He shook his head quickly, panic glazed his eyes and a deep blush siphoned into his cheeks.

'It was nothing mum.'

'Putting a lad in hospital isn't nothing Russell,' she said softly, 'come on, you can tell me anything you know.' She added with her maternal smile that he trusted.

He could feel the frustration starting to build again and he didn't want to shout at her, he wasn't like his dad, not where she was concerned.

The child pulled away from her and held his head with a hand on each temple and he shook with anger and rage.

He stood up and she could see the same anger in his eyes that he had inherited from his father.

'It's because I'm different mum, because I have this skin, the others all laugh at me, they all call me names.' He shouted.

'Oh Russell, I wish I could help you, why didn't you say something before it got to this point.' She held him tight and kissed his forehead.

'It'll be alright son, I'll make it better.'

'How mum?' He questioned. 'How are you or anyone else going to make this better?' The teenager held out his hands. 'Are you going to make this disappear? Can you make me better? No you can't, why even try to make me feel better about it.'

He turned his back on his crying mother to look out of the window and watch some youngsters on the street kicking a football between them.

'You know they're right, don't you, when they call me a freak I mean. You know he's right too, when he says I should have been aborted, should never have been born.'

The shocked mother looked at her son, disappointment, torment and resignation flashed over his face.

'No Russell no, they are all wrong, if they could only see what I see. If they could look behind your condition and see what a loving caring child you are then...' she stopped.

He smiled at his mother.

'You're wrong mum because you only see what you want to see, you don't know me anymore. You don't know what dark thoughts fill my head. I'm angry and bitter and now I don't want to be anyone's target any more. Andrew got what he deserved and some of the others will get theirs too.'

He turned to her and held her hand.

'But you. You deserve better than this, better than me and certainly better than him.'

'What do you mean Russell, better…?'

He didn't let her finish, the young Russell Lattimer stormed from the room, out into the street

The adult Lattimer observed from behind the white net material cover the window and saw their fear of him on the other children's faces.

Still fuming, the youngster stopped in front of one boy.

'Give me the ball, I want to play.' He demanded.

The boy held onto the ball, refusing to give in to him.

'You know what happened to Andrew today don't you?' He said quietly to the terrified child.

He nodded.

'Do you want the same?'

He grudgingly relinquished the ball to Lattimer, he and the other children then ran away from him.

From today, no one is going to bully him. Not one person is going to call him a bad name ever again. Today Russell Lattimer decided his own path in life.

Even through sleep Lattimer was aware he was dreaming, he was not surprised when he felt the room spin again, flashing past the court case in which he was acquitted of any wrongdoing by a sympathetic jury, and at school some things had changed, other kids became frightened of crossing him.

When the adult Russell Lattimer looked again he saw the child was a little older, maybe in his final year at school and a party was organised, as is the tradition.

He, of course, had no intention of going, only to watch others having a good time with their friends or dancing with girls. Then one day at lunch, about a week before the party, as he sat alone eating the sandwich his mother made, a girl approached him in the dining room.

'Russell... I... err... are you going to the party on Saturday?' She shyly asked him.

He sat up, shocked by the question.

He looked behind her to see if anyone was watching or laughing, but no one was.

He looked up at her.

It was the first time she had ever spoken to him, even though they shared an English lesson, but he never noticed her before now.

'I wasn't planning to go, why?' He asked wary of the motivation behind her enquiry.

Her face had reddened as she approached him, but now she was almost purple.

Lattimer studied her as he waited for her soft voice to speak to him again.

Her name was Sonya, a mixed race girl with mocha coloured skin, which looked smooth and inviting to touch.

Her dark hair was straightened from its normal wave of curls and down the side of her cheeks she had signs of side burns growing and above her plump kissable lips sat the impression of a moustache.

His mind was not on the additional hair on her face; it was on how lovely she looked, how her smile warmed him and how he wanted to dive into her eyes, which were like two pools of chocolate sauce. He wanted to swim inside her soul.

Sonya held her head high.

'I was wondering; would you take me to it please.' She added a smile.

He thought for one second of her proposition.

'Why me?' He questioned suspiciously.

She shrugged her shoulders.

'This isn't a wind up, is it Sonya?'

She shook her head and grabbed one of his sore covered hands. She held on to it, not pulling away, although he tried to at first. However, the softness of her touch was something he had only felt from his mother's hand, yet this was different, this was a girl touching him and he liked it.

No, he loved it.

'I don't think you're as bad as people say you are and besides who's going to ask me out? Look at all this hair!'

She bowed her head with slight playful embarrassment and they both sniggered.

'But you're so lovely Sonya, even with the hair. Yeah all right, let's do it.' With his heart racing and palms sweating, he smiled at her.

'We can be freaks together.' She added with a smile.

That night, Russell went home happy, he had got a date with a real girl and he couldn't wait to tell his mum.

He put his key in the door, it didn't fit.

He tried again. The key definitely did not fit.

He rang the bell and used the ornate, pseudo Victorian door knocker.

There was no answer.

He looked through the window and saw nothing between the holes that formed the white net curtain.

The room was empty of everything, furniture, pictures and the television had gone. The panicked boy turned around. The car was gone and by his side he found a cardboard box and two bags.

Inside the large brown envelope attached to the box was a note to him and some money.

'My darling Russell, I am sorry but your father has sold the house. We have gone and I can't tell you where because he won't tell me. I have packed some of your clothes here and have left you two thousand pounds in cash to start you off.

I'm so very sorry son.

Mum.'

An explosion of anger ripped through his body, as it went far beyond any control he had. The front door flew open, relenting to his determined kicks, splitting the frame.

Every child, especially a son, should be able to look at their own father and see him as a hero. Russell Lattimer had only a coward for his, a weak man who had no time for his only son and didn't have the courage to help the child.

He stormed around the house calling out for his mother, but there was no answer. He looked out of the kitchen window and saw the garden had been freshly manicured and the patio had been cleaned of weeds. It also looked as though some of the slabs had been relayed, but he didn't recall there being a need for it.

A deflated Russell walked out from the empty house and took only the money, leaving everything else behind when he walked away.

At Sonya's house he told her what had happened, her parents were kind enough to take him in and there he stayed for three months without incident.

The love between the teenagers grew until Sonya was eventually ready to go the next step with him.

They had the house to themselves, her parents had to go away for a family thing and when he entered her bedroom, he knew she was naked under the duvet.

'Hello.' He said softly with a big smile.

Sonya smiled back.

'We don't have to do this you know.' He reassured her.

She nodded her understanding with the same smile and slowly removed the cover.

It was the first time Russell had seen anyone naked in real life and even though she was a little overweight and hairier than he expected most women to be, for him she was the most beautiful girl in the world.

He began to unbutton his shirt.

This also was going to be the first time she would see a man naked and the excitement grew in them both. He moved to the bed and removed the shirt, discarding it on the floor as he lay next to her.

Her hands immediately retracted away from him, he looked into her eyes; they showed him that she was repulsed by his body, disgusted by the touch of his flaking skin on her smooth hands and body.

Russell Lattimer had again been made to feel like rubbish by someone he loved. He didn't say anything to her, he didn't have to. He knew she loved him, he also knew how his problem had this effect on people.

He left her that day, never to return.

Chapter Ten

The white, candy floss clouds floated in the cool blue early morning sky, their whispery tails becoming tinged orange from the sun, as the bright ball of heat pulled itself over the horizon. Its invisible rays warming everything they kissed and with the opening of windows and the movement of people going about their business, Launceston woke to yet another beautiful day.

In the room once occupied by the late Robert Garforth, Celeste Baker stirred from her slumber with the sudden realisation of where she was.

She sat bolt upright and instantly an excruciating pain flashed through her body. The muscles in her neck had become twisted and stiff from sleeping in an awkward position in the empty wardrobe.

Groaning a little as the tight pain stabbed at her nerve ends, restricting her mobility to small careful movements. Celeste managed to keep the volume of her complaints low, so no-one outside the room would hear her as she moved.

After a while, the pain subsided and creeping over to the washbasin she stayed below the edge of the filth-covered window.

With great effort, she held on to the white china sink, hoping it would take her weight as she pulled herself up to look at herself in the broken mirror fixed to the wall.

Her face was still so badly swollen and bruised and at first glance she was quite unrecognisable, even to herself.

Her body was so very stiff, not only from the night's cramped sleep, but also from the beating she had endured and yet she managed to be more than a little shocked by her reflection.

The reverse image looking back upset her, it caused tears to well up and she felt the tickle of them behind her eyes.

'Come on girl, you've a job to do, so no feeling sorry for yourself Baker.' She whispered to the malformed doppelgänger who was looking back at her.

She needed to get out of the room and quickly, before someone found her. Still staying low, she crept to the door and placed her ear to its cold, painted wooden surface.

The sensation caused her body to shudder slightly, as she began to listen.

When she was sure there were no movements in the hallway, Celeste slowly opened the door wide enough for her to peek through the small gap with her good eye.

With Garforth gone, she had no-one she could really trust, Celeste Baker was completely alone and so very desperate for help.

'This is as good a time as any to call in any favours owed,' she thought to herself.

Thankfully it was clear on the outside of the room, it would seem luck was on her side and in one swift, but painful movement, she was out; shuffling along the corridor and on her way to the servant's quarters.

Unfortunately the quarters were situated on the lower floor, making it difficult in her weakened state to navigate. Add to that, the corridor overlooking the courtyard did not make it safe either as she limped her way along the hallway. The balconies of the upper floor were open to all sides of the square below holding little or no hiding place. If anyone below were to take the trouble to look up they would surely see her.

Fortunately, the luck she had with her remained, as not one person milling about below, chatting or going on patrol, looked up.

She watched from behind a pillar.

No one bothered to look up! Under normal circumstances this sort of complacency would have been reported and Celeste Baker, the Enforcer, would have had no compunction in dishing out the appropriate discipline or punishments. They were all taught to be vigilant at all times, no matter where they were.

But she wasn't that person anymore, so she carried on evading everyone, until she had eventually made it to her destination in one piece, without being detected.

She slowed her pace as the last door to open loomed, she prayed it was not locked as she began to carefully turn the highly polished brass doorknob.

Much to Celeste's relief it twisted in her hand and as quick as her body allowed, she quickly stepped inside closing the door behind her.

Inside the room, a surprised Marta Brunning spun around to see what she thought was a raging vagrant running at her.

The filthy tramp, with a dirty hand out-stretched, trying to grab at her. Marta gasped, preparing to scream, but like a frightened rabbit in the headlights of an oncoming car, she remained quiet and still.

Celeste took this time to place an encrusted hand over Marta's open mouth, just before the frightened woman found the ability to make, what would have been, a very loud terrifying yell. The last thing Celeste needed right now was someone raising the alarm, alerting others to finding her here and the thought of knocking Marta out for a while crossed her mind as one option, if the sound carried on much longer.

'Shush Marta, it's me, Celeste.' She whispered while taking off her cap then looking at the door, making sure no-one else came in. Marta realised it was her old friend, back from the dead and her eyes widened even more than before.

Marta stopped the noise and placed her hands gently on Celeste's and softly tugged at them, but only when Celeste was sure it was safe did she remove her hands, allowing Marta to breathe and talk.

'Oh Celeste, you're alive, we were told that you had been killed. What's happened to you? What have you done to your hair?' Before Celeste answered, Marta grabbed hold of the troubled woman and held on to her tightly.

'No time to explain Marta, I need your help, I want to get in touch with the resistance and please don't say you don't know who they are, because I know you are involved with them.'

Marta jumped, more than pulled herself away at the revelation of Enforcement having knowledge of her participation with the dissidents. It seemed as shocking as the first sight of a beaten Celeste storming into her room.

'But how? I thought I had been so careful.' Marta replied quietly.

For a moment the two women remained silent, they simply looked at one another, both thinking of what was going on and what the consequences of this discussion would be, for Celeste she also thought of how crazy her life was getting.

Time was ticking by and that was a luxury Celeste Baker had very little of. She grabbed Marta's hand, 'Please Marta, please help me do this, it's important to me. It's important to Launceston. I want their help, but I need your help in getting to them.'

Marta thought of what she should do and finally, Celeste released the soft hand and looked into her eyes.

'Look Marta, I'll be honest with you. I want to kill Lattimer,' she coldly added.

Marta's eyes widened again, but this time her mouth opened at the same time and when the words finally sank into her confused head a second later, she snatched her hand away from Celeste.

'You are joking, right?'

'No Marta I wish I was, but he's gone too far,' Celeste held out her open hands, 'innocent people are being killed for the smallest of reasons and the flimsiest of excuses.'

Marta turned her back on Celeste and looked out the window.

'You know Robert is dead, don't you?' Marta announced.

Celeste nodded to herself and whispered. 'Yes, do you know what happened to him?' Celeste asked and looked at Marta, who still had her back to Celeste. She saw the back of Marta's head as it shook a negative reply.

'You know something Marta; I think Lattimer had something to do with that too. Look, I found this in Rob's D.I.A.L.' She took the polished silver ingot from the pouch and asked Marta to look at it.

Marta twisted her upper body to take the ingot.

Celeste watched her reaction closely.

The small piece of metal seemed to make her uneasy as she examined it.

She seemed to conclude the risk Celeste was taking just by being here, was too great for it to be anything but serious and eventually she agreed to help.

***

Russell Lattimer woke with the rising sun shining over the town and onto his face. His only movement was the slow opening of his eyes, the rest of his body remaining quite still. He remained like that, allowing the memories of yesterday to climb back into his foggy head, reactivating his increasingly depressive state of mind.

Going through the details of these latest events, the troubled leader tried to find a link, a possible connection between them in some way.

Firstly, the resistance, these were an ungrateful group of people who seem determined, for reasons unknown to him, to interfere with his plans. However, for sometime now Lattimer had been very successful in controlling them, but their numbers kept growing.

It appeared, as soon as he stopped one of these bastards, there were another two waiting to take their fallen comrades place. Moreover, the resistance had suddenly become more active in recent weeks and had turned out to be a lot more troublesome than he cared for.

He determined that he had no choice, they now had to go.

Secondly, the people of the town were also becoming more defiant to his edicts, the use of punishment squads had increased of late. Disobedience was now so high, even the most loyal of Enforcers were beginning to test his authority and a good example of that was Celeste Baker of all people.

How dare she question assignments given by him?

'Who the hell did she think she was,' he thought with a tinge of anger moving around his chest as he lay in his bed.

He sharply turned himself over with his scab covered back facing the sun. He looked at the empty pillow on the other half of the bed and reached out his hand to stroke it.

Poor Celeste, she was such a lovely girl and in time she would have made a fantastic nurse, he thought, 'maybe even a wife,' he said aloud.

He sighed as this idea floated around his head.

Lattimer felt disappointed, as yet another opportunity for him to find a companion, had just passed him by.

His ever worsening mood increased.

Overnight he had somehow managed to mentally justify the murder of Robert Garforth, as well as rid himself of any feelings of regret or remorse he may have harboured. He woke this morning depressed, but with no feelings of guilt.

His twisted mind had theatrically distorted the fearful grimace on Garforth's face into a smile and then a laugh. Lattimer remembered how, just before the maddened leader plunged the knife into his students neck, Robert Garforth was actually laughing at him.

Last night he retired full of confusion, but today, he was comfortable at putting the deaths of the two promising students down to their own failures.

Then it suddenly dawned on him, it had been a while since he had killed anyone by his own hand. He had almost forgotten the intoxicating, euphoric feeling of the absolute God-like power that rushed through his whole body at the moment of taking a human life.

Picking himself up from the bed, he left dried blood stains on the sheets. It was his own blood, seeping from where he had scratched at his body, opening the sores as he slept. He walked naked into the shower and as the water played on his skin, he noticed more blood.

It was all that was left of Garforth and had remained in the shower from last night, as if he needed any reminding.

Stretching out he rubbed hard at the dried stain on the white, glass tile with his soaking wet hand.

The blood loosened and streamed down the wall swirling into the drain.

Now every sign of Robert Garforth's murder had disappeared and only one witness remained. He was very confident she was going to stay very quiet about that.

Lattimer continued to shower.

He then shaved and he loved how smooth his face felt after a good groom. It was in stark contrast to the rest of his skin. He splashed some cologne that stung as he applied it liberally across his cheeks and neck.

He dressed in his usual choice of a clean, white linen suit after which he made his way to sit at a large, dark oak dining table.

It had already been set for his much anticipated breakfast. For Lattimer, it was always a lavish affair, compared to the rest of the population of Launceston.

The kitchen knew in advance what he wanted and as today was Tuesday, he eagerly awaited the delivery of four rashers of grilled, smoked bacon, not crispy but definitely well done and it had to still be sizzling on his plate. These would be joined by two eggs, lightly poached and not broken, seated on top of two slices of wholemeal bread, toasted golden brown. This would be washed down with plenty of fresh, steaming hot, black coffee.

The serving woman knocked then nervously entered the room. She felt it was better for her to leave her trolley outside in the hallway, as she worried that the clattering of plates against the metal lids may disturb him.

She served him and signs of her nervousness of being alone in his company were clear, making it obvious she had heard about the murder of Garforth. Silently she busied herself around him, only glancing at her leader when he mumbled to himself, as a passing thought frustrated his thinking, or he would slap the side of his thigh while giggling to himself now and again.

His behaviour this morning, was more erratic than she had seen before, making her even more jittery than usual. She had difficulty in holding the plate still in her shaking hand as she placed it in front of him.

Finally she was done and could not get out of his presence quick enough. The old woman breathed a great sigh of relief when she pulled the door behind her, leaving him alone with his thoughts and whatever demons he had in his head.

The Elite Enforcer forgetfully picked at his meal and breaking the egg yolk with his knife, he watched as it spilled its oozing yellow contents over the toast and onto the plate.

In his mind the yellow had turned red.

He stopped and stared into space, just as he usually did whenever he became troubled and deep in thought.

He was lost in a world of his own and it was only a knock at the door that brought him back to earth.

Lattimer looked over at the door and blinked.

'Come!' He shouted loud enough to be heard from the other side of the panelled heavy door. The man with one hand confidently strode into the room, still dressed in the same black uniform he had worn the night before. His presence was in stark contrast to the glaring white of the room as he crossed to the table.

Archer approached the table and stopped abruptly, about a metre from the edge and saluted.

'Sir, we have taken a man into custody, he was picked up last night after he was found breaking curfew.'

Lattimer raised his eyebrows in surprise.

'Someone else has had the balls to disobey me Daniel!' he exclaimed while shaking his head.

Archer was careful to choose words which would cause the least aggravation to Lattimer.

'Yes Sir, but he is an outsider.'

'An outsider you say?'

'Yes Sir… err… It's Maitland.'

Lattimer's eyes widened, his jaw dropped open, as he sat for a moment in utter disbelief.

'Maitland.' Lattimer placed both hands over his mouth as if he wanted to capture the words as they fell out.

'What the hell is he doing here?' Lattimer snapped as he stood enraged at the news.

'I don't know Sir, he won't talk.' Archer lowered his head, ashamed that the tried and trusted, well used methods of getting information he personally devised, had no effect on their overnight guest.

'He's been going through induction all night but refuses to talk. I have come here directly to tell you.'

As Lattimer listened he became both agitated and exited, impatiently he waved his hand to silence his visitor.

'OK, Daniel, keep him where he is, but don't kill him. No, don't you dare kill him. I want to be able talk to him myself.'

The one handed man acknowledged the instruction from his boss with a silent and deliberately exaggerated nod.

Without looking, Lattimer returned it.

'OK, I need some time to think, Daniel. Have him ready for me, tomorrow afternoon, in the penthouse. I have to go to Tintagel to discuss our losses.'

The man in black again nodded, turned and began to leave.

'Oh and Archer,' Lattimer's voice became calm again and he sat back in his seat.

The man stopped and turned to look at the despot.

'The next time you speak to me you will not tell me anything, you will inform me and make sure you have a clean uniform on, there's a good chap.'

Archer looked down at his uniform and seeing a small amount of blood glistening in the sunlight he deflated slightly.

'Yes Sir. Sorry Sir.' He replied meekly.

Lattimer saluted with a gesture of his hand, indicating to Daniel Archer he should now leave the room. Within five minutes of Archer leaving, Lattimer had made his way through the door at the foot of the castle and walked through the well maintained garden, leading him to the base of the Kernow wall.

It was only here that Lattimer was permitted entry through the gateway, but only under armed guard and he was escorted to and from his pre-arranged destination.

The treatment of him not being trusted and the looks of suspicion that came from the guards, always made Lattimer realise that in Kernow, he would be a little fish in an extremely large pond. It was not a feeling he liked, as it always reminding him of the old days.

He looked up at the towering, featureless, drab grey structure and a sudden feeling of insignificance washed over him. He dismissed it as he finished his journey to the gatehouse.

Lattimer took a black metal key from a pocket inside his white suit and inserted it into the awaiting hole in the door. He turned it anti-clockwise and smiled when it made a satisfying clunk.

Removing the key with one hand, he pulled on the handle of the bare wooden door with the other.

It freely opened at his touch.

Lattimer entered the wooden gatehouse and when he emerged on the other side he looked at the flag of a white cross on a black background.

The flag of Saint Piran stood proudly, displayed for all who entered the gatehouse to see.

The monochromatic pennant dated back many centuries. It had become a sign, an iconic representation of how Kernow had always been an apolitical part of England, no matter what those governments thought. It is a symbol the people not only embraced, but also protected as part of their identity and heritage, never more strongly, than in the years following 2012.

These visits were the one thing Lattimer knew always lifted his spirits; he was still smiling when he sat and almost blended into the white fabric sofa, in what he called 'the waiting area'.

While he sat in silence, waiting for the guard to take him the rest of the way, Lattimer played out his misguided plans in his head.

He envisaged a new goal for him to reach; a dream, that once inside the wall, he would quickly rise to an important position within whatever Government there may be, eventually taking the country as his own.

The Elite Enforcer must have dozed off because he woke to find himself in the back of a solar powered vehicle with two guards either side of him.

'Technology is a most fantastic tool,' he thought as they drove, almost silently and at breath taking speed towards his appointment.

***

Celeste had remained alone pretty much all day in her friend's room with Marta Brunning returning at regular intervals to make sure her guest was comfortable. On one visit Marta had brought some food and drink with her, for which Celeste was eternally grateful.

Marta's mood seemed more and more up-beat with each visit, giving Celeste the impression her friend was seeing this as some sort of adventure, brightening up her otherwise boring and humdrum life.

For Celeste, it was fast becoming a nerve racking game of cat and mouse, one she wished was over or more correctly, a game she wished had never started.

There was no one the ex-Enforcer could really rely on and all the while she was in this room, a feeling of vulnerability quickly built inside.

Sitting on Marta's bed her adrenaline waned and as she thought about the things that had happened Celeste's mood worsened and self doubt entered into her mind.

'What now Baker?' she quietly asked herself as she lent backward to allow gravity to take her down to meet the comfort of the soft mattress below. She used the time to reflect on the whole situation again.

Since she could remember, she had always felt out of place, even in the compound amongst the others of her class. She never really had a sense of belonging that she so longed for. However, she always had a sense of purpose hiding inside her; it was something she was never sure about, until now that is.

When a passing thought of Robert Garforth ran through her mind, she allowed a tear or two to fall, but once those gates were opened, a torrent of emotions flooded out.

In just under a fortnight she had gone from star pupil to outlaw. She had been beaten, abused, rescued and finally abandoned, all in a few days and a sobbing Celeste Baker fell into a sound sleep.

***

Jon Maitland was exhausted and completely disorientated by this latest and possibly most thorough beating he had ever received. It finally ended when the one handed Daniel Archer returned to the room.

Fortunately, the strong hot smell of chilli powder was still in the air, as it masked the smell that was coming from the prisoner, who was still tied to the chair and was so weakened by the torture, that his bodily functions were no longer controlled by him.

Between the chilli powder 'bed bath' and the workout the goons had given him, Maitland was feeling tremendously hot and even though he was sweating profusely, he shivered. It vaguely felt to him like he was suffering from sunstroke or some kind of intoxication, though he had no recollection of having had any alcohol.

The room was still spinning, with his whole face feeling heavy and unsteady on his shoulders; Maitland knew that if he were able to stand, he would certainly fall over.

Perhaps they had used a drug mixed in with the hot red powder. He just didn't know, nor did he actually care.

With a simple nod, Archer was able to dismiss the tired guards, who were just as thankful for the break as Maitland, and as they closed the door Archer pulled out a chair to sit directly in front of his prize captive.

With folded arms, Archer sat opposite Maitland, simply looking at the now harmless Reaper.

The two remained like that for some time with Daniel Archer patiently observing and making notes, trying to join bits and pieces of anything he might recognise or regard as important, as he listened to the disoriented prisoner.

Maitland disjointedly moaned and groaned through his dry, swollen lips, while his bloodied head bobbed and lolloped loosely on his shoulders.

Daniel Archer needed to know why Maitland had turned up at Launceston, after all everybody had an agenda, a motive to do or be somewhere, so why would Maitland be any different?

Archer remained seated, silently watching his captive.

An hour had passed since the end of the beating and Maitland started to regain a modicum of lucidity in his mumblings. He screamed out time and again and Archer thought he heard the names Laura and Emily.

Maitland shouted the word 'no' so many times, as though he was begging someone to stop whatever it was he could see behind those closed eyes, as he relived some terrible incident in the past.

Still concentrating on his prisoner, Archer stood and walked over to a table. He picked up a jug of water and began to pour the ice-cool liquid into a glass.

Maitland's sense of hearing was not impaired as he reacted to the recognised sound of flowing water. He tried to look through his swollen eyes in the direction of where he thought the sound was coming from, but he struggled to focus on its source.

Archer smiled. 'Would you like a drink of water Mister Maitland?' he asked rhetorically.

Maitland began to smack his dry, sticky lips together. He then used his tongue to force them open and gasp what sounded to Archer like 'Water... Water.'

Archer returned to his seat.

He placed the glass of refreshing liquid to Maitland's mouth and almost on contact tiny lumps of dried blood detached from beaten lips and sank in the clear glass, creating a maelstrom of pink and red as they disintegrated on their decent to the bottom.

Not having the sense to care if the water had been tampered with, Maitland took a large sip and allowed the tasteless substance to swirl around his mouth and quench the dryness. As it sloshed about his mouth, the blood washed away and he swallowed hard.

The water was so refreshing as it travelled down his arid throat and Archer permitted him to take another bigger sip.

The sip turned into a gulp until finally, he had guzzled the contents completely.

'Now Mr Maitland,' Archer said, taking the glass away, 'we need to clean you up, tomorrow you have an audience with our leader, Russell Lattimer.'

Maitland started to come round a bit more, enough to understand what was being said to him at least.

'Do you understand me Maitland?' Archer enquired as he studied the wreck of a man sitting in front of him.

Maitland made what Archer took for a nod.

The Enforcer brushed his broad smile with the stump at the end of his arm.

'OK, that's good, now I'm going to cut your ties, but I don't want you to do anything rash, like trying to attack me, understand?' Archer was speaking slow and precise. 'You're in no fit state to fight anyone Maitland.'

Only when Archer was sure he would be safe did he commence cutting the ties holding Maitland's limbs. His left arm was released and Archer backed away from Maitland a little, just in case the prisoner used what little fight remained in him.

Archer crouched low and proceeded to release the right arm and Maitland obediently remained in the same position, trying to make sense of what was happening.

The Enforcement Officer stood up after cutting the final tie and moved his chair back into the corner where it had come from, he called out to the guards and instantly they re-entered the room.

'Take him to the infirmary, tell them he meets Lattimer tomorrow, I need him awake and talking, but he is not to have access to anyone else. Do I make myself clear?'

***

A startled Celeste jumped up far too quickly from her slumber, becoming dizzy and making her stumble as Marta rushed back into the room.

'Celeste, are you OK?' Marta asked as she rushed across the room to help her unfortunate friend.

'Yes I'm OK. Thanks.' Celeste softly whispered holding onto Marta's outstretched arm.

'Good, now come and sit down, I've some good news for you,' Celeste was guided back to the bed where they both sat down; 'you're in. I've spoken to my people and I have told them everything you told me. They are, of course, suspicious, but they're prepared to listen to you.'

Celeste managed a faint smile accompanied by a nod.

'Come on, we need to clean you up and then we will go to meet them,' it seemed more good fortune had just landed on Celeste's lap, 'but before that I'm taking you to see a friend of mine, she's a nurse.'

Celeste shot her a worried look.

'She's OK I promise you and you do need to have that eye seen to.' Marta held out her hand to gently stroke Celeste's face but the thought of the pain caused by her touch made Celeste jerk herself away from the soft hand.

Feeling a little more dejected by this rebuff Marta stood and quickly moved to a cupboard. She opened it and inside she found some clothes, her spare uniform which she took out and abruptly passed to Celeste.

'You can wash in the basin and change into these.' Her tone had cooled and she threw the clothes onto the bed.

'I'll be back for you in twenty minutes, you know, when they are all eating supper.'

Celeste thanked Marta and stood as her 'Good Samaritan' left the room.

Catching a glimpse of herself in the mirror ubiquitously fixed over the basin, Celeste was again surprised at the shock she felt at seeing her reflection.

She began to undress and her body fought back with agonising pain when she made sudden movements, like the raising of her arms. Getting out of these rags now seemed almost impossible and as soon she started to remove her clothes, Celeste realised just how filthy she was and even though she had showered at the house, the stench of the past week or so was still about her.

Limping over to look at the full length mirror, she saw how the bruising had made a fantastic tattoo of blacks, purples, blues and yellows covering her entire body.

Her inner thighs ached terribly, but the pain she felt over the rest of her body made it somehow less noticeable. Scabs had now formed over cuts, her wrists and ankles still were chaffed raw from the shackles.

She was a shocking sight, but at least her eye was at last showing signs of opening, with a glint of light getting through.

Moving to the sink, Celeste began to wash.

Chapter Eleven

Maitland groaned more than a little as he bounced on the bed, having been dropped onto it by the heavy-set goons. They moved away looking at one another with satisfying grins, as they had to remain in the room, they stood at the end of the bed with their arms folded.

He could hear them being reprimanded by the, rather well rounded, pudding of a nurse, while other nurses began to examine and clean their new patient. The orders from Lattimer were to ensure Maitland did not talk to anyone and that included the staff. The guards watched as the medical staff busied themselves around their prisoner.

If any rumours got out that he were here in Launceston, it would only be seen as encouragement for the resistance to become more active. Besides, if he was here working for, or with, the resistance; his capture would make for good propaganda in helping to crush those that are actively against Lattimer and his plans.

'What have you idiots done to this poor man? He's been nearly beaten to death, you know you Punishers go too far sometimes, you know, just too far. Who is he? What has he done?' The Matron cheerfully fussed over him, while aiming the quick fire questions and reproaches at the two silent and slightly embarrassed guards.

They had to cut Maitland's clothes from his body, which as they were new to him, he somehow regretted, although the thugs had re-dressed him only minutes before delivering him here.

The nurses gave him what little medication they could afford and when they had finally done all they could to make him a little more comfortable, he was left to rest in the medical bed.

The small amount of sleeping draft seemed to be working, he started to relax and throughout the rest of the day he drifted in and out of consciousness.

He was not sure of what was real or a dream.

For a moment he was back with his beloved family and he really could smell her cooking, hear their laughter and singing, but then the sounds faded into the screams of those so cruelly lost to him.

Suddenly he was flying and he landed in some place where he had just saved a young woman from being attacked. Maitland could still see the blood of a man running down his hands as he looked at them, but it was suddenly his blood and it was him being beaten.

Maitland slowly became aware of his surroundings, the noises and smells of a hospital were universally unmistakable, no matter where you were, even in this world, a hospital was still a hospital.

The instincts he had honed and relied on for so many years returned to him. He kept his eyes closed trying to remain completely still, giving his audience the impression of still being out cold.

Only after a few minutes of listening did he carefully and exactingly open his eyes, but just enough to see what was happening around him.

Uniformed nurses were silently walking around the room and he could only hear and feel the matron gently tending to his medical needs, as she had with so many other uninvited visitors to Launceston, he thought.

Moreover, it was up to her to make sure this particular VIP, yet another victim of a punishment gang, was treated well and she made sure that all of her patients were treated the same, no matter who they were, or what they had done wrong.

Perhaps it was something to do with the Hippocratic Oath these nurses had to take, or maybe if he did happen to die while in her charge, she knew it wouldn't be too long before the same fate befell her.

The threat of death is the incentive keeping her concentration focused.

At the foot of the bed, all he could see was the folded arms of one of the guards; he knew the other was standing next to him with his arms folded as well. Maitland also knew they both had the same miserable grimace on their ugly faces as they silently kept watch.

A sudden and excruciating pain shot through his body, he had trouble telling where it hurt or where it come from, but it caused him to wince and the matron noticed.

'Ah you're awake, good.' She was a middle-aged woman who, in her younger days may have been attractive enough to some, but the ravages of time, babies and poor diet had taken their toll on her. She was a large woman that could even be described as rotund. She was remarkably assertive with her barking constant orders at the staff and as expected they reacted like sheep that were being chased by an obese member of the canine species.

Maitland was sure, by the look on some of the nurse's faces, that the woman was not popular within their ranks.

Matron left his bedside for a moment, only to return with two other nurses and all three helped Maitland move into an upright position, an exercise that was carried out in complete silence, except for the moans and groans of the battered and bruised patient, as he was pulled from one to the other.

They finished with their fussing and she ordered the nurses away with just a look, this left the Matron to smooth out the bed alone. She stood with her back to the guards, taking hold of Maitland's wrist.

'My, you have been busy with that.' She commented about the scars on his wrists, then looking down at the traditional nurse's watch pinned to her buxom right breast hemmed into her slightly too small uniform, she quietly monitored his pulse with her soft gentle fingers.

Maitland looked up to get a better view of the serious Matron and she diverted her eyes from the face of her watch to the face of her patient.

There was a definite hint of a smile on her tiny mouth set in her ballooned checks, she then added a wink.

The small room had been painted grey, probably the only colour they had, as it was the same as the room where he had received his beating; only these walls were free of his blood.

They obviously did not want him on a ward; that would be far too public and much too easy for him to make his escape. As he lay there, he could see the windows had been barred from the outside.

'I see you have met my husband. How are the eyes? Still burning?'

Maitland remained silent but his eyes suddenly darted back to his carer and his look said it all.

'The chilli powder, it's one of his favourite methods, you know, ever since he accidentally rubbed some into his own eye, while he was cooking us a meal one evening.'

There was a boastful tone to her voice at the cruelty that the one handed man could inflict on a person.

'Oh it was a lovely meal.' She sighed as she fussed over him some more. 'You know, I think he gets a bit jealous of uninvited strangers, especially those who are fully equipped.' She gently touched his hand to demonstrate her meaning. 'It's a good thing you have me here. You know, to make you all better I mean.'

For a second he thought he was still dreaming but continued to look at her completely amazed in what she was saying.

'You know, he hurts you, they bring you here. I fix you up, then they take you back, where it starts all over.' She remained smiling and friendly in her manner as she spoke. 'It's the best of both worlds here, pain and pleasure in the one place.' She finished bustling over him and sat on the edge of the bed.

'Now, why don't you tell me, you know, what you're doing here?'

He looked at her, the continued use of 'you know' every time she opened her mouth was beginning to grate on him.

He remained silent.

He had no answer for their questions. Well, not the answer they wanted, because he genuinely did not know why he had returned.

'Still not ready to talk then eh? OK, suit yourself,' she said, still sickeningly chirpy, 'you had better get some rest, I'll be back to see how you're doing, I'm off to cook a lovely meal for when my Danny gets back from work and who knows, if you really are a good boy I may even give you a, you know, special treat.' She gently touched the blanket where his manhood was and still smiling she stood, winked at him again and then left the room for him to be alone with the two ever vigilant guards.

Maitland sat in bed in utter disbelief before he looked at the bigger one of the guards and playfully blew him a kiss. The brute's face showed his disapproval and complete contempt as he took a small step forward, but the other, slightly smaller guard placed a hand on his arm to hold him back.

Deciding to sleep Maitland smiled and lay back down; after all he was in no real state to do anything else at the moment, even if the Matron had, you know, other things on her mind.

***

Celeste Baker sat on the bed waiting for the return of Marta Brunning. For the normally active Enforcer, this inactivity only helped to slow time down to a snail's pace, making seconds seem like minutes, with the hours becoming excruciatingly boring.

She was not used to idly lazing about, nor did she like it, as it allowed her to think. So she busied herself around the room and curiosity got the better of her. She started to look around, searching cupboards, drawers and even under the bed, not looking for anything in particular, just being nosey and she found nothing.

In fact, there was so much nothing it seemed impossible, not a single item of interest or out-of-place. Marta had remained as dull as when she was a novice officer. There were no clues to her personality and this troubled Celeste.

She sat watching from the bed as dusk turned to night on the other side of the glass window. The door finally opened and Marta popped her wide eyed face through the gap wearing a huge smile.

'Celeste, come quickly.' She ordered and without a second thought Celeste got up and followed.

Once again she was sneaking around the corridors and passages of the Reformation Centre, but at this time of the evening it was quiet with not too many people about to cause the girls a problem. Mercifully the stillness made it a little easier to escape and at last they were through the hidden door, out in the cold night air; scurrying along the dark streets.

Celeste turned her head to watch the door as it clicked shut. The sound of an alarm bell began sounding distantly in her ears accompanied by the question, 'Was that a little too easy?'

There was no time to wait for the answer, it was curfew and they needed to be off the street and out of sight as soon as possible.

She followed Marta as they quickly and silently moved in the darkness, hiding in shadows at the sound of nearby Enforcers. Finally they arrived at a small detached cottage, it looked ancient; maybe two hundred or more years old, she followed as Marta darted around to the back door.

She confidently rapped on the condensation frosted window of the back door and without waiting for anyone on the inside to answer, she opened the door.

Marta entered and ushered Celeste into what turned out to be the kitchen of the house.

It was warm and stuffy, as none of the windows were open to allow for any type of ventilation of the heat from the wood burning stove.

The cream appliance was covered with pots of boiling water, happily steaming away with their lids wobbling from the bubbling and foaming liquid being boiled.

The presence of two dark oak beams that were tied to the bare, red brick walls made the ceiling seem lower than it really was. The room appeared smaller than it should have been. This illusion was helped by the dull and dirty walls which had remnants of cream coloured plaster here and there and the badly cracked, dark red flagstone floor looked just as greasy and filthy as the walls.

It was a depressingly drab room.

Whoever lived here tried to add a bit of colour and cheer by placing photographs in frames along the shelves, intermingled with the cooking utensils and pots stacked on an old wooden dresser.

It looked to her that the dresser had been painted some time ago with the same magnolia paint as the walls.

Soon the two women were greeted by another.

She was in a nursing uniform and Celeste assumed it had not been long since she had finished her shift.

'Ah, there you are. Come in won't you? Please sit down.' She smiled as a nervous Celeste was gently directed to a brown wooden dining chair.

Celeste obeyed and followed her to the chair and sat at the table.

It was laid out with what should have been a clean, white tablecloth, but was instead, covered with old stains, which in turn was covered in an assortment of medical equipment and potions, alongside the vegetables and what looked like lamb chops on a plate ready for the pan. Apparently this nurse was preparing to make the evening meal, as well as preparing for Celeste's visit.

Even though this was not the most hygienic treatment Celeste had received in her life, this medic was surprisingly well equipped considering it was black market medication and the pain was so much she would accept any treatment right now.

'Well my dear that eye looks very nasty indeed, what happened to you?' the jolly medic asked.

'I... Err... tripped over and hit my face when I fell down some stairs.'

'Oh dear, it looks painful, what's your name my dear?'

'I'm... Linda.' Celeste lied.

'Well Linda, let's have a closer look at that eye of yours shall we?'

Celeste again obeyed and slowly reclined her head back to allow the examination to begin. Her whole face was still so very tender, she was still reluctant to let anyone touch it and Celeste screamed out as even more pain covered her face.

The nurse didn't use the well trained, gentle touch Celeste had expected. Instead she opted to force the eyelid open with her thumb and forefinger a little more than it naturally would have done with this type of injury.

There was a definite smile of sadistic satisfaction on the face of the medic as she pulled away from her patient. She wasn't sure, but Celeste formed the opinion the nurse was almost in a moment of sexual excitement.

'It's OK, you know, it's nothing to worry my dear. Here put some of this ointment on and wear this eye patch for a few days. It will soon be as right as rain and open again.'

Celeste took the items and applied them as instructed.

'Then you can come back and, you know, we can have another look at it, to see how you're doing.'

Celeste's face throbbed hard at the pain and while the nurse began to clear the table of the medicines, she chatted some more.

'Where did this happen to you Linda?'

'It was at my house, I was running when I tripped.' Celeste noticed the nurse look at the watch pinned to her uniform for the third time in less than five minutes. That distant alarm that she could hear was getting louder. Celeste looked around the room to see if anything was amiss.

There, on the dresser.

The line of smiling faces looking out from the frames. One of the pictures, Celeste recognised a face.

Celeste suddenly stood up.

'I have to go now.' She was still looking at the photo of Daniel Archer with his handless arm draping around the large woman while he kissed her bulbous check.

The nurse smiled. 'Go where Linda?' She put an emphasis on the name. Celeste looked at the door from where she entered the house. It was now being locked by her so-called friend.

'I am sorry Celeste but I had to, you see it is my duty, isn't that right Auntie?'

A dumbstruck Celeste stood frozen in time at hearing the revelation. Marta Brunning was related to Daniel Archer, a fact that even Enforcement didn't know. As far as Celeste was concerned, Marta was a normal girl, she had almost grown up with her and besides she was part of the resistance.

Celeste looked at the Matron who had a large grin as she gently nodded confirmation to Celeste.

'But why Marta? Why didn't you tell me? I thought we were supposed to be friends.

Marta walked over to Celeste and gently stroked her face, she was not going to take no for an answer this time and touched the damaged face with her shaking fingers.

'So did I, but I wanted us to be so much more than friends,' Celeste frowned trying to work out what was happening, 'but you spoilt that when you chose Amber. How could you pick that red headed bitch over me as your lover?'

'But Marta you never said anything to me. You were always interested in Robert. When you failed at being an Enforcer, you were sent back to serving, that's when you moved out of our room.'

'I didn't fail, I asked to go back, I asked because of you! Because I couldn't bear to see or hear you and her together, but when the time came I fixed her didn't I!'

Fury enveloped Celeste as her heart fell into her stomach, her body twitched in frustration and she sat down, unable to react at what she was hearing.

She could feel her heart breaking again at remembering the loss of her beloved Amber.

'You're to blame for Amber leaving me, leaving Launceston. You're the one who reported our other friends, had them killed.' Celeste started to shout at Marta.

'How the hell can you put this down to me Celeste? This is entirely your fault for lying to me, for making me feel foolish and no good.' Marta shouted back, her face twisted and tears falling, 'when we heard you had been killed I grieved for you, but I also thought it was no more than you deserved.' Her tone softened as she continued, 'but then you came back, alive and well and you came to me for help, I thought it was my birthday, you had come back to me.'

'Don't flatter yourself Marta, I only came to you because Robert was dead.'

The nurse gently interrupted.

'Now, now, don't fight my dears. Marta your uncle will be here soon and we'll, you know, leave it to him to take very special care of Miss Baker here. Lattimer is going to be so pleased that, you know, you're alive and well Celeste. Yes, yes, he also thinks you're dead you know.' The nurse added.

Panic painted Celeste's face as her two captors began to laugh and guide her into the living room where they all sat quietly. She had to look at her captors with their smug faces smiling like Cheshire Cats, awaiting the return of the man of the house.

Chapter Twelve

Daniel Archer walked away from his office upset, he was not so much annoyed, it was more that he was frustrated and mainly at himself for once again being reprimanded on his appearance by Lattimer.

Archer rubbed his stump remembering the triviality that cost him so dearly. 'I should have learnt that lesson the first time,' he thought.

The day had been an unusually long and particularly tiring one for him, what with Maitland turning up out of the blue and not talking, then the soiled uniform and finally the trouble he had to sort out with the farmers this afternoon, taking his day into the night.

Still at least the rest of his limbs were intact and he was now on his way home to his beloved Annie. He could rely on her to cheer him up, she always knew how and as he walked along the street, he played out the welcome scene in his mind.

On opening the door, he would be greeted by the smell of home cooking as it wafted up his nose and instantly warmed him, his brain would turn the aroma into a waterfall of saliva erupting from the glands in his dry mouth and the gastric bubbles would form in his stomach in preparation for the wonderful food. She always cooked up a feast did Annie and as it was Tuesday that meant his favourite would be waiting for him, some delicately cooked, young and tender lamb.

Archer imagined the perfectly cooked, pink lamb on a plate with new potatoes still steaming from being boiled, lightly covered in a sprinkling of chopped chives that sat on their soft, tan skins as a knob of butter melts into the bed of carrots and peas.

All the vegetables would have been freshly picked from their garden that day and all would be cooked to perfection.

Then after the main course, maybe some apple crumble and custard for afters and talking of pudding, his wife would be waiting to give him a great big cuddle and a tender kiss, while on the table the feast would be laid out ready for him.

He would sit down and smile at the offering, then at his wife, before taking hold of the tall glass of room temperature, red wine that was standing guard over the delicately decorated china plate with the twenty four carat gold rim.

The evening would be full of conversations about how one another's day had gone and, no doubt, the topic of Maitland and any success she may have had in getting information from him would crop up.

After all of this, she would run a shower for both of them and bed would follow.

Mmm bed, the place where they have the most glorious of love making sessions. Annie Archer may well have been a large woman, but she was still so tremendously flexible and so very willing to pleasure him, in every way he could imagine. The thought of this brought a beaming smile to his face and he found himself having to adjust his arousal so he could walk a little easier and maybe a little quicker.

The problems of the day had held him up and made him later than usual and when he arrived home he opened the door while calling out.

'Hello Annie, it's only me.'

'We're in here Danny, but close your eyes before you come in. I have a big, you know, surprise for you.'

'OK my love, I'm coming in.' He chuckled to himself, already his mood had started to lift.

In his eagerness to get in, he didn't realise there was a lack of aromas from the eagerly awaited meal and with his eyes closed and his hand reaching out, Daniel Archer entered the living room and was greeted by the soft chubby fingers of his wife's hand as she guided him to the settee and gently pushed him down by his shoulders.

She sat down next to him and excitedly held his hand, telling him to open his eyes.

After a moment of quickly blinking several times to clear his blurred vision, Daniel Archer saw his wife sitting next to him with a huge smile, while his niece stood by the door and she too was smiling.

'Hello you two,' he said, 'oh, we have an unexpected guest my sweet.' He added as he saw the beaten woman seated opposite him.

He leant across to kiss his wife's cushion of a cheek.

'Oh yes Danny, a very special guest, go on take a closer look at her.'

He turned his face from his wife to study the woman in all her battered glory.

With his mouth open, he couldn't take his eyes off her.

'Oh my dear Annie, where did you find her?'

'Well Danny,' she giggled, 'the funny thing is, you know, she sort of came to me for help with her eye. See, she's wearing the patch I gave her.'

Annie Archer giggled again, amused by the whole situation. She then flung her arms around her beloved husband adding, 'Lattimer is going to be so pleased with you Danny. First, you know, getting Maitland and now Baker.'

Celeste reacted at the mention of Maitland's name which, the ever observant, Archer noticed.

'So you've met our Mister Maitland Celeste and did he do all this to you my dear? Did he try to kill you?' He was now sarcastically throwing Celeste a lifeline in order for her to justify her recent activities.

'Uncle, she told me she wanted to kill Lattimer and that she wants the resistance to help, she even has one of their ID keys, she said Garforth gave it to her.'

Celeste shot a look at her old friend, only now realising just how evil the niece could be with this her final betrayal.

Excitedly, Archer nodded.

'So you're working together then? You and Maitland I mean, not you and...,' he dangled his fingers, loosely gesturing toward his niece.

Celeste remained silent, her thoughts focused on how the hell she was going to get out of this mess, more so now that she had found out Maitland was in Launceston.

Analysing the situation and allowing her training to take over her knee jerk feelings. Her finely honed instincts started to kick in. She calmed herself and began to weigh up her captors, judging the opposition by their individual abilities and what level of threat they were going to be.

She raised her hand to her mouth and let her finger gently tap her lips. It looked to others like a nervous habit, but it helped her think.

She suddenly realised, in the excitement of finding her, they hadn't restrained her. She could not believe it; they had made a school-boy error in forgetting to tie her up. It was an oversight by them that she will turn into a big mistake. A slip-up she was going to take full advantage of.

They were showing her more civility than she expected or deserved, but it also showed they did not see her as too much of a threat as they all carried on as normal.

Celeste began to score each one in reverse order of threat level as she studied them.

The traitorous bitch of a niece was not going to be a problem, even in her condition. Celeste knew she had spectacularly failed at becoming an Enforcement Officer, no matter how Marta wanted to dress it up and Celeste felt sure Marta had done little or no fighting since.

Yes Marta was going be the last to be dealt with.

Now then, Annie Archer, the nurse from hell and because of her size, Celeste assumed the nurse's reactions would be slow and besides it would be a pleasure to take that smug smile off her face once she saw her beloved Danny disposed of.

However, because of her love for 'dear old Danny', her reactions were unknown, therefore difficult to judge, so Celeste would have to be ready for anything.

Then there was Daniel Archer, the leader of this particularly unsavoury pack of wolves. Celeste studied him as he lovingly interacted with the two women and she remembered he had been one of her tutors.

She knew that even with his disability, he could be devastatingly accurate with a gun, a knife or even a punch from that stump of his.

He would definitely have to be the first to go.

'I'll prepare some dinner, you know, now you're home love, sorry it's a tad late.' Annie said to her husband, as she got up and without looking at Celeste, moved to the kitchen.

The smiling, rosy-cheeked, pig of a woman called for her slimy, snivelling, low-life of a niece to help and after looking at Archer, who nodded his approval, Marta also left the room.

Celeste's stomach was tightly knotted, as she fought hard to control the hatred building inside. Her hands were restless, looking for something to hold and they twitched a little as she sat looking at Archer.

He sat opposite her in quiet contemplation; the digits of his remaining hand were clasped around the stump where his other hand should have been. It reminded Celeste of how the fingers of a mount on a ring would hold on to its precious stone.

Archer enjoyed that the fact she was uncomfortable with her situation and smiled as he watched her small but significant twitching.

'Come on Baker, you know that anger you're feeling should be harnessed don't you?' He questioned. 'You know by concentrating your energies and directing it to the task in hand, you might escape this mess.' He laughed at his own suggestion.

Her hands were now shaking with rage, so much so, she had to hold tightly to the arms of the chair to help it abate.

Since she had been left alone with him, Archer had not taken his eyes from her. He was amazed and fascinated that she was alive, albeit beaten.

He smiled at her and she knew that by her appearance he too assumed she was little, if nothing, of a threat to him and still her hands held on tight to the chair arms and there she sat trembling with rage.

'It's so wonderful to see you alive and almost well, Celeste. Now, are you going to tell me what happened?'

'This you mean?' she asked pointing at her face, 'oh just a little present from Lattimer in the form of a punishment,' she replied, trying to make the tone in her voice sound as calm as possible.

'Ah, so the body Garforth found at the house was in fact, the Punisher,' Archer laughed again, 'poor Robert, he thought the body was you, he rushed back thinking his best friend had been killed and he was in such a terrible state you know. You're not much of a friend though, are you Celeste?'

She frowned at the blatant disrespect he showed to her dead friend. Archer instantly stopped laughing when he menacingly pushed his face close to hers.

'Can I assume by the tone you have adopted Baker, you blame Lattimer for all this?' He pulled away and sat back again. 'So let me see if I can get this right, according to your logic it must be Lattimer's fault that you disobeyed his orders, making him feel he had to send to you a gift of a punisher?'

Celeste remained quiet, bitterly looking at him as he continued to bait her.

'Please feel free to correct me if I am wrong.' He opened his arms to accompany the invitation.

She continued to stare at him, wondering where this conversation was going.

'Well if that is the case, then maybe it's your fault Garforth is dead. Perhaps it was your actions, or maybe inactions, that led Lattimer to cut the throat of your beloved friend.'

Her eye widened as the truth fell from Archer's mouth. The truth that Lattimer killed Robert himself, there was also venom in his voice as he spoke. He was really enjoying the torment he was putting her through.

Silence fell in the room while each of them thought.

He snapped around to look at her.

'Why did Garforth not see you at the house Celeste? Where were you? Hiding or held captive by Maitland perhaps?'

Sitting in physical and mental pain as he spouted off his thoughts, she was resolute he would not goad a reaction from her, especially now she knew he was right about Garforth.

But no matter how much it hurt right now, she had to concentrate all her efforts on getting out of here and the sooner the better.

Celeste mumbled as he spoke and did not answer.

There they sat; captive and captor, both remaining quiet until the niece returned to the room.

From the corner of her eye Celeste watched as Marta began to lay four dinner places. She then lit the stumpy, mismatched candles standing in the discoloured, silver plated candle holder and placed it in the middle of the table.

'It looks like you're going to be staying for dinner my dear,' he smirked as he sat in the chair, 'you're in for a treat tonight Baker, my Annie is a marvellous cook; oh I do hope you like lamb.'

Marta smiled at the compliment and her Uncle responded with another wink and a lift of his eyebrow that told her to return to the kitchen.

Once again the two remained in silence for a while. Archer suddenly stood and moved to a small table where a bottle of whisky and several empty mismatched glasses stood. He picked up the bottle, removed the lid and poured a small amount into two of the glasses.

He walked back and handed one to Celeste while he took a large sniff at the other.

Suspiciously, she hesitatingly put her hand out in acceptance of the much needed alcoholic stimulant.

Her hand still shook with anger, but she managed to put the drink to her lips using both hands to empty the glass dry in one swift gulp.

The strong alcohol caught the back of her throat making her choke and she felt the liquid warming her as it travelled down. The effects were almost instantaneous as the liquid flowed through her, the courage increased.

Her shaking subsided a little. The thought of killing another person had always felt wrong to her, but she always did what she had to. Tonight though was going to be seriously different. Tonight's killings would be in self-defence, even if it was going to be cold blooded and now premeditated, it was not murder.

Looking into the bottom of the empty glass for possible resolve, Celeste knew she had no choice, she was fighting for survival and passing the empty glass back to her subjugator, her decision was made.

He took the glass and moved to pour another drink for them both and returned to his seat.

'Well now, Oh by the way, did you know that we have our mutual friend here?'

Her face had no choice in showing her surprise.

'Yes, yes, he's in the infirmary where my lovely Annie has been looking after him. So what do you propose we do about this situation of ours Baker?'

216

She shrugged and took a mouthful of the refilled whisky.

'You do realise that with Lattimer under the impression that you are dead, I could do pretty much anything I wanted with you and get away with it?' He looked her up and down and he rubbed his chin while licking his lips. 'Mmm, in fact that's not such a bad idea you know? I've always thought you would be so good, in the right situation of course.'

'You know you're so right Danny boy, in fact you are spot on,' she was smiling at him with her upper body slightly bobbing, 'but how about, when she comes back in, I tell Nurse Annie what your plans are eh? What do you think she would say to that Dan?' She replied, repulsed by the idea of him even thinking about touching her.

He sat forward a little, looked back at the door to make sure no one was listening and then he whispered.

'Go right ahead Celeste, you see... Annie would love to have a crack at you too.' He laughed raising his glass in a toast; 'to Lattimer' he said throwing his drink into his open mouth and draining the glass of its contents.

On lowering his head he was dumbstruck to see the muzzle of Robert Garforth's gun pointing at him. He dropped the empty glass from his hand and it hit the hard floor and shattered into pieces, at the same time as the loud explosion of the gun sent a bullet flying into the skull of the now deceased Daniel Archer.

Celeste watched in, what seemed to her to be, slow motion as a small hole suddenly appeared in the middle of

Daniel Archer's forehead, which was soon followed by a trail of blood, slowly trickling down from the hole onto his face. Finally, a split second later, blood sprayed from behind his cranium, covering the chair and wall as the back of his head exploded.

He didn't seem to react at all to the fatal impact; he just sat there, with a stupid look of shock on his face before he collapsed in a heap on the floor.

The large woman came rushing in to see what all the commotion was about, only for her to be met by the gun's hot muzzle kissing her fat, reddened cheek.

With the gun in her face and the body on the floor, she was shocked into a sudden and most welcome of silences. At last the smug bitch was lost for words.

With a finger on her own pouting lips, Celeste used the gun to direct Annie Archer to sit down in the same blood soaked chair her husband had recently, but fatally vacated.

Naturally the woman became visibly upset at the sight of her husband who had folded onto the floor, dead as a door nail. She lifted her hand from the sofa only to see his blood covering it and she began to sob. Without pity Celeste watched as the woman's tears rained down the fat cheeks.

Celeste felt every bit of the extreme pain caused by the metal poker Marta Brunning had swung to hit her arm, but instead of dropping the gun, as Marta had predicted, it made the trigger finger unintentionally pull on the weapons firing mechanism.

There was another percussive bang and Annie joined her dearly departed husband on the floor in death, with a hole on one side of her temple. In all the commotion, Celeste had forgotten about the niece. Marta had followed her Aunt into the living room and Celeste had underestimated the turncoat's courage, as Marta realised what was happening and armed herself with the brass handled rod of black iron and began attacking Celeste.

It just goes to show that anyone is capable of anything under the right circumstances, but seeing the contents of her relative's heads splattered everywhere, Marta froze and a well placed punch to her temple from Celeste, stopped her from screaming.

Marta fell onto the other two bodies.

Standing over the unconscious niece, the victor was still so angry at the girl for her spying and lying. So, she was to blame for so many deaths, but more importantly the disappearance of Celeste's beloved Amber.

Tonight, for only the third time in her life, Celeste Baker killed with intent, with murder in mind. It was cold calculated and with a single bullet sent from under her chin, up into her brain, Marta Brunning finally got her 'just deserts'.

As an Enforcer she had been expected to kill.

Tonight she had no legitimate reason, other than murder, other than her own survival and looking at the lifeless bodies, she began thinking about how Maitland must feel.

She was walking in his footsteps now and she questioned herself, had she begun to turn into a lonely, uncaring monster like him? Like Lattimer? No, this is different, she had a cause and this was the effect.

It had nothing to do with ego or control, only survival.

Celeste stood, made for the door and in a whisper she departed the house, making her way in the darkness towards the infirmary, to find and rescue Jon Maitland.

Chapter Thirteen

Russell Lattimer closed the door behind him and returned the lock to its closed position. He then pocketed the key in the inside of his white suit where it had come from and he smiled. These trips to Kernow always made him up-beat on his return and especially today, as the result of the meeting had been better than anticipated.

After they discussed the problem of the resistance making a stand and the notorious Maitland having unexpectedly turned up also causing a 'modicum of grief' as Lattimer put it, his mind was a little easier now.

As far as his contacts were concerned, the problems he was facing were exactly that, his problems. They are internal issues for him to resolve without their assistance.

This part of the outcome did not please him, but the mere fact they understood, took some pressure from his shoulders. They accepted his explanation only on the condition that he would ensure it would never be repeated and they would still take delivery of a new consignment within a week.

As the town leader walked back to the castle, he allowed himself a wry smile of victory in the glorious mid morning sun; he was famished but happy.

Before entering his room, he ordered another breakfast from the kitchen as his first one had been rudely interrupted and not finished, and then took the opportunity to freshen up.

While waiting for his sustenance, he sent a messenger to demand that Daniel Archer urgently present himself, the two of them had a lot to talk about, as Lattimer was in a quandary. How was he going to squeeze more from the people, within a week and without them turning against him?

A quick, delicate solution was needed and Archer was always so much better at this sort of thing than he was.

Lattimer was halfway through enjoying his third cup of wonderfully aromatic, sweet, hot, black coffee when the messenger returned with the news, announcing the demise of the entire Archer family.

Exploding with rage, Lattimer threw the half empty coffee cup through the air, sending its scalding contents over the guard as he cringed, while the steaming hot liquid ate into his flesh through his uniform.

Lattimer stood up, his fragile mood immediately changed from one of quiet contentment, to a maelstrom filled with anger and hatred. He violently pushed the breakfast table over, sending the cutlery and plates of food scattering noisily, as they spilled onto the white floorboards.

'What the hell do you mean they're dead? Do you mean all of them? All of them are dead?' He questioned.

Three lives had been lost, three people with whom he had been close for many years, were now gone. They could have been considered the nearest thing to a family he had ever known.

His brain pounded with pain.

Lattimer could never have been accused of ever being sentimental, though his concern was more to do with the fact his plans were unravelling faster than he could now think.

He simply was no longer in control of the situation.

'No! Where's that bastard Maitland? Where the hell is Maitland?' He screamed at the cowering messenger, who was still fighting the pain of being covered in the hot remnants of coffee.

'Maitland is still in the infirmary Sir, still with his babysitters,' the guard nervously replied.

Lattimer stared at him for a moment, but then he began to erratically pace up and down the room, while pondering his options, as he whispered to himself through gritted teeth.

'Not Maitland, not fucking Maitland.'

He stopped and turned to stare at the view from the window.

Looking down at the Launceston roof tops, he decided he had now had enough; he needed to be in the Penthouse, overseeing the conception of a new plan.

Lattimer breathed deeply a couple of times, managing to calm his anger a little, at the same time he remained agitated as he turned back to the messenger.

Lattimer shook his finger as he spoke.

'You, go to the infirmary, tell the guards there to take Maitland to the detention block and secure him. Then I want you, not anyone else! Just you! To gather as many people as you can find, tell them to meet me at the Penthouse at midday and no later. Do you understand me boy?'

The messenger nodded, gave a weak salute and then ran out of the room, grateful that he had only received the scalding coffee and not the same fate as Robert Garforth.

Lattimer continued to look from the window, his mind racing at a thousand thoughts a second, trying to analyse all the evidence at once.

'It had to be the resistance,' he heard himself conclude aloud. It was the only rational explanation he could come up with.

Today, he decided he was going to make sure those bastards understood what retribution meant. Today the resistance would finally be crushed once and for all and he was going to have to take personal charge of the operation. It was the only way he could ensure his orders were going to be followed, to the letter.

Continuing to pace around the room, Lattimer craved revenge like an addict craved his fix, he was going to give them real retribution and he would only be satisfied when their heads lay on real silver platters in front of his feet.

Lattimer concluded that he had been too lenient, for far too long, now it's 'no more mister nice guy.'

***

'Get up. Get up now, you're coming with us,' one of the thugs guarding Maitland ordered. Bleary eyed and groggy, he was still half asleep when he felt his legs being pulled off the bed to hang over the side. He then was lifted by the arms and as his bare feet made contact with the floor, the coldness startled him awake.

Automatically he moved to an unsteady standing position.

'What no breakfast? Not a very good service is it?' He quipped through a yawn while trying to put on the dark blue overcoat that had been thrown at him. When Jon Maitland realised what was happening, he once again engaged himself in trying to goad the two Neanderthals into a fight, but neither of them reacted this morning.

Maitland looked at the guard's features, which were boxer-like and noticed that they both had more of a serious look than before, something had obviously happened while he slept.

'So where's that fat nurse? Why isn't she here to look after me?' He asked as he placed each foot in the neatly arranged shoes below his bed.

The guard he had mockingly blown a kiss to, moved forward and gave Maitland a quick jab that he felt deep into his ribs. It forced him to groan in pain and he quickly exhaled all the air from his lungs, as he collapsed back onto the bed.

'Shut the fuck up arsehole, you're to follow us.'

A winded Maitland carefully stood up. 'You only had to say.' He coughed and hobbled slowly over to the door the other guard was holding open.

It was a tight squeeze, as he had to push past the hefty man to get through the door and for a fleeting moment, Maitland thought about running.

Instinctively the thug grabbed Maitland's arm as if he had realised what was on his prisoners mind and began to push Maitland out of the room. Maitland was walking too slow it would seem, or they were in a rush, either way all three were in the corridor quickly making their way towards the exit.

As they passed the wards, he noticed that all seemed strangely quiet, especially for a hospital. As they walked through the corridor further, he realised no one was talking or taking any notice of him and his escorts. Even the nurses seemed to be purposely busying themselves, trying to ignore the trio as they progressed, uninterrupted out of the hospital.

***

After she had spent the night hiding in the bushes of a garden, Celeste arrived outside the infirmary. The sun was peaking over the horizon and in the grounds she found a quiet corner to place herself, just where some rubbish had been piled up. She settled down behind some discarded boxes, relaxing while she settled down for what she expected was to be a long wait.

She carefully watched the comings and goings of the people for hours and was nearly caught twice when someone decided to add to the rubbish around her.

Suddenly a youngish man, dressed in the green uniform of a novice Enforcer rushed inside. Celeste slightly shifted her position to get a better view of the doors he had just gone through. She rubbed at her tired eyes and watched the front door. Had she guessed right? Was this the messenger for Maitland's guards? 'Robert you were right, Lattimer was so predictable', she whispered.

Celeste's stiffening muscles reminded her that it was around her sixth hour of waiting, when the doors of the old college accommodation block were violently flung open. First the young man rushed out, running back to where he'd come from and a few minutes later, one of the guards urgently strode out into the yard.

He quickly scanned the area and made a hand gesture behind him.

A dishevelled, injured, limping Maitland emerged being 'assisted' by another of the guards.

So Maitland was here, albeit battered.

'Well Mister Maitland, I think it's time for me to return the favour and save your sorry arse.' She quietly said to herself, but now was not the time, there was little she could do in her current condition and deciding to remain hidden, Celeste waited until they had gone.

She watched the trio disappear into the detention block which, thankfully for Maitland, was only a short walk across the grounds.

Celeste sat back behind the discarded rubbish and took stock.

Maitland was alive.

Archer was dead.

She was alive.

Lattimer was alive.

Alive and well with at least fifteen hundred men and women protecting him, all of whom awaited his command. Her thoughts swam around and feelings of inadequacy tried to erode at her confidence, she was unable to do the job at hand. The odds of her surviving, let alone having any success, were ridiculously low.

This whole situation was completely crazy, so there was only one crazy thing left for her to do. It was insane at the very least and surely would certainly mean suicide at best, but it just might work.

Chapter Fourteen

A group of fifty-one men and women sat around the stuffy room situated on the upper floor of the Penthouse.

All were wondering why they had been summoned and only Lattimer had that answer. He watched the people as they settled down, he had thought someone was bound to ask why they were here and he needed to give them a convincing reason.

The reality was, he needed to quell the discontent that was spreading around the town, like a pollutant; an epidemic that was fast becoming out of control.

He was not used to things being out of control, it was something else he didn't need right now. No, what he wanted was for things to return to normal, what he needed was for everything to be back under his control.

Lattimer was getting hot and scratched at his neck as he looked at the faces of those gathered, all loyal, all willing and all unquestioningly obedient.

He stood up, still silently looking around at the faces of the expectant crowd. His eyes were wide, his facial expression was harshly set to emphasise the serious nature of the meeting.

The crowd fell silent.

'Thank you all for coming at such short notice; I am sure you are all more than busy enough to not be troubled by my issues.' His voice was deep, calm but stern, as it always was, just for added drama. He waited for a split second then continued.

'You have all heard that Daniel Archer, his wife Annie and their niece Marta, were executed last night in their own home.' He tried to sound as solemn as he could, after all he had just lost a friend. The crowd made their expected and obvious noises of disapproval.

Lattimer decided to pace around.

'We have evidence that proves the resistance was responsible for this atrocity,' he looked at the floor while he added another silence.

'My friends,' he lifted his eyes to them, 'it would seem these people are getting more audacious in their endeavours, their tenacity is showing no limits.'

There was another pause.

He then stood proudly, almost to attention.

'Daniel Archer was more than just a friend to me, as he was to some of you. He was my second in command, my confidante and a leader among men. He was like a brother to me.' Lying had become easy to Lattimer, he'd gotten used to it, so much so, it was now first nature for him to say and do anything, in order for him to make people believe what he said was the absolute truth.

230

Noises of agreement sounded from the gathered crowd and he stopped his pacing and folded his arms over his chest.

'Also this week comes the sad news that both Robert Garforth and Celeste Baker were cruelly taken from us.' Gasps could be heard from the crowd. 'They were killed in separate incidents, while carrying out their duties and again they were both murdered by the damned resistance.'

For a moment his eyes genuinely glazed over, as a rare flash of real emotion rained over him at the thought of losing Celeste.

'I ask you all, when is this going to end? Are they not going to be satisfied until we are all destroyed? Have we learnt nothing since the double whammy?'

The sharp imagery of never seeing Celeste again, caused a lump to develop in his throat and this in turn made him croak a little as he spoke. He choked on his words, this time not on his lies, but real feelings of loss.

He grabbed the glass of water from the table and swallowed some of the liquid.

It loosened the lump and allowed him to continue.

The crowd looked at their leader as he stood in front of them, showing he was as vulnerable as they were, when it came to dealing with a loss.

Somehow it made him more humane.

'How is this going to help us meet our aims for getting into Kernow?' he asked them rhetorically. Oh how he could not bear dealing with fools right now but Lattimer continued.

'Look, let me put this as simply as I can for you; these people are threatening the very reasons why this community was built, they want to stop us, they want to destroy everything that we, no…, they want, to destroy everything that you have made possible. My friends they are laughing at us all.'

Each person in the room began to mutter and fidget.

Their agitation increased.

'So is it fair that these crimes are allowed to go unpunished? Is it right that these so called 'freedom fighters,' are fighting against the very freedom I have promised we will all have beyond the wall in Kernow?'

With the rallying of their spirits, the noise in the room increased to an almost unbearable level, which of course cheered Lattimer; it was how he wanted it and would make what he had to say next a little easier.

'Friends I do not want revenge, no, no, no, I want justice. Justice for you and for your hard work, for the sacrifices you all have made.'

There was a concern in his voice, contradicting the contempt he was feeling for most of the people looking at him.

'As your Elite Enforcer it is my duty to ensure the safety of every person that resides here and I intend to find these bastards, not for what they have done to me, but because I want to cut them down where they stand.'

His statement sent a ripple of mixed emotions through the crowded room, which he ignored and continued. 'We must be allowed to continue our journey into Kernow unhindered, but first we need to replace the goods that were destroyed.'

An old man seemed to take forever in picking his skeletal frame from the chair he was sitting on, the whites of his leaf green eyes, were turning the same colour yellow as the remaining trio of his monolithic teeth, his jaw involuntarily rose and fell with age, his raised his infirm aged hand, that also shook, as he lifted it above his balding head.

'Lattimer,' he raspingly called out and the people around him began to quieten, 'you have known me since before the big one two and you were there when my family left me for a better life in Kernow.' He wheezed and coughed a little before he breathlessly continued, 'I have worked hard all these years only because I want to be with them.' His whispering voice was allowed to travel around the room, as all present remained silent.

Russell Lattimer studied the wrinkles on the elderly face; trying to connect one of the many forgotten names scrolling through his thoughts and squinted a little before he recognised him.

'Archie Leach,' gasped Lattimer, 'it's been a while since we've met. I am so sorry, ashamedly I didn't recognise you, one of my oldest friends. Rest assured old man you will see them soon, I promise you that, I promise that to all of you here.' Lattimer shouted.

'No you misunderstand Elite Enforcer, I will not be joining you or my family in Kernow; for me it's too late,' the old man's wheezing worsened as he spoke. He held out his wrinkled hands, they continued to tremble, 'as you can see I am not long for this or any other world, except wherever my maker decides to send me. I am dying Russell, with only weeks to live and I wanted you to know, all I have, I now turn over to you, to use in getting whoever you can, safely into Kernow.'

Lattimer raised his hands to cover his open mouth, giving the feigned looked of shock a more dramatic emphasis. 'Oh Archie I am so sorry to hear this sad news, but also I am or should I say, we, are all enormously grateful for your gift. You have humbled me.'

Around the room, the tremor of applause surrounded the old man as he heavily returned to his seat. This was followed by an aftershock of others clambering to offer their similarly generous assistance, until Lattimer held his hands up to quieten the crowd.

'I just don't know how to thank you all, really I don't. These gifts you have made today, will go a long way in making up the deficit of the lost merchandise; I am deeply moved by your loyalty'. He moved to sit down facing the group, 'however, we still need a way forward, first we need to resolve the problem of the resistance. What are we going to do about them?'

Lattimer smiled as he looked around the room to watch the faces before him, fill with passion and pride. Opinions and options began to fall from their moving lips.

'Kill them all!' Was the shout from someone in the crowd. It made Lattimer smirk.

It was the response he was hoping for.

'If only it were that simple, but I promise you, these problems will not happen again, not one single person will hinder us, because I am prepared to do whatever it takes to stop these low-lives. You can trust me to devise a plan to ensure your bidding is done and it will be completed tonight.'

Lattimer shouted across the baying voices.

He once more motioned to the crowd.

'Thank you all for coming and for your suggestions. I will think about what you have said, but before you go, I want the following people to remain.'

He began to point out the people, whose names were on a list he had created during the meeting.

In the end, a mixture of fifteen men and women remained in the room while the others were dismissed to await further orders. The group pulled up a chair and each sat in front of their leader, eager to listen to what he had to say to them.

Lattimer stood and he remained silent as he examined the faces of the chosen few before him. He looked into their eyes to see if fear, bravery or stupidity was present in any of the individuals. Finally, he was satisfied that all he saw was blind obedience, the pre-requisite he needed, now more than ever and in abundance.

Obedience!

It was just how he liked it.

'I'm sure you are all wondering why I have asked you to stay behind.' Again he sat in the chair at the front of the crowd. 'As time is of the essence, I'm going to be brutally frank with you. Each one of you possesses a certain... err... skill... yes skill, a good word for it. These skills are the very things I need to utilise tonight. Look around you and see that even though you all look different, know that inside you are all the same.' He explained while gently tapping the side of his left temple.

They looked from left to right, expressions of recognition on some faces while others were complete strangers, but they all had an air of pride, of arrogant smugness, as they sat listening to their leader pile on the flattery.

Lattimer knew by simply massaging people's egos, like blowing smoke up their arses, to coin a phrase, he could get them to do pretty much anything he wanted.

'You see, I know that all of you are killers, not simply killers, but killers who enjoy killing.' There, he said it, he'd let the genie out of the bottle and while he smoothly ignored the shocked looks, he continued.

'I have decided that tonight I need you all to carry out an act. An act so disgustingly terrible, that normal thinking people would be revolted and sickened at the mere thought.' Confusion filled the room.

'This act, if carried out properly, is designed to eradicate the resistance completely and because of its nature, it's an act only you can carry out.' The faces in front of him soon had smiles on them, soon to be unfettered psychopaths smiles, broadening as the words from Lattimer began to sink in.

'Though you must also be aware and realise that after tonight, you will not be allowed to join us and live in Kernow. For that reason alone, I will allow each of you to choose if you want to do this or not.'

Everybody in the room was aghast and as this last detail became understood, they simultaneously erupted with excited questions aimed at Lattimer.

He put up his hand to induce the silence he needed to continue.

'My friends, before you decide on anything, I want you to know that you are the best. That you are the only ones I can trust for this most important of endeavours. It's for the survival of Launceston and will ensure our future.'

The group were silently thinking.

'Look, you all know in Kernow there is no place for people like you, not now and not in the future. This is why I ask you to do the unthinkable; this is why I ask you to make the ultimate sacrifice, not for me but for everyone.'

One woman stood up. 'What's in it for us Lattimer?'

'Simple. Tonight you are free to do whatever your sick minds and urges want you to do. There will be no-one around to stop you. There will be no repercussions and your families will be saved.'

He remained silent, waiting for signs of anyone deciding not to participate, in the simple but sick and devastatingly efficient plan of his.

He was taken by surprise when not one of them said no and as Lattimer remained seated, he went through his plan of action with them. There were a few questions asked and he answered them as frankly as possible.

Then the newly formed team excitedly vacated the room, leaving Lattimer pleased with himself for coming up with such a fantastic plan.

This time, his mind was far too occupied for him to feel the slightest bit of the loneliness, as he kicked around a tin can, for inspiration in his head.

Lattimer walked out onto the balcony and as he watched the people below milling about their business, unaware of the atrocity that would befall their town at midnight, he absentmindedly played with his damaged locket, imagining that some of the faces he was looking at, belonged to the very people who were working for and with the resistance.

Were they laughing at him behind his back, mocking him from below, as they planned their trouble, just as Garforth did? Well, by tomorrow morning there would be few less of these bastards to worry about and then it would be Lattimer who was laughing.

A misplaced sense of pride, made him smugly turn his back on the crowd and he returned to the Penthouse.

When he pulled aside the curtain to enter the room, instantaneously he knew something was wrong, as a putrid smell hit him hard. He rushed into the room, his knife drawn in one hand and a handkerchief in the other, covering his mouth and nose. He looked around almost in a panic and was surprised to see somebody had a damned cheek, to not only let themselves into his office without permission, but also drape their sorry, stinking carcass over his desk and sit in his chair of all places.

'Who the hell are you? And what the hell do you mean by coming in here like this?' Lattimer shouted at the uninvited guest. Rage immediately flooded his mind, as he sped across the room with his knife poised high above his head.

This sudden change of mood made it easy for him to kill again. As he got to the edge of the highly polished dark walnut desk, he managed to come to an abrupt halt. He swung his arm down hard, aiming for the skull of the disgusting sitting duck.

At that moment Celeste Baker lifted herself and felt the contact of his hand closed around the bone handle of his steel knife, as it brushed against her hair. Fortunately she had managed to avoid the sudden, fatal contact with the sharp instrument.

She reeled back in the chair, her good eye was now wide open, shocked at his violent over reaction to her being there. She lifted her hand and stroked her hair, trying to remove the sensation of his hand sweeping past her.

The tip of the knife embedded itself into the lovingly maintained, highly polished console and Celeste sat back in the luxuriously padded, swivel chair looking at him through her open brown eye.

Lattimer's mouth literally fell open, his lower jaw hung in mid-air. She could almost see the slow process of recognition begin to sink into his confused, disbelieving brain cells. He stepped back a little from the desk, not quite comprehending exactly what was happening here.

After a thousand ideas had flashed through his mind he concluded that he was perhaps hallucinating, or he was being haunted, then again, maybe he had finally gone out of his mind, flipped his lid.

He guffawed and giggled as he turned away, then wagged a pointed finger at her. 'But you are dead; you're supposed to be fucking dead.' He hissed as he bent towards her, 'how? What?' His emotions had instantaneously run the gamut from elation and shock through to anger, guilt and finally settling on surprise.

A wry smile almost appeared on Celeste's face at seeing the control freak, uncontrollably freak out, but that

240

would have been no help to her. She stood as quick as her aching body would allow and attempted a salute.

'No Elite Enforcer not dead, just injured Sir.'

Lattimer had remained standing, with his mouth wide open again as he looked at her.

'What happened to you Baker?' he whispered with a puzzled expression in his voice and on his face.

Oh, how his mind must be turning somersaults, she happily thought, as she tried hard to keep any of the bitterness she was feeling from emerging as she spoke. She started to recite her well rehearsed explanation of the fictional events leading her to this moment.

'It happened a few days ago Sir, at the house. It was Maitland. He had somehow found the house and broke in. He was after information and kept asking questions about you Sir and when he didn't get any, he killed the punisher you had sent.'

Lattimer remained in shock, he sank slowly into the chair opposite where Celeste stood and indicated Celeste to sit back down.

'The bastard then turned on me and did this Sir,' she said, as she returned to her seat. Celeste lifted the eye patch to show him the damage to her eye, 'he knocked me out and when I woke I was in the barn, where he had tied and gagged me. After a while I heard Garforth turn up, I could hear him calling to me, but I just couldn't answer him, I couldn't let him know or warn him about Maitland.'

She found it easy to inject some panic in her voice.

'Then, as fast as Robert arrived, I heard him run back out of the house.' Celeste looked at Lattimer to see if he believed her story and she could tell he was trying to connect, what was being said to him, with what he already knew.

'That was when the animal set the house alight. I had to sit and watch as he burned the house down and I think he didn't care if Robert was inside or not. I guess Maitland's timing was just a little too late because I heard Rob run back into the forest.'

Celeste wiped her dripping nose on her sleeve, stopping a runaway tear from landing onto the desk. She was trying to be as convincing as possible about her distress.

'Maitland left me there, in the barn, trussed up like a chicken Sir.'

Once more she scrutinised Lattimer's face as it contorted, due to his thoughts and the onset of another itching attack from his psoriasis.

'I don't know where he is now Sir, but I understand that he was looking for the resistance. I think he wants to kill you Sir.' She added, knowing the Elite Enforcer's paranoia would get the better of anything logical that may be true.

It worked, it got him, hook line and sinker.

'I managed to loosen the ropes enough to get free and get here to warn you and Robert as soon as I could.'

She stopped talking; expecting some kind of angry eruption to take place, but Lattimer remained quietly seated, allowing his consciousness to drift through a million scenarios.

'You're here to warn me? Warn me about Maitland? He's here is he? To kill me you say?' While he rambled on, Celeste remained silent, enjoying every second of watching him squirm, while he tried to assimilate her unwelcome news.

After a moment she broke the heavy silence.

'Are you OK Sir?

Lattimer's mind suddenly snapped back into the room, his face calm and non-readable.

'Me? Oh I'm fine Baker, just fine,' he chirped with a convincing smile as control, once again, reigned over him. 'Are you OK my dear? You look like shit you know, even though it is damn good to see you alive and well.'

There was a definite chuckle in his voice.

'Tell me Celeste, what are your thoughts about this Maitland fellow?'

'You want my thoughts Elite Enforcer?' she snapped at him, she surprised herself at just how angry she felt at being asked such a blindingly stupid question.

'What the hell does it matter what I think? Look at me! Look at what he's done. I'm hardly going to give him a raving report, now am I?'

'Yes, yes of course you're right Celeste, a silly question really, but you've heard the folklore, you know the rumours about this Maitland chap, how he seems to be hell bent on spreading anarchy and mayhem everywhere he goes and right now my dear, he's here in Launceston.'

She nodded vaguely, still reeling from his question and wondering if she should believe his explanation. 'Does he know I'm lying,' she thought to herself, 'or is there something else?'

'I only wanted your opinion on how we might prepare for his arrival, that's all, I mean you have been up close and personal with him, but also I wanted to know if he reminded you of anyone.'

With a quick glance he gauged her reaction, as the look of hurt appeared on her face.

'No sir, no one at all... err... why, should he have?' She questioned.

Lattimer smiled a little and rubbed his face as he looked down at the desk. 'No not at all my dear, it was another silly question.'

He then noticed the gun on the desk.

Celeste had kept it to hand, just within her reach, in case she needed to get to it in a hurry.

'It belongs to Garforth' she explained, 'he dropped it at the house; I'm going over to give it to him as soon as I can.'

'Oh no, Garforth, you don't know do you?' He looked into her uncovered eye while leaning forward. 'I am so sorry my dear, but I have some sad news for you. You see, Robert Garforth is dead.'

Celeste feigned surprise and sorrow, well enough for Lattimer to believe it. 'No, it's not possible Elite Enforcer. How? When did it happen?'

'I don't really know,' Lattimer again lied, 'he was on duty, out on patrol when it happened. Someone, maybe even Maitland, had surprised him it would seem? They simply cut the poor boys' throat.'

At least that bit was the truth.

She buried her face in her hands, not really having to force the tears to flow. Under these circumstances, that was not difficult at all.

Celeste stood up.

'I'd better go see Nurse Archer Sir.'

'That's also going to be a bit difficult my dear, I'm afraid she too is dead.'

He pulled back and became a little more nonchalant as he continued, 'as is her husband Daniel Archer and their niece Marta Brunning.' Celeste continued with her feigned surprise.

'You see it would seem that our Mister Maitland has been a busy boy Celeste.' He raised his eyebrows, as if to impose his theory on her, to somehow, force her agreement.

245

'Look Baker, why don't you just go to the hospital wing, get yourself sorted and we can continue this discussion later or maybe tomorrow even, once you have rested properly of course.' Without waiting for an answer, he got up from the chair and called out to the guards, while Celeste turned her back on him, her hand reaching out for the gun.

'Err… You won't need that my dear, just leave it there would you and see to it that you're in your uniform tomorrow.'

She hesitated for maybe just a little too long, she didn't know, finally, she left the gun on his desk, disappointed an opportunity had just passed her by.

She left the room.

'Celeste, you have no idea just how good it is to have you back' he called out just as she closed the door behind her.

'Wow! This is an interesting turn of events,' Lattimer mused aloud; he clapped his hands together excitedly. Celeste Baker turning up alive and with a story about her encounter with Jon Maitland.

For a constantly suspicious Lattimer, her appearance raised more questions than answers. Where was his merchandise? Did the seemingly 'un-talkative' Mister Maitland take it, before he set the house on fire? Was it destroyed in the said fire? Are Maitland and Baker now in cahoots?

Now that would be interesting, he smiled.

Immediately he wanted to speak to Maitland, but now was not the time. Time was a commodity that he did not have in abundance, so that particular meeting will just have to wait. Maitland was out of the way, safe and sound in the detention centre where he can wait; Lattimer had more pressing issues like leading the fight in the eradication of the resistance.

Chapter Fifteen

Celeste did as she was instructed and escorted by the guard, she quietly made her way to the infirmary. The silence from her escort, was only interrupted by the occasional tutting sound he made, when he had to slow his pace or stop for her to catch up. He was becoming pretty impatient with her lack of speed as they walked, but she didn't allow his petulance make her go any faster, instead she slowed even more, so she had to put up with his churlish noise-making and used the time during the walk to digest the conversation with Lattimer.

So, Maitland was here and she knew Lattimer was lying about many things, but did he believe her story?

They arrived outside the infirmary.

She looked over to where she had earlier placed herself only, to see the makeshift sanctuary of piled up rubbish that had hidden her so well, was now gone. The guard walked ahead, opening the door for her, not through gallantry though, he was in a rush and anything he could do to speed up her progress, he would do, short of actually carrying her.

Celeste looked at him, as he stood all masculine and in charge, while impatiently waiting for her to climb the steps and finally walk through the doorway.

As she entered the hospital lobby, the smell of disinfectant engulfed her. It reassured her that in here, she would receive a more hygienic examination, than she got from Annie Archer, in her filthy kitchen. Although Celeste had to admit, the ointment and eye patch given to her, seemed to be working. When she lifted the patch to show Lattimer, she saw light and shadows, a sure sign that her eye was slowly improving.

The young nurse gently examined the eye and Celeste could again, just make out that light was getting through. The soft touch of the medic's fingers stroking at Celeste's tender skin reminded her of Amber.

Celeste closed her eyes.

Her heart reminded her how it had been shattered, on receiving the note, Amber had left behind. It told her simply that she could no longer stay in Launceston and that was it. No reason, no forwarding address, no clue as to why.

As far as Celeste was concerned, they were happy together and had been from the first night they were united in passion. Celeste had been in enforcement for three years when she and Amber had worked closely on the project. Tonight they were coming to the end and the mood was of relief, more than anything. It meant Celeste would be allowed out into the field at last.

It was late in the evening and they had made their way into the dormitory. At the bedroom door they looked at one another and smiled the last flirty smile of the day. For Celeste, it would be the last of the flirting for ever.

The silence between them was not awkward, just long. She nodded a final good night to the red head and held out her hand to turn the handle. Amber grabbed her shoulder and pushed her hard against the door. Celeste looked shocked but couldn't say anything, as her mouth was now covered by Amber's soft lips pressing into hers.

After a few moments Celeste felt the pressure on her mouth ease off, as Amber slowed down with her kissing. She found her eyes were closed and their tongues were now dancing with one another, as the tender finger tips of Amber's hands excited her checks.

Her own hand had moved up Ambers back and she was stroking the shape and line of her spine, as the other then gave up the door handle and finished off fondling that mop of flaming hair at last.

As they pulled away, there was no shock, no feelings of shame or remorse between them, but they both remained silent, wiping their own mouths from one another kisses.

'Well, you only had to ask you know.' Celeste said.

'No I couldn't, you might have said no.'

Celeste smiled as she peeled herself from the door, moving closer to Amber.

'I could never say no to you.'

This time she initiated the kiss.

It was slow, tender and very, very soft.

But with Marta's confession still ringing in her ears, Celeste now knew Amber was chased from Launceston and could be anywhere by now, that is, if she was still alive.

After the examination was over, the nurse advised Celeste to continue using the cream and keep the patch on for just a few more days.

Then the two women talked about her other injuries, but Celeste didn't want to talk about that, she attempted to steer the conversation round to Maitland.

Celeste tried to push the medic to reveal any information she might have about him, however, the nurse was obviously under orders from Lattimer to remain silent on this particular subject and finally, she discharged Celeste, sending her to the dormitory block.

Escorted by the same guard all the way to her own room, Celeste thought how obvious it was that Lattimer did not trust her, but then, he didn't trust anyone and with her sudden reappearance, Lattimer was even more on his guard.

Apprehensively she opened the door to her room and entered. She fully expected the room to have been completely emptied of her possessions and it was, but it was still a shock to see it completely bare.

'Where did all my things go?' She asked the guard as he began to leave. He stopped and turned to her. He shrugged his shoulders and flashed a knowing smile, then left.

The door closed and she heard the sound of the key turning in the lock. She walked over to the wardrobe and pulled the doors open. A solitary wire coat hanger swung on the otherwise empty clothes rail. Celeste grabbed at it to stop its metallic rattling from interrupting the silence.

Looking down at her D.I.A.L., at the bottom of the wardrobe, she saw on the door, a tiny red dot. It would have been totally inconspicuous to anyone, but to her and Garforth it was the sign, that a message from Robert was inside the little black, metal box.

The excitement and anticipation she began to feel, caused the adrenaline to once more pump around her nervous system; injecting some much needed energy into her body. She felt her pulse begin to rise just as quickly, as she fell to her knees to hastily open the door.

Inside, she found two letters.

One of which, she picked up.

It was from herself to Robert, she had placed it there some time ago, it must have been about two weeks now, explaining to him her actions in saving the young family.

As she examined it, spinning it over and over in her hands, a puzzled look contorted her face, as she turned it over to see it was still sealed, why had it not been opened? But then the other letter, the one from Robert to her, had caught her eye and dismissively she replaced the first one and took out the other.

Pulling at the edge of the white envelope, she discovered it had been attached to a package. Celeste grabbed at it with both hands and scrambled to the bed.

252

On the front was the note, a single word scribbled on it, 'Celeste.' There were no humorous quips about the number thirteen this time and it could only mean the contents were more serious.

She quickly ripped the letter from the brown paper package and lifted the flap of the envelope, to remove a single leaf of white paper from inside.

'Celeste.'

She settled on the mattress to read the neatly spaced hand written note.

'I have tried to anticipate every possible move that maybe played, in this game you and Lattimer appear to be playing. Now you know I am not a mind reader, just a great strategist and if I am right, which I normally am, then you are now locked inside your room and there's a guard placed outside.'

She looked at the door, as if to confirm what was written was correct, she smiled. He may not have been a mind reader, but he did a damn good impression of one in these matters.

Celeste turned back to the note.

'One of the problems of having a structured regime like the one we have, is that up to a point, it all becomes especially boring and very predictable to someone like me.'

Celeste's smile remained at his apparent lack of modesty and she continued reading, 'and if I am right, then you really are going to need this package. I have tried to get everything I think you will need, to give you a head start.

Firstly there is a gun, it's only a small one, but in your hands, I know it will do whatever job you need it to. I could only get a small amount of ammunition as well, so use it wisely. I also managed to get you some master keys for the Centre, these will unlock only some of the doors to the compound and finally, I have also got you a few medical supplies.

All of which will come in useful at some point, if you have any chance of escaping that is.'

Celeste stopped reading again, this time to open the package and still with excitement, she ripped off the wrapping to see what, the ever efficient, Robert Garforth had left for her.

There was the gun with twelve bullets. It was a small, black metal handgun with a wooden handle.

She picked it up and played with it.

It wasn't a weapon she was used to and as she handled it, she decided, although it was lightweight, it was usable.

Returning the weapon to the box, Celeste picked up the small bunch of seven shiny, metal tag-like pieces, each with a different letter stamped on the circular end, while the toothed edge, had different ridges cut into them. The letters were A through to G, so all she had to do was insert the correct key with a letter, that corresponded with the lock buried in a door and it would open once she turned it.

She then saw the small medical kit. It was more like a first aid kit than anything else, but it would help.

She placed them all on the bed and turned her attention to the letter once more.

'So there you have it Baker, hopefully you will make good use of them and they serve you well, because I don't know if you, or even me for that matter, are still alive. If we are, then I am sure we are going to have a good laugh over this sometime in the future, but before I sign off, I want you to know something.

I love you Celeste. I always have and before you say anything, I know you don't see me in that way, but if I don't tell you now, in this letter, I have a strange feeling I'm never going to have chance.'

She stroked the words 'I love you' by softly running her finger over them while the slight, but increasing sting of tears veiled her sight.

Celeste smiled thinking about Robert, thinking about how she felt about this, his inevitable confession. She had always known he had felt something more than just friendship toward her, but seeing it in black and white somehow rammed it home and perhaps under different circumstances she might have felt the same, who knows? Once more her attention was directed back to the letter.

'There, I've said it, well sort of and now I have to go but with the hope of seeing you again, of seeing you alive. There is a very small chance that I'm wrong about all this of course, but I doubt it. If I am wrong then just ignore this letter and live a long and happy life. Take care, Rob.'

A tearful, but smiling Celeste finally allowed the letter to fall softly onto the floor. Until this moment, she had never even entertained the notion of have a relationship with a man. Though she was sure if it were to have happened, Robert would possibly have been at the top of her list.

Now, however, was not the time for the sentimentality of 'ifs and buts', she needed to get out of here and try to free Jon Maitland.

***

The Reaper was taken to his cell, with the guards going through the same routine, with one of them opening the door with the other 'helping' their prisoner inside, with a not so gentle push.

Once he hit the floor, they closed the door on him and he heard it lock from the outside.

He looked up from his resting place and spoke.

'How the hell do I get out of here?' He asked himself aloud as he looked around the surprisingly spacious room.

There was a violent bang on the door, followed by the raised voice of an irate guard, shouting at him to remain quiet. This proved someone had to stay on the other side of the door, 'thus making any escape harder', he thought.

The presence of the guard outside the cell, also gave Maitland the idea, that maybe the room wasn't secure after all.

He stood and twisting his neck, as if he was performing some strange exercise routine, Maitland began to look around the cell, trying to find any possible weaknesses he might be able to take advantage of.

He was still in a lot of pain, but was able to hobble about slowly and a close examination revealed the walls were indeed constructed from metal panels, just as he thought. He ran his hand over the weather beaten surfaces, the cold, hard, grey skin, reminded him of the exterior walls of the warehouse's that were built back in the old days.

He vaguely recalled that there used to be an area of warehouses just outside Launceston. That must have been where the material had been scavenged from, when they built this place.

He was slow and deliberate as he walked about his cell while randomly tapping at the structure with his knuckles, testing the solidity of each of the grey monoliths. They all sounded solid, certainly solid enough to hold him, especially in his current condition. He noted tack welds in place where the walls met one another and where they met on the ceiling and the floor.

This place was definitely made for holding, not escaping.

Maitland quickly weighed up his predicament.

He was locked up in a sealed metal box that had no ventilation grilles or windows, it would appear the only way in or out, was through the door.

Feeling a little defeated, he concluded the door was the only weak spot in the room, so he started to walk over to it and take in every inch of its hard grey painted surface.

As he got closer, nothing in particular jumped out at him, while he examined the gap between the frame and finally the mirrored glass panel.

'Move away from the door now.' An anonymous, but stern voice bellowed from behind it.

Maitland stopped and slowly backed away, just as he was ordered, but his focus remained on the door. He noticed the lack of welds to hold it, there were just three silver hinges and they didn't look particularly strong.

Then it hit him; he realised the door was not made from metal but wood and the reflective glass panel, which had been placed into it, was so obviously a viewing panel.

It was yet another Cycloptic eye, this one being a two-way mirror with someone watching him, spying on his every move. It was also another weakness in the door.

He thought he might be able to crash through it, once he regained some real strength. But until then, he moved to the bed and in his usual position of one of his hands raised behind his head, he reclined and there he waited for whatever chance may be presented. After all, he was in no rush whatsoever to go anywhere, especially now he was due to be taken to Lattimer. Besides, maybe he could goad this 'Elite Enforcer' or one of his guards enough to push them to kill once more and carry out his execution.

So he quietly waited alone with his thoughts, going through scenarios, attempting to foresee every eventuality, staying like that for several hours until the guard finally delivered some food to him.

The sentinel entered the cell with a gun in one hand and a tray of food in the other. He had a miserable look on his face with slight signs of nervousness, as he looked over at the bed,where his un-stirring prisoner now lying on top.

Maitland thought he was miserable because he pulled the short straw and was allocated babysitting duties, or because it was he who had to deliver the food, just like a good errand boy.

Looking up from the bed he smiled. 'Ah, room service at last. You know I'm going to have to tell Lattimer about being starved half to death, before he's even had a chance to talk to me and what would he say to that?'

The guard seemed immune to the glib comment and simply dropped the tray on the table without taking his eyes off the relaxing prisoner.

He then moved backwards away from the table, with his gun constantly trained on his prisoner. He stopped when he reached the closed door and placing his free hand behind his back he blindly searched for the handle.

'Err... would you like me to get that for you?' Maitland asked politely, with a bit of a grin, as he swung his legs over the side of the bed. The guard did not answer and finally opened the door with his free hand after groping about for the handle.

As the door opened Maitland noticed that it swung outward and unless there was somebody hiding behind the door, it seemed it was just this solitary, but unhappy guard, to keep him company. Once in the hallway, the guard closed the door and again locked Maitland in.

The inviting smell from the hot meal filled the room. Maitland's stomach began to rumble and bubble in a chorus of gastric readiness for the most welcome of sustenance, no matter what was on the menu.

Maitland carefully rose from the bed, gearing his body up for more agony. To his surprise he found that, after all the rest he had been allowed, he was in a lot less pain than he expected and he relaxed the tension in his muscles.

After staggering towards the table, he stood over the metal covered plates of hot food, unable to decide whether he was going to eat it, or just admire the layout, just as a patron of the arts would salivate and postulate over a Turner or Picasso.

In the end, art had its place and it wasn't in his stomach. He opted to eat and as he sat down he looked towards the viewing panel. Maitland imagined the nose of the hungry and miserable guard pressed up against the smooth cold glass rectangle, involuntarily licking his lips at the sight of the low-life prisoner tucking into a freshly cooked meal.

He winked in case the guard was watching him and then turned his eyes back to the table. He didn't know which he was going to enjoy more, eating the food or the thought of the torment the guard was being put through. He smiled mischievously at the thought of both these ideas.

A hungry Maitland then turned his full attention back to the tray, with its three plates and metal lids, with a small amount of aromatic steam escaping here and there.

Still in a playful mood and with the greatest of exaggeration, he closed his eyes and sniffed at the wonderful aromas. A muffled groan came from behind the door, confirming the guard's presence and curiosity and again Maitland allowed himself a smile, but it became a little broader, with the knowledge of the torment he was causing on the other side of the door.

He opened his eyes.

There was a white envelope poking out from under a condensation covered bottle, of what he took to be beer. A surprised, confused look appeared on Maitland's face, as he picked up the paper.

There was no writing anywhere to be seen on the outside, so he turned it over a few times, just to double and treble check, but all he could see was the damp ring where the cold beer had sat, weeping away its moist jacket.

He opened the unsealed paper wallet and took out the note, carelessly discarding the envelope onto the floor as he unfolded its contents.

The handwritten note started, 'My dear Mister Maitland.'

He quickly scanned the sheet to the bottom to see the signature of Russell Lattimer. 'Curious', he thought and he began to read the note from the beginning.

'My dear Mister Maitland. How good it is of you to take time out of your busy life to come and visit my little town of Launceston. Unfortunately, I am unable to meet with you today as I had planned, purely because official pressures mean I have to deal with several problems of dissension and mutiny, of which I am under the impression that you sir, may have something to do with.

Rest assured though, by tomorrow morning your journey here will have been a complete waste of time for us both. Not to worry though, we will still have an opportunity to hold an open and frank discussion sometime tomorrow, perhaps in the afternoon.

So until then, please accept this glorious meal, knowing it could well be your last, at least, here in Launceston anyway, kindest regards, Russell Lattimer.'

Dissension, mutiny and a last meal, an interesting and very definite choice of words, thought Maitland.

'I wonder what he means by that?' He said aloud.

After hearing his stomach complaining once more, he screwed up the note and contemptuously threw it at the door, then lifted the lid off the nearest plate to him.

It was time to turn his attention to more important things; himself and he got great pleasure as he watched a plume of steam erupt from a china bowl when he removed the metal lid.

Drips of condensed water fell onto the floor from the edge of the aluminium ring as he held onto it. He found the bowl filled almost to the brim, of what he took to be a delicious smelling vegetable soup. It was a thick and creamy broth. It looked like a real bone sticker start to the meal.

Placing the lid on the floor by his foot, Jon Maitland pulled the thin metal handle sticking out of the steaming pool. When he lifted the utensil, he watched as thick dollops dropped from the edge of the spoon, back into the pool of nectar, leaving little craters as they made contact with the surface.

He took a large mouthful and cringed.

Feeling like Goldilocks tasting her porridge that was too hot, it burnt his mouth and throat when he swallowed. It was a painful, yet wonderful experience that was all too quickly over. Within minutes, the bowl had been emptied and he couldn't resist, he just had to lick it clean! He then took a small swig of the cold beer, to wash it down.

If this was to be his last meal on this earth, he was going to enjoy it. He sat back on his chair letting out a loud, satisfied burp, while adding a quiet 'excuse me' to it. Then, without cleaning his mouth from the moist beer, he focused on the large lid that he hoped covered just as large a plate, of whatever was going to be beneath it. Although he would have been happy just to continue with the soup; he joked with himself, that he would force the rest down as he lifted the lid.

Again he saw a plume of steam erupting, this one, however, disappointed him slightly as it was smaller than the first, but the sight of the food being revealed with what looked like steak; a thick juicy rump, with its darker brown lines where the red flesh had sizzled on a barbecue griddle, soon dissolved his disappointment.

He saw how the juices from the meat still flowed and mixed in with the sauce, where it had been laid to rest on the plate. The slab was accompanied by a small gathering of baby carrots, looking sweet and tender bathing in their glazed coating next to a generous portion of fresh peas which, by the smell of them, had been minted along with the five baby new potatoes. These had a knob of butter placed on their light brown jacket, which was still melting, allowing the chopped parsley to swim about the plate.

He decided not to waste any more time by teasing the guard or himself, not because he felt pity, this time he just couldn't wait to tuck into this fantastic meal.

Picking up the cutlery, he pushed the prongs of the fork into the steak, forcing the three sharp points in to penetrate the brown flesh and then with the serrated edge of a shiny steak knife, he began to tenderly, but firmly, cut into the fibres, until he separated a morsel.

Maitland lifted the mouth-watering chunk, it was pink on the inside and cooked almost to his preference, but he was in no position to have preferences. He put the piece of meat in his mouth and chewed on it until it disintegrated.

He found it was cooked to absolute perfection and reluctantly he swallowed, making him want more. The end of the main course came and this plate was also systematically licked clean and with another swig of beer followed by a quieter burp, he lifted the final lid.

There was no plume of steam at all and even though water from the condensation still dripped from the lid, he knew the contents would, at best, be at least warm, but the sight of the small sponge pudding covered in a creamy, smooth, yellow custard, more than made up for the lack of heat.

Oh, this was definitely a meal fit for a king, or an execution and as last suppers go, this one was probably the best he's had and it would have been rude not to eat it all.

Chapter Sixteen

Midnight very quickly arrived and Lattimer, along with his hand-picked team of psychos and sociopaths, were not only ready to begin the annihilation of the resistance; they were high on the euphoria of being set free to live out their most deranged and sickening fantasies. Not one of them seemed to be shying away from the task at hand.

Much to his own discomfort, Lattimer had chosen to dress in the same black uniform as the others. This, of course, caused him some embarrassment as the dark material highlighted white. But he wanted to show some solidarity with this brotherhood that he had brought together.

The mood of the group was one of nervous exhilaration, it somehow reminded him of when he was back at school and the class was treated to a rare field trip.

Each member of the team openly showed their eagerness to do their duty, no matter how sickening. For Lattimer, as long as it resulted in the resistance being finished off once and for all, he would be happy.

In recent weeks he had begun to crack down on the dissidents and no matter how big, no matter how trivial the trouble they may have caused, his retaliation was quick and always harsh. The Elite Enforcer was utterly merciless in his hysteria, with no one ever escaping his backlash.

Tonight the enforcers were being sent into the heart of the resistance camp. Weeks before her untimely death, Marta Brunning had already set up a meeting. It would be a time and place when the resistance members, would all be under one roof. It was simply a case of going into the house and erasing them, but her murder had caused Lattimer to suspect they knew of the plan. He wondered if it was maybe he and his team, who were now walking into a trap.

No matter though, it all added to the excitement and besides, he would be sending in cannon fodder first, just to be on the safe side.

Each member of the team had their own targets to engage, Lattimer watched through the door as he opened it slightly. Some of them had combined forces for their tasks.

He himself, had chosen four of the fifteen to accompany him to complete his duty and for the last two hours the whole group just sat in the room, some sitting alone, visibly making mental notes on how and what they were going to do, while others began to regale one another with tales of their past lust and destructive exploits.

Lattimer silently entered the room; everyone looked at him, he could feel the tension. It was as thick as the condensation that had formed on the windows.

Finally, the midnight deadline arrived and he nodded.

It was game on for them and they all stood, picking up their belongings to leave the penthouse quickly, calmly and quietly.

A proud Lattimer stood shoulder to shoulder with his men and he couldn't help but admire the attitude they were showing, each was still loyal to him, everyone was more than willing to follow his orders to the very last letter.

Everybody moved out into the street and after splitting into groups, they headed to their pre-ordained targets.

It took around ten minutes for Lattimer and his team to find the house he was looking for. The shutters were closed tightly against the windows, but he could see little glimpses of light escaping through, from the small gaps in the weather beaten wooden panels.

Lattimer raised his hand and the group of five silently stopped as one. Silently he pointed to the first two men; the gesture was an order for them to move to the back of the house. There they would wait for his signal. He then directed the other two to the front.

He was cold and excited while checking the street, to make sure it was clear. It was only a puff of warm air that streamed from his pursed lips that indicated, it was him the shrill whistle came from. It was the signal. The stereo reverberations of both the front and back doors simultaneously being smashed to pieces, brought a smile to the leaders face. The four men ran into the house, shouting orders and waving their guns around at the people inside.

Lattimer's wait was rewarded when he heard the satisfying screams and shouts from the occupants, as they found themselves being trapped in the house.

He turned the signal into a tune and whistled to himself, as he slowly sauntered to the front. He was remarkably calm and relaxed and by the time he got to the hole, that was once filled by a door. He folded his arms and leaned his back against the wall and waited some more.

A terrified woman soon ran out from the house, she was screaming as she ran past Lattimer, heading out onto the dark street, but Lattimer's reaction was swifter than her running and he managed to get his foot to make contact with her leg.

The look of surprise on her face, humoured him even more than, seeing her body twist and turn in the air, as she attempted to regain her balance.

He giggled loudly when she finally hit the ground, shoulder first which was then followed by her face scraping along the hard ground of the pathway. There she remained, out cold and motionless.

Her breathing was still fast and heavy, not that Lattimer bothered to check and still whistling, he waited for a further five minutes for the noise to dissipate before he entered.

The house was a mess and by the look of it, most of which was not made by his team.

'Don't these people have any self respect?' He asked himself walking along the filth covered hallway.

He made his way into where the confused, frightened people were rounded up like sheep, huddled together in the centre of the living room, trying to protect and gain comfort from one another.

The armed men were smiling and laughing, as they took great pleasure in pushing their guns hard into their victims, while they circled the frightened group.

Lattimer began to remove his gloves and he too circled the penned in prisoners, but he looked at their faces, trying to pinpoint the leader.

One of the held men kept an eye on Lattimer as the Elite Enforcer circled, buzzard-like, while toying with the gun in his hand.

Lattimer stopped and turned to face him.

'You! You seem to have a problem with me.'

The man got to his feet, while struggling to pull his hand away from the woman he was cradling in his arms. Anger and hatred shone in his eyes, which soon extinguished when Lattimer took a swing at him with his hand.

The thump loudly echoed around the room.

Lattimer's aim, as always, was spot on.

His fist hit the side of the man's temple and as he fell to the floor, Lattimer brought his knee up, making contact with the falling victim's face.

After the noise of bones cracking, blood began to pour from the olfactory organ. The crowd gasped and the woman screamed as she grabbed onto the now unconscious prisoner.

'OK you!' He pointed to a young girl. She seemed to be about eighteen or nineteen, with pretty dark eyes and unattractive short hair, a boyish look he thought. 'Take the children to the reformation centre and make sure they all arrive safely, otherwise you will suffer the same fate as the rest of this scum. Do I make myself clear?' He ordered.

Instantly she become hysterical and Lattimer raised his hand, smartly smacking the back of it across her perfect, soft yet innocent skin.

He pulled his stinging hand back and looked at his knuckles. Her blood remained on his skin and it looked like someone had painted a stroke of red paint on him.

Immediately she was stunned into silence, he pulled her hair and directed her contorted and wide eyed face to show her just what he had done.

He then licked her blood from his hand.

She could feel the pain in her lip, after it burst under the sudden, powerful pressure from the violent contact.

Within seconds it was swollen and bloody.

Menacingly he pulled her closer to his face.

'I asked you if I had made myself clear, now give me an answer you ignorant bitch.' He gaspingly whispered through his clenched teeth.

It made him splutter spit on her face and hair. She was crying again and her face still twisted in fear and pain, but he felt her nod under his hand and he let go of her hair.

'Good, good, now go.' She looked at the group in abject fear, as she wiped her face from the blood and tears.

'Oh and when you've finished that little chore for me my sweet, I want you to go to the castle and wait for me in my room.'

When the men from Lattimer's team laughed and cheered, her face turned ashen with disgust and in desperation she ran from the room to collect the children.

The dull, staccato thud of her speeding footsteps on the bare, wooden steps could be heard in the room, as she ran up the stairs. Lattimer followed the sound with his eyes and imagined her collecting the crying children from where ever they were. He gave a small smile when he heard them as they hurriedly ran out into the night. He laughed as he heard the children's terrifying screams at the sight of the fallen woman. It appeared she was still unconscious on the ground.

A sneering Lattimer then turned to the remaining group, huddled even tighter together.

'You see how easy this would be, if only you followed the rules and did as you were asked, like my new little friend.'

All of them were too frightened to respond to his statement and remained helpless to stop what was happening.

Lattimer smiled a friendly smile.

'Well now, here we are,' still holding his gun he clapped his hands together in pretend joy, 'shall we get down to business then?' he slowly began to circle the group once more, 'so, who is going to tell me what the plan is tonight, Eh?'

The group remained silent.

'OK, let me see if I can loosen a tongue or two.' He whispered into the ear of one of his guards, the armed man suddenly laughed, he nodded vigorously and without looking the manic guard grabbed the nearest woman by her hair and dragged her screaming from the group.

One of the prisoners instinctively stood up and tried to grab onto her, fighting to stop her from being taken.

Lattimer moved in quickly and kicked the 'would be' hero, hard on the side of the leg. A loud crack was heard as the joint in his knee shattered.

The man lay writhing in agony and without warning Lattimer, pulled the gun and without a second thought, not even with a bat of an eyelid, he pressed the barrel of the gun hard against the man's temple.

A loud silence screamed from everyone in the room.

He looked up and smiled at them.

He pulled the trigger.

The click of the metal hammer smashing into the empty chamber broke the silence.

Lattimer's men gave out a loud, if belated, laugh.

'Now be a good boy won't you and sit up. I want you to watch something. I want you to learn just how a real man behaves, with a disobedient woman.'

He looked up to his man and nodded.

The screaming woman struggled hard, fighting against the hand that reached and grabbed her, just because she was the closest to him, and as he began to rip at her clothes, her squirming protests made him stop, only to slap her around, making her a little more obedient.

She gave up her struggle and he ripped off the rest of her clothing, revealing her naked body for all to see. She tried in vain to hide her modesty, but all that did was antagonise the man further and he hit out at her once more.

Lattimer kept watching the reaction of her friends and smiled his sick smile.

The other women screamed their protests, crying for her their 'sister', feeling her every violation as their own. They cradled into one another, not wanting to watch the debauchery of their friend.

A raging frustration was building up within the captured men, which was becoming more visible, as they impotently looked on, while this evil man humiliatingly did whatever he wanted to this woman.

Finally it ended with the Enforcer standing up and Lattimer applauding his man. The Enforcer mockingly bowed to his captive audience, he was out of breath and laughing, leaning over her for a final humiliation as he spat in her face.

274

Picking up his gun from the floor, he joined the others as they patted him on his back and cheered, while the woman remained lying on the floor where he had discarded her, staring into space, shocked into silence.

She didn't even flinch when his spittle impacted on her reddened cheek.

'Very good, excellent in fact,' Lattimer smugly looked around, 'now, is anyone going to tell me who the hell is in charge here?'

A man stood up slowly.

'I a…' he began to say.

He was not allowed to close his mouth to finish the word 'am' and with his mouth still open, a bullet from Lattimer's gun flew past his lips, only to emerge from the base of his skull and embed itself into the plaster of the wall behind.

Instantly lifeless, the body fell heavily onto the people huddled on the floor. Some screamed out again, while others tried to remain quiet, but all were startled by the sound of the gun going off and the body falling on them. The noise also brought the naked woman round and as she scurried to crouch in a corner of the room, she began to sob hysterically.

Lattimer continued.

'No. That is not the right answer. Would anyone else like to try?'

There was no reply coming from anyone now. The only sound was just the sobs and mumbles of fear and anger. Lattimer became more frustrated at the lack of interaction.

He began to scratch at his skin.

'OK, look, it's easy. I'm the one who's in charge here, me, not you, or you.' He swung his gun hard into the heads of whoever was closest.

The loud thud of metal hitting skulls made a blood curdling sound.

Pulling a chair over he sat himself down in front of the group, staring at them with his crazed eyes, scanning the cowering group of people.

'Let me ask you resistance scum another question, which one of you idiots, is responsible for bringing that murderous bastard Maitland here?'

Two of the men quickly looked at one another.

Lattimer noticed their reaction.

'Do either of you have something to say?'

One lowered his gaze, while the other stood. 'We... we are not in any resistance and it was not us, who sent for Maitland. We didn't know he was here.'

'LIAR!' shouted Lattimer and another bullet entered another man's body, instantly killing him.

Lattimer turned to the other man and a faint glint of recognition tapped in his memory.

'You, you were in the square today, I saw the guard hit you.'

He nodded to Lattimer.

'Well, are you going to tell me the truth?' Lattimer asked, while pointing the gun into his face.

Through pure fear the man lost control of his bladder before he spoke.

Lattimer looked down at the dark stain as it grew around the man's groin of his trousers. He shook in disgust.

'I... I... I'm Mike Spencer and we are telling you the truth Mister Lattimer. We did not call for Maitland.'

Lattimer sat back, thinking aloud.

'But Mike Spencer, Maitland killed Russell Archer and his family. Wait a minute, no he didn't. Maitland was locked up wasn't he?' Lattimer moved forward again, looking directly at the terrified man, 'so who did kill Archer then?' he demanded, as he raised his gun and pushed it into the soft flesh under his prisoners chin.

Mike Spencer was still shaking and stammered. 'We... we did not have anyone killed. We are not the resistance, you think we are.'

Lattimer lashed out hitting Spencer in the face.

'Don't you dare tell me what to think! I tell you! OK?'
Lattimer's breath became fast, 'What about Marta Brunning?
You thought she was one of you? You thought she was a
member of the resistance and when you discovered she was
the niece of Daniel Archer, you had her killed and in cold
blood too. You had them all killed, because of her betrayal.'

Spencer shook his head continuously. 'No Lattimer,
not us. I swear we are not the resistance, we have gathered
here for peace. We didn't even know about Marta and her
family, until the news broke of their deaths.'

Anger shook Lattimer to stand, he wildly shot at
Spencer, but his aim was off and this time he hit an arm. The
pain forced Spencer to fall into the others and there he stayed,
holding his wound, screaming in agony.

'If you're not the resistance then who the bloody hell
are you? Why have you all gathered here tonight?'

Spencer looked up at Lattimer.

'We are all the children of God. A God that you tried
to ban, we have gathered here to pray, we have gathered to
reform the church, that you so despise.'

A surprised, confused and angry Lattimer remained
silent, as he stood listening and working out his thoughts. He
seemingly wanted to say or do something, but stopped himself
and he then turned to leave the room and the house. He spoke
as he passed one of his men.

'Enjoy yourselves boys.'

Lattimer left the house, to the cheers of joy and screams of fear in equal amounts.

Outside the house he put on his gloves and brushed off the blood and stray flakes of his skin and before walking off, he spat on the still unconscious woman.

His walk back to the penthouse was a troubled one, as his victory was incomplete, but there would be time enough tomorrow for him to hear Maitland's side of story, 'before I kill him that is', he thought.

Chapter Seventeen

With a large swig of the beer, Maitland finished his meal. His belly was satisfyingly full and as he sat back he reminisced on how he hadn't had a meal like that in such a long time.

He moved from the table back to the bed and threw himself down on the mattress, as he lay in his usual position, he began to drift off.

He was quickly at the point of being half asleep and half awake, tonight he found, he was only too willing to float in the sea of blackness. For a reason that was beyond him, he began to allow the lost, painful memories of his adored wife and their beloved child come into a neural existence.

His sleep was troubled as usual, while the guard smiled as he watched his prisoner toss and turn from one side to the other. Maitland placed an arm over his closed eyes, then turned his face into the mattress, both, a futile attempt to block the images that were being painted in the front of his mind's eye.

Why had he really returned to Launceston? What possible reason did he have coming back, to where it had all gone wrong for him? What did he think was going to happen?

As he began to fall deeper into sleep, his mental time machine took him again on a journey to the past, taking his mind to an uncomfortable place.

Maitland was surprised to find, he was completely aware that he knew he was asleep in his cell, but his surroundings had changed. The cell had gone, dissolved from all existence, he had returned to an earlier time, eighteen years earlier, but he was still here, in Launceston.

Looking at his desk calendar he saw that his consciousness had taken him back to 2016, four years after the big one two. It was a time when he had been a little more productive, than he was today.

It was an important day or him, it was the final construction phase of the Kernow wall.

Jon Maitland was the chief engineer responsible for the construction of the wall and he had volunteered to stay and finish the English side. It was the promises made to him and the others, of a guaranteed place in Kernow, but only once the wall had been completed.

It was too attractive an offer for him not to accept.

The authorities had made an agreement, an area of Launceston, would be temporarily allocated to construction workers and here he was able to live with his wife and their child, safely protected by the armed Kernow forces.

The arrangement was made in return for the promise of trading licences being put in place, but that promise would be broken after tonight.

Three of a Kind

The Maitland family unit was in this compound, it was a small two bedroom affair, laid out on two floors with a tiny rear garden, where Laura grew their own vegetables. Jon always admired how his wife had done such a wonderful job in making the place a home for them, especially under the circumstances; having armed guards there all the time.

Maitland looked down at his hand; it was resting on a garden gate, their gate. He lifted his arm to look at the watch, which had suddenly appeared on his wrist, it was the one Laura had got him for his first father's day. He touched it and smiled at the lost treasure and with that smile, he went on to follow his usual routine when he arrived home from work.

Dressed in his dark blue business suit, Jon Maitland continued through the gate, he was to be noisily greeted by a small bundle of energy called Emily running up the path, giggling as she called out to him.

Tonight his pride and joy was dressed as a pirate.

Her ever resourceful mother had made the costume from an old, frilly, dress shirt she had found and altered. She added a black scarf that was tied around Emily's head and the little girl held in her hand a wooden sword with a gold painted handle. To finish off she wore an eye patch over one eye, leaving her piercing blue eye shining in the evening sunlight.

The eight year old ran as fast as she could, culminating with her jumping into the air. It was the perfect end to almost always a bad day. This tiny ball of giggles and laughter, was the perfect antidote for all the poisonous people he had dealt with.

Recently he and his colleagues had been approached, by some of the less than honest members, of the Launceston Enforcement Office. They piled pressure on them, wanted him and his team to build a secret tunnel in the wall, allowing an undetectable passage to and from Kernow. The devious bastards wanted to open a route for the highly profitable trafficking of merchandise and people.

But Maitland was an honest man, a man with integrity and deep rooted morals and principles. The, then Elite Enforcer, did not expect he could not be bought or compromised, nor did he expect that Maitland, an engineer, was anything of a fighter. However, he vehemently defended everything he believed in and even under the threat, from this so called Elite Enforcer, he still refused to comply.

As far as Maitland was concerned, within a month he and his family would be building a new life in Kernow. Jon Maitland would be safely watching his family grow; perhaps they would even have a son, while he left this filth to remain here, rotting away in their own sordid juices.

At the sight of Emily, the tired engineer's spirits lifted and he dropped his bag to the floor, just in time to catch his now airborne daughter. They both laughed and giggled as she landed in his strong safe embrace and she kissed her father as many times and in as many places over his face as she could.

'Ha, ha, ha, hello Em and M, come on now, you know you're not supposed to be out of the house at this time of night don't you?' He looked at her happy, angelic face. How could he ever really get cross with her?

'But Daddy, you're home at last and I've missed you so much.'

They laughed again and he knelt to return her feet to the ground. As he released his arms, she grabbed one of his large hands with her tiny fingers and proceeded to drag him up the pathway to where Laura was waiting.

'Mummy, Mummy, Daddy's home. Put the kettle on love,' the child tried to deepen her voice wanting to mimic her father. He picked up his bag and willingly allowed himself to be pulled toward the house to be greeted with just one more kiss.

The tall, slim, dark haired woman with eyes that changed colour from brown to green depending on her mood, stood with her arms gently folded as she leant against the door frame. She was smiling at the antics of the two most important people in her life. As he moved closer to her she pressed her lips against his, slipping her hand up to the back of his neck to gently stroke his short brown hair.

Maitland wanted to stay in this dream. He wanted to remain in this lingering memory of his beautiful wife and wonderful child.

Tonight, he just didn't want this to end.

'Yuk' shouted little Emily and screwed her face up before running back into the house.

'Hello you,' he said as their faces separated. 'I've missed you too much you know.'

He started walking into the house and as Laura took hold of the door to close it behind them, she looked through the decreasing gap, just to make sure no one was there.

Maitland turned to her, he was smiling still. 'Still expecting trouble love?' He asked her.

Laura shook her head. 'No not really Jon, I think it's more of a habit now, take no notice of me love.'

'Laura, it's OK to worry, but don't let it take you over, it's all going to be fine, I promise. This area is well guarded and we're not going to be troubled by the Elite Enforcer or his men.'

She smiled, trying to show she was reassured, as they walked into the kitchen where she placed the kettle on the hot stove.

***

Celeste Baker chose not to dress in her uniform as instructed by Lattimer. Instead she remained resolute in her complete defiance of the twisted leader and his wishes and while she remained in her room, the foundation of a plan began to form in her thoughts. A plan to remove Lattimer from power, but it meant she needed to get the help of the resistance. Somehow she had to convince them to help her in the rescue of Jon Maitland, because he was going to be the key.

The first step though was to get out of here and find them, so she picked up the keys Garforth had left for her and slowly turned the lock in the door, trying to keep the mechanism quiet as her hand turned the key over.

Unfortunately the lack of speed in the turn, did little in her avoiding detection, the sound of metal scraping against metal was followed by the loud clunk of the lock disengaging, echoing down the hallway and at this time of night, even the slightest sound becomes amplified.

Disappointed in her attempt at a stealthy exit, she prepared herself for the inevitable attack by the guard waiting outside the room and cautiously she opened the door.

'Damn' she thought, just as expected the guard was there and pointing his gun at her.

Moving her focus from the weapon to his face, she saw that here was yet another of Lattimer's predictable puppets. By the gormless look on his face, he came with the brain capacity to blindly follow whatever orders he was given and without question.

There he stood in the doorway, with his gun in hand and a sneer on his lips, as he blocked her exit. He looked her up and down, implying the question, 'what did she think she was doing.' But he had mistakenly underestimated her small, battered stature as not being a threat to him.

Celeste returned a sarcastic smile a moment before she smashed the solid handle of her gun, on to his forehead, with all the force she could muster.

The impact caused pain to shoot through her hand and up her arm, as a fleeting look of surprise was stamped onto his face, just before he fell forward to sprawl out on the floor in front of her.

She bent down to look at him and slapped his face, just to make sure he was out cold. There was no reaction from the sleeping heap of thuggery.

He was too large and too heavy for her to move and so literally she walked over him and hopped off when she reached the hallway, just as a young child would jump over a sandcastle on the beach.

Once clear of the room she was able to continue through the hallways, eventually finding her way out onto the dark streets. A steaming vapour emitted from between Celeste's lips when she exhaled a deep breath in the still night.

It must have been somewhere between midnight and one in the morning she figured. The early morning sky was covered in a deep black, velvet blanket that had been sprinkled in diamond tears, sparkling as she walked away, leaving the Reformation Centre behind.

As she travelled she heard a noise, again she looked to the shadows to hide her from whoever or whatever approached.

As the noise got closer, she could see it was a group of children moving quickly toward her. They were crying as they ran and as they came into view, Celeste saw that their faces were filled with utter terror.

She put her gun away and slowly stepped from the shadows.

'Hey, hey, what's going on here?' She held out her hands to show she had no weapons. The whole group stopped, cowering and cuddling one another.

The injury on the older girl's mouth looked sore and was still bloodied. 'I'm sorry, but we can't stop, its curfew!' she said quickly looking around, worried that someone would see them, 'Mister Lattimer ordered me to get the children to the reformation centre before he gets back.'

'Lattimer? Did he do this to you?' Celeste asked pointing to the swelling. She nodded while her hand tried to cover her mouth. 'That would explain the lip, so he's coming back here, from where?'

'From killing our parents! Him and his men are holding them back at the house.' She said it in such a matter of fact way, like it was an everyday occurrence. Then a girl, not much older than the children she was escorting, tearfully explained what had happened.

'So, that's why there are so few Enforcers about tonight.' Celeste observed.

The girl nodded, 'I then have to go to the castle, to wait for Mister Lattimer to return from...' She went quiet, realising she was about to repeat herself and both women shared the same disgusting thought of what might happen to this innocent young woman, if left alone at the hands of the vile Lattimer.

Celeste raised her hand to her mouth with the sudden realisation that the families were the so called resistance, she had been looking for.

288

'Tell me where they are; I need to get to them. I can help them.'

Reluctantly the girl gave Celeste the address.

'OK, look, go to the centre, take the kids there, but you must remain with them. Do not go to the castle, is that clear?'

The girl shook her head 'I can't, Lattimer will kill me when he notices that I'm not there.'

'It's going to be OK, I promise, as long as you do as I say, you'll all be safe and hopefully so will your families.' The girl tried to smile a little, nodding her understanding of the instructions. She hurriedly rounded the children up and they continued on their way, while Celeste Baker began to move as fast as she could, following the directions given to her.

It wasn't too long before Celeste slowly sidled up to the house, knowing full well that Lattimer and his men would still be inside. She remained in control of her nerves by feeding off the anger, that had hitched a ride with the adrenalin, as it flowed in her system. She waited, hidden from view of the house, to see what was happening.

Shivering in the night air Celeste listened to the screams and shouts, as gunshots shattered the silence of the night. A dark figure then appeared where the door used to be, he was exiting the house and as he moved further out into the street, he seemingly placed his hands into what could only have been gloves.

She watched carefully as he walked out onto the street and finally recognised the shape as, Russell Lattimer.

He left the scene and as usual he left his men to finish his dirty work, slowly he walked towards the castle. Celeste imagined he was wearing his usual smug look on his face, as he disappeared from view.

Baker carefully crept over to the house, making sure he did not return.

Walking up the path she checked the woman on the floor, she was breathing but still unconscious. She left her and cautiously entered through the broken front door.

The hallway was in complete darkness, except for a shaft of light emanating through a gap in the door, that had been left slightly ajar. The air was filled with the noise of shouting, screaming and cheers coming from the occupants of the beyond.

Celeste was experienced enough to know what was happening to the people in there and she readied her gun, taking up a position where she could spy on the only part of the room that was visible through the gap.

Inside, she clearly saw the backs of two of the enforcers, they each had a gun in one hand, but they were held loosely by their side. However, in their other hand, each had a woman who was struggling and screaming for help.

Everyone she saw seemed to be watching something, some sort of action happening, just out of her field of vision, it was after another blood curdling scream that Baker steadied her nerves and finally decided to attack.

The people in the room stopped to look round as the door abruptly swung open, they watched as the woman with the eye patch dived into the room, shooting the first two Enforcers in the back. The dead men instantly dropped to the floor at the same time as Celeste landed on her knees, from her airborne entrance.

The people in the room were stunned into silence; the screaming she heard was from herself. The pain of making such an entrance could not be ignored and as she looked around, the people were as still as statues.

Celeste got to her feet, trying to compose herself.

'Hello boys, having fun are we?' she quipped, addressing the last two Enforcers.

They were unarmed, out of breath and one was busying himself by taking turns in showering blows onto Mike Spencer, as the other held the defenceless man down. They stopped and before they could get to the guns lying on the floor, Baker shot one of them in the side of his head while the other took a hit in the neck.

The pain had affected her aim, but no matter, as both Enforcers dropped to the floor. One dead, the other writhing about as blood exited from his body from the open jugular.

The first part of her plan was complete, the group was finally free and now they owed her.

'Thank you, thank you so very much my child, but who are you?' The injured and naked Mike Spencer asked as he stood up and cleared his mouth of the bloody debris by spitting on to the floor.

'I'm Celeste Baker and some of you may know me as an Enforcer, but no more.'

'Lattimer's prize student? Who hasn't heard of you?' One of the women cried out. 'Have you come to finish us off?'

'No, no, look around you, I'm not here to kill you, I'm here to save you,' she answered while putting her gun away 'but also I need your help.'

'Why? What do you need us for?' Everyone seemed to be finding their voice now and the questions were flying thick and fast, until Mike Spencer managed to push himself forward.

The amount of suspicion and distrust she received from the group was understandable.

'Because I want Lattimer dead, that's why.'

'Why on earth should we trust you, let alone help you?' Mike asked calmly.

'Because Lattimer did this to me,' she pointed to her face, 'because he destroyed my family, because he made me destroy other families and now I want to destroy him.' Bitterness was present with each syllable she spoke.

They all looked around at one another.

'I need to get Maitland out of the Detention Centre and I can't do that alone, not like this. Please help me.'

She looked at the faces, all were showing fear and not one person was willing to even comment.

Frustrated, a pleading tone came to her voice.

'Look. I did not kill these Enforcers for nothing and I certainly did not save you, only to have you killed,' they looked down at the bodies, 'please don't make it that I have again killed for no reason. Don't turn me into Lattimer. I'm no longer in his service.'

Surely the speech must have been proof enough for them to, at the very least, begin to trust her?

It was certainly proof enough for the man who had just been attacked and beaten. Mike Spencer put out his hand to shake hers and finally introduce himself.

'Celeste, I am The Reverend Mike Spencer, but you have to understand, we are not the resistance Lattimer thinks we are. We're just trying to follow our beliefs, attempting to worship our god.'

Celeste looked blankly at the man.

'You're a priest, a clergyman?' she asked with surprise.

He lifted himself proudly.

'Yes.'

'So how is your god going to be of use to me?' She asked.

'It is said that he moves in the most mysterious of ways.'

She sat on the floor, deflated and defeated.

'Baker, we need to get out of here, we need to find the kids.' He said.

Celeste vaguely nodded her understanding. 'You don't need to worry about them; they're safe in the Reformation Centre.'

Mike Spencer sat next to her and the others dispersed to tend to the injured.

'Look Baker, we can and will help you to a point, but we do need to have someone look at our wounds first.'

'But isn't killing going against your beliefs?' She asked.

Spencer smiled and held her hand, 'I haven't always been a Priest you know; besides you're the one who wants to kill him, remember?'

Her thoughts began to brighten.

'Well then Priest, if all goes well, I promise you that by tomorrow, either that crazy bastard Lattimer will be dead or this crazy bitch will be. Either way you'll all be free.'

Chapter Eighteen

With increasing clarity, the recurring nightmare of the screaming woman and terrified child jumped back into the thoughts of Jon Maitland with such veracity, it startled him bolt upright and fully awake from his unusually deep sleep.

Blurry eyed, he looked around just as he usually did, making use of the part of his brain that he trained to be his guard dog, making sure he was really awake, and checking it was just his nightmare.

He was alone and so very tired of re-living the same scene, every time he closed his eyes.

Since his cell had no windows to see the outside world, he had no idea of how long he had been asleep, nor did he have any idea as to what time it was. Then seeing the note from Lattimer he had discarded was still on the floor, he knew no one had been in to clean up.

As a double check he looked at the table. Yes, it was still covered with the dirty plates from the meal that he really enjoyed.

Maitland stretched his fatigued body out, adding a loud yawn for the benefit of the guard outside. He found he was bored to the extreme still being incarcerated in the cell. He was fed up of waiting for the 'all great and powerful' Russell Lattimer to show his face.

The prisoner had decided he was in no mood for sitting about any longer. No, for him this part of the game was over. He sat on the edge of the bed trying to think of something, anything that he could do to escape from here. It was time for him to be free, or die in the attempt, either way his patience had worn just a little too thin.

As he slowly attempted to stand on his unsteady legs, Maitland felt the strength returning to the muscles in his body, he was hoping he was steady enough on his feet for a change, as he took a step, then two more.

Ah success, the room did not spin, the pain in his torso and arms had become a bit more bearable and after a minute or two of walking around, he was feeling confident, as he targeted the only weakness he could find in the room.

The door, with the nosey guard on the other side. He strode over to it with urgency in every step, as he called out.

'Guard, are you still there?'

'What the hell do you want Maitland?' came a suspicious and disgruntled reply.

'What time is it Guard?'

There was no reply.

'I asked you what time it is.'

'Shut up and go back to your bed, you're not supposed to be talking.'

'Ok Guard, tell me about Lattimer then?'

'What's to tell? He's in charge and I follow whatever orders come from whoever is in charge and those orders are to keep you quietly and safely locked up in here.'

Maitland pulled a face as if to say, fair enough.

'So you used to be a soldier then?'

'No, a security guard and nightclub bouncer.'

Wow, a completely honest answer for a change, 'maybe there is hope for humanity after all', he thought.

'You know I want to kill him don't you?'

'Yeah I heard about you and what you've done here and there. Thought you'd be bigger somehow.'

Maitland snorted a little. 'Yeah, I get that all the time,' there was a pause in the discussion. 'So tell me how I can get to him. Tell me how I can get out of here without having to kill you first.' Maitland placed his face firmly against the cold, hard mirrored glass surface, hoping the guard was looking at him.

The ever vigilant guard shouted from the other side of the door.

'Maitland, stop this and go back to your bed, now!' Tiredness, frustration and anger were loaded in the guard's plea like a command and Maitland knew he had finally got the bite he wanted. Now it was time to land the fish.

'Why don't you come in and make me?' Condensation covered the glass panel, as Maitland spoke, but only a loud bang on the door, which made Maitland blink, was his reply.

'Well come on then boy, open this door,' Maitland pushed at the handle.

To his amazement the door opened slightly.

It wasn't locked after all.

Carefully, he pushed at the door with both hands and this time a little harder, just to test how far it would go without being interrupted.

The door willingly and smoothly swung fully open, stopping only to return to its closed position, all thanks to the help of the built in self-closing mechanism.

He saw the hulking guard, with a shocked expression then move closer to the door, ensuring it closed properly.

'Go back to your bed Maitland. Don't make me shoot you.' Panic filled the instruction.

Maitland smiled.

'Now I doubt you're going to be doing that are you?' Maitland shouted as he kicked out with all of his strength at the wooden barrier. The door repeated it's only function and quickly swung open on its hinges. That was until the hard edge hit and buried itself into the forehead and nose of the guard. It seemed he got a little too close for his own good. With blood flowing down his face, the guard dropped to the floor, jamming the door closed.

Maitland heard the thud of the guard hitting the floor and saw the door being slammed closed with a bang. He had to push hard from his side, to open the door wide enough to allow him to leave.

'So, you are alone,' he said as he bent down and pulled at the guards lapels, raising his head up to talk to the dazed and injured man, he asked, 'come on, tell me, where can I find Lattimer?'

'Penthouse.' Mumbled the guard just before passing out.

'You're not going to be of any use to me, are you?' Maitland said as he slapped the dazed man's face and dropped him back to the floor. The guard had dropped his gun and Maitland picked it up, walked along the corridor towards the exit and out into the compound.

As the escapee walked away, the guard began to come round a little. His groggy instinct was to go after him, or at least alert others, but he decided it would be better for him to stay exactly where he lay, after all he wasn't going to be the one that got the legendary Jon Maitland killed. Not before Lattimer had a chance to speak with him anyway. He settled down and remained on the floor, bleeding as he watched Maitland exiting the building, into the night.

Once outside Maitland abruptly stopped, his eyes adjusting to the lower light level, as he looked around at the dark horizon. He was trying to see if he could find the silhouette of the castle.

'Well Mister Lattimer, it would seem when you scratch the surface of this perfect little town of yours, it starts to show the cracks beneath.' Maitland thought.

Cracks in Lattimer's façade, that Maitland wanted to chip away at and cautiously he continued his walk through the cold yard, he slowly became aware of the lack of guards and considering this part of the compound was the prison, he expected to find at least a whole garrison of personnel guarding the place.

Was this more failings in Lattimer's charade? He questioned. Maybe they were on their way to let Lattimer know his prize prisoner, was now free and making his way to the Castle, but this time it was Maitland who wanted to talk to Lattimer.

***

Celeste Baker found herself having to carry out a forced entry to the Penthouse, an act that was definitely not one of her better ideas, but at this stage in the proceedings, she had little choice and even less to lose.

Lattimer was going to have her killed for the murders of his men anyway, let alone breaking into his offices. Being in the suite felt completely alien to her, it was the first time she had been alone in here and in complete darkness too. She was silent and listening to the distant sounds of the building creaking and groaning, only added to her nervous state. All of her recent actions went totally against what her training had taught her.

She wondered where it was coming from.

'What the bloody hell are you doing in here Celeste?' She quietly asked herself, as she stood with her back against the door listening to hear if anyone had followed her in.

It was a habit of hers, even though she knew she would not be disturbed with Mike Spencer watching her back outside, she still felt it wise to be careful.

With only the light of the moon climbing through the window, reflecting off all the white surfaces it touched, to light her way, her eyes quickly adjusted to the darkness.

'Now to work,' she determinedly whispered and began to search the first room. She was hunting for anything that may be of help, in the rescuing of Maitland from his incarceration and the toppling of the crazed Lattimer.

She found, such was the conceit of the madman, he had left his desk drawers unlocked. She was surprised, he genuinely thought no one would dare invade his office space and after several minutes of a simple search, Celeste found nothing of use to her, except Garforth's gun that she had left earlier.

'Oh yes, that will do for starters,' she said smiling as she picked it up, checking the chamber to see if the bullets had been removed or not. Her smile remained, as it still contained the six tiny messengers of death, and after replacing the hammer carefully, she placed it into the brown canvas bag, which she had the foresight to bring.

Continuing the search, she checked cupboards, filing cabinets and drawers, all without any success and when all of the obvious hiding places had been exhausted in this room, she moved to the doors that lead to an inner room.

Celeste cursed under her breath when she found they were locked. 'Why would it be locked when nothing else is,' she wondered as she grabbed the keys from her bag. It was difficult to read the lock ID in the dark and so she tried all of them. On her fourth attempt she matched the corresponding key and swiftly entered the room.

It was filled with row upon row of shelves, shelves that were filled with books. Celeste had never seen so many books in one place, outside the library of the Centre.

She approached the first rack and twisted her neck to get a better look at the words written on the spines. She ran her fingers gently across the print; they all seemed to be political. There were books covering old Westminster, the history of English politics over the years and so on. The books in the next rack covered subjects of religion and sociology and the next rack was filled with books about the arts.

She slowly walked around, awe struck as the books seemed to cover every subject imaginable, cooking, animals, farming.

She finally ended up looking at a brown leather armchair; next to it was a small table, with an open, green leather bound book on top of it.

She sat down and picked up the tome.

'Brave New World' by Aldous Huxley.

The old yellowing sheets of paper emitted a smell that reminded her of vanilla and it was tinged with a fruity, almond scent, that was followed by the smell of mushroom. It was not a bad smell and it somehow had a warming, familiar feel to it, akin to fresh bread being baked.

After removing her nose from the pages, Celeste replaced the book on the table and decided the room was pretty much everything you would expect a well-to-do tyrant to have at his disposal. All of it was nice, of course, but there was absolutely nothing, useful to her, whatsoever.

She was getting agitated at the fruitless search. No matter where she looked, there was precious little of anything that she could use. The situation was leaving her disappointed, 'what self-respecting dictator didn't have hidden secrets?' Celeste thought, as she left the book room to return to Lattimer's desk and poured herself into his chair.

She remained there for a few minutes, looking at the shadows, trying to put herself into his shoes, trying to think like he does. 'Come on Russell, tell me, where would you hide things?' She said aloud.

Suddenly there was a twitch at the curtains on the French doors, it caught her eye and she spun to scrutinise the white, heavily lined drapes leading to the balcony. She watched the curtains as they made a definite movement, somebody had opened the door from the outside and that somebody was now entering the room.

Her heart began to race, pumping more adrenaline into her bloodstream and around her body. Somehow though, she remained calm, listening to the rhythm of her heart, as it pulsed in her ears.

Without showing any signs in her actions of the panic she was feeling, Celeste slowly retrieved the gun from the bag and pulled back on the hammer, until she heard the reassuring click as it locked into place.

Celeste, despite her impaired vision, squarely aimed the cocked pistol at the material as it billowed in the night breeze.

She watched with curiosity as a single foot, wearing a black shoe appeared at the hem of the curtain. This naturally, was followed by another. The whole thing was becoming too surreal and it would not have surprised her if a peg leg had followed, but what are the chances of Lattimer's office being broken into twice on the same night, at the same time?

'You can stop right there.' Her voice carried all the authority she could muster.

'I've got a gun, it's loaded and I've got it pointing directly at you and I can and will use it.'

There was a hesitation from the intruder.

'May I suggest you come in from the cold, close the door and get to your knees.'

There was no movement, no reaction.

'Now!' She sternly added.

After some unseen movement from behind the curtain, there was a click of the door being closed. She did not blink her stinging eye as she closely watched the pair of feet walk into the room, lifting the curtains from the door to slowly reveal who the mystery guest was.

At their limit, the heavy white sheets of material eventually stopped and gravity took over, helping them to fall quickly back into their original position, fluttering slightly as they came to rest covering the French doors.

A man was standing in front of her, his back was turned and his hands were raised.

He stood, silent.

'I said on your knees and turn around, I really don't like shooting people in the back.' A recollection of Marta's death flitted through her mind. That was the exception, she thought, and watched as the uninvited guest obeyed and got to his knees.

Her mouth was dry and she had to lick her lips. There was a slight shake to her hand and as he slowly turned to face her, she reaffirmed her aim.

'Well I must say you do look remarkably well, for a dead woman that is and a hell of lot better than when we first met,' Jon Maitland smiled at Celeste as he spoke. 'Not sure about the eye patch thing you have going on though.' He joked.

'Oh my God, Jon Maitland. I was just about to come and get you out of gaol.'

He looked down at the floor, then glanced back at her while opening his hands, as he gave her 'a what now' look.

'Oh Sorry yes, please get up.' She said as she released the hammer and placed the gun back in the bag.

It was a sign to him that he had her trust.

Maitland stood and moved to occupy the chair opposite Celeste and there they remained quietly looking at one another for a moment.

'Perhaps you now want to talk to me Mister Maitland,' she finally stated.

'Looks like I have no choice in the matter Miss Baker, but first, suppose you tell me some history of what's happening here and who the hell this Lattimer is. You know he's blaming me for your death, don't you?'

'Not any more he's not, he knows I'm alive, but he does think you did this to me and that you have his merchandise, you know the boxes at the house, oh, he also thinks you're here to kill him.'

'I wonder how he came to that particular conclusion.'

Maitland added with another smile and the two talked for some time, with questions being asked and answers being given.

Back and forth the conversation went, each trying to gauge the other's motives, seeing if they could work together, until Mike Spencer came rushing in, holding aloft an old, dirty cricket bat as a weapon.

'Baker, are you OK? I wondered where you had gotten to, so I came looking for you and when I heard voices from in here, I thought Lattimer had caught you. I figured you were in trouble, but I can see you're all nice and cosy.' He was panting with fear.

Celeste laughed a little. 'No, it's OK Mike, I'm fine. Sorry I forgot you were outside, come in. You had better meet Jon Maitland. Maitland, meet the Reverend Mike Spencer, he thinks a lot.'

The clergyman opened his mouth to speak, then forgot to close it, standing with his hand out while Maitland pumped the outstretched limb in greeting. 'Pleased to meet you Reverend Mike Spencer.'

'Mike, Mike... err... are you OK?' Celeste called out.

The star-struck man nodded; then he quietly sat on a nearby chair while Baker and Maitland continued with the history lesson.

After two more hours, Maitland had a better picture of the trouble he was in, as more pieces of the puzzle began to fall into place.

'So that's it really,' said Maitland, 'Lattimer's off his head, completely crazy and out of control and we have to get rid of him.'

With her one good eye, she looked directly into his eyes. 'But the question I have for you Mister Jon Maitland is, will you help me to get the town away from him?'

He sat back in his chair and thought for a second.

Then he grinned.

'Wouldn't miss it for the world Baker, but before we go, put the kettle on love, I'm gasping for a cuppa.' He shot a wink at her.

She quickly looked at him, her face turning serious for a moment.

'What did you say?

'Err... I just asked for a cup of tea that's all. Why?'

'Just a touch of Déjà Vu that's all. I've been having it a lot lately, its nothing I guess.'

A council of war had just formed and unbelievably the three of them sat about drinking tea and discussing plans, in the office of the man they were plotting against. Celeste, Maitland and the Reverend Spencer finally agreed that the best way to deal with Lattimer was head on, once and for all. It was to be a confrontation like no other and for Maitland, there was no time like the present.

Celeste turned to Mike Spencer. 'Priest, I need you to go into town, you're to get as many people as you can and be sure you are all ready in the square at the usual time of Lattimer's sermon. I think with Maitland on our side, you may just get to see your miracle after all.'

The priest nodded, but before leaving, he lowered his head and, clasping his hands together, he said a prayer for them all. Out of respect Celeste copied him, while Maitland looked on with zero interest in the proceedings.

Chapter Nineteen

It must have been around five in the morning when Russell Lattimer, feeling almost victorious and jubilant, entered his living quarters within the empty castle. He had gotten used to there being nobody to welcome him on his return home from work, but tonight he was expecting the young woman from the house at the very least.

She had obviously disobeyed him and absconded, 'and who could blame the poor girl,' he thought, sniggering to himself, knowing full well he did actually blame her.

Her absence infuriated the hell out of him; how he despised the emptiness that surrounded him and he sat for a moment, trying to relax in silence while the whistle of temporary tinnitus rang in his ears.

He reclined, trying to relax and allow that exhilarating tingle that came during and after another murder, to dissipate, but it was making him restless and agitated. This in turn aggravated his psoriasis and made him have to scratch his skin raw.

Finally, banging a clenched fist in frustration on the table, Lattimer jumped up from the seat and called out to a guard outside.

'Bring my nurse here, tell her I need her potions and tell her it's urgent.'

While he waited he removed the uncomfortably tight, black uniform. When he undressed he saw the large dusting of dead skin cells that covered the inside of the dark material. Disgusted with himself he threw it to a corner of the room, where it would stay for the servants to clean up in the morning.

Lattimer entered the shower and turned the taps.

The water cooled and cleansed him from the clothing and finally he rinsed the soap, with the dead skin, sweat and blood of the murdered again being flushed once more from his body.

After drying, he prepared for bed.

This normally meant he would be getting naked between the cool, white cotton sheets alone.

He smiled as the tired nurse meekly entered the room.

Clare Adams was shaking with fear when she entered the room and her heart sank even further, when she found Lattimer was already laid out on the bed.

He moved from his repose to leaning up on an elbow. This way he could see who it was that had entered and for a split second he hoped it might even have been the young woman; perhaps she was just a little late, but no.

'Ah Nurse Adams, it's you,' he announced coldly, 'please do come in, come in. As I recall we have some unfinished business to attend to.' There was a slight disappointment to his tone, for a brief moment he thought he would have had the pleasure of both women, at the same time of course.

She looked at him, pleading with her eyes for him not to do this to her again.

'Oh, you forgot?' He quizzed, 'but surely you didn't really think I would let you slip my mind, did you Clare?' he smiled a little 'never mind,' as he dismissed the smirking guard and continued with his diatribe. This time he spoke in a mock, childlike voice adding a petted lip just for effect.

'Oh Nurse, I have a pain and I think it needs kissing better,' he reclined back on the bed and opened his gown to reveal his grotesque manhood once again.

Clare froze where she stood.

Disgust painted her face and her hesitation made him look up again, this time with complete and utter contempt for the woman and the terror he was causing.

Then, through gritted teeth, he repeated his demand.

'Nurse, I said I have a pain that I want you to kiss better. I suggest that you get that beautiful mouth of yours over here and I do mean now woman!'

The petrified nurse had no choice, she had to obey the pig and reluctantly she walked over to him while slowly undressing.

***

After the Reverend Spencer left the Penthouse, Celeste Baker and Jon Maitland made ready and quietly walked from the Penthouse to the castle. He followed her as she led them through the streets, avoiding as many of Lattimer's guards as they could, only killing those they felt necessary. It wasn't long before the duo slowly approached the ancient building from Castle Dyke.

They watched quietly, as a lone guard stood at the entrance. After a few moments he was joined by another and they seemed to share, what Maitland took to be a joke, as he saw them both laugh.

The guards slapped one another on the back, moved apart and took up their positions quiet and relaxed.

Through improvised hand signals a silent conversation took place between Maitland and Celeste. The signals were understood by one another and they both agreed on which guard they would take on. Maitland raised his hand and after a count of three, they rushed to the doorway, with one going right and the other left.

Maitland despatched his guard quickly, by simply breaking the poor man's neck, with an anger filled, but unnatural twisting of his head.

His surviving partner was too slow in reacting, having seen his friend lying dead on the floor, giving time for Celeste to sidle up behind him.

She swiftly placed her left hand over his mouth, followed by her making a lightning quick and deep incision into his neck with her knife.

With the slicing of his flesh, came the severing of the artery buried in his neck. Celeste tightly held on to him when they both fell to the floor. She wrapped her legs around his waist, with her hand still gripped tightly over his mouth. She desperately tried to stifle his screams as they remained on the floor.

With the guard on top of her fatally entwined, Celeste was fighting to hold on to him. She managed to manoeuvre herself from below him when she felt his strength dwindling.

At last she straddled him, breathing heavily enough for both of them, then the guard lay dead.

She stood up and was still gasping for air when she looked at her jacket. It was covered in his blood and quickly she took it off, discarding it in a nearby bush.

Celeste stood in a thin, white vest top and ignored her shivers, while Maitland leaned against the door with his arms folded, an impressed look on his face at her abilities. He was right, she could look after herself.

She grunted at him as she cleaned her knife on the grass and then she opened the door to the castle, gesturing for the smiling Maitland to enter first.

He slightly bowed and accepted her offer.

They made their way to Lattimer's bedroom, again remaining in complete silence.

***

Lattimer's other arm was bent over the top of himself, his head resting in his open hand.

He voiced his enjoyment with a moan and couldn't think of a more perfect way to end the day, than in the company of a beautiful woman.

Suddenly the door to the room burst open, making the quick witted, but outraged Lattimer, brutally push the choking nurse away.

'For fuck's sake, am I ever going to get any type of sex from this or any other woman this week?'

He turned to see the barrels of two guns pointing at him.

Jon Maitland and Celeste Baker stood side by side in the doorway.

'Ah Lattimer and I see you're still awake, good' Celeste said, 'for a moment there I was worried I might have to disturb you, but I can see you're disturbed enough.'

'This is the famous Russell Lattimer?' questioned Maitland, 'at last we meet, I've heard so much about you Russell that I feel I already know you. Judging by the note I got with that fantastic meal, which I must thank you for by the way, you want to talk to me and it seemed rather urgent too.'

Maitland, with Baker by his side, walked into the room and they moved to either side of the bed.

Lattimer quickly sat himself up and began scratching at his skin and rubbing his face.

'What the! Who the hell do you think you are?' Lattimer spluttered. Then on realising who his unexpected guests were, he very quickly quietened down.

The distraught, naked woman finally registered with Maitland and he realised what was happening to her. Behind the tear filled grimace, he noticed a resemblance to a face he had recently met.

'You, are you the mother of Maria and John?' He bluntly asked.

She nodded.

'Do you know where they are now?'

She looked at Lattimer, 'He told me he has them, in the Reformation Centre.'

Maitland shook his head, 'No, I met them the other day, up by the old quarry; I gave them a horse and a gun. Do you know where they would have gone?'

Her whole body was now shaking with rage and anger, with excitement and shame, but she managed to nod to him.

'Good, good. They're great kids; I wouldn't want anything to happen to them. Baker, give the lady a hand to get dressed would you, I want a quiet word with Lattimer.'

Celeste nodded, immediately helping Clare from the bed and retrieving her clothes, they headed out of the room.

Maitland strolled over to the bed and Lattimer's hand smartly disappeared under his pillow, but by the time the panicking leader swung back to face Maitland, a closed fist, containing the handle of a gun, smashed hard and loud into his skull.

The collision between soft flesh and the hard edge of the solid handle, left Lattimer with a large gash in his scalp and the start of a massive headache, which increased, with the thunderous concussion as Lattimer's gun rang out.

The explosion momentarily deafened all of them and instinctively they covered their ears. Maitland turned to the door to see the nurse's mouth open with no sound coming out. It was a moment or two later her high pitched scream seemed to grow louder, as his hearing level returned to near normal.

Maitland then looked to where he could feel a pain and he saw a trail of the red, thick liquid, slowly trickling from a hole that had suddenly appeared in the bicep of his left arm.

He touched the blood with his right hand and rolled it between his thumb and finger as though he was checking its viscosity. Curiously, he pressed at the rim of the small circular wound, the touch made the pain in his arm increase and he winced.

Angrily he glared at the shocked Lattimer, whose own blood was running from the gash in his head down his cheek.

Maitland took the smoking gun away from Lattimer's trembling hand, as easily as he would have with a naughty child and a toy.

Celeste had busied herself by grabbing the arm of the now hysterical nurse and continued escorting her into the other room.

Maitland turned his back on the bleeding, naked leader to watch the women leave.

Maitland thought for a moment, then, still with his back to Lattimer, he said.

'You know Lattimer; you're not the nice, friendly chap you pretend to be, are you?' He moved away from the bed a little, 'now I'll ask you again, why do you want to talk to me?'

Maitland returned his gaze to Lattimer.

They looked into one another's eyes, sizing one another up.

'So you're the great vigilante Maitland, eh?'

'That's me.' He curled his mouth and shrugged his shoulders, 'I'm The Reaper and wherever I go, death soon follows, so you had better keep that in mind Lattimer.'

A small glint of something began to sparkle somewhere in Lattimer's thoughts, but it was not clear.

'I seem to know you, do I know you? Have we met, Maitland?'

Maitland pulled back, averting Lattimer's gaze to search his own memory, checking to see if there was any recollection of his adversary in there.

Nothing.

He returned a blank expression.

Lattimer put his bloodied hand in the air and motioned that it was not important at this point.

'Maybe it is just the stories, no matter. But what does matter is what you did with my merchandise, you thieving bastard.'

'And what merchandise would that be?'

'Don't you dare play games with me Maitland, not now and certainly not here. You know full well what merchandise. I want my stuff and I want it now, do you understand me, NOW!' He began shouting.

A bemused Maitland thought nothing of moving closer and lashing out at his enemy again. The white sheets became increasingly stained, as yet more of Lattimer's blood splashed onto them, all thanks to another well aimed pistol whipping from Maitland's hand.

With yet another wound in his head, Lattimer sat, oozing the red body fluid.

'Don't raise your voice to me, you're in no position to be giving me, or anyone else orders, is that clear?' Maitland's eyebrow rose.

Lattimer nodded while holding his head from the blows.

He gestured with his hands for Maitland to stop any more attacks.

'OK, OK, but look here you fool, that merchandise is important to me right now and I want it returned intact. Look Maitland I'll make sure you get what you deserve.'

The cornered, scheming dictator stammered as he attempted to negotiate.

'Sorry Russell, I really don't know what the hell you're talking about, looks like you got the wrong man.'

Lattimer had remained on the bed and in the same position, but his eyes wandered everywhere. To Maitland it looked as if he was reading from an invisible book, but he knew the man's mind was busy trying to collate the various pieces of information he had just been given.

There was a moment of complete silence.

Lattimer lifted a finger in the air.

'For arguments sake Maitland, let's say I believe you. It begs the question, what the hell are you doing here in Launceston? And what about Archer and his family? Did you have to kill them?'

'Archer? Nope. Wrong again. I didn't meet Archer until he ordered his goons to turn me into a spicy meatball, after which, I was introduced to his very strange wife. In fact, I don't know anyone here anymore, let alone kill them or have them killed.'

'You've been here before then?'

'Oh yes, a long time ago, but that's all academic Lattimer. You need to answer me now and tell me why you want to talk to me?'

Lattimer ignored the question, his mind was occupied with trying to work out what Maitland had just said, or more to the point, what he was not saying.

'If not you, then who?' he whispered.

His hands danced in the air, he was moving pieces of invisible information about, blocks of dates, names and places cross referenced with deeds done, finally putting them in one order and then another. Suddenly, the eyes of the maniac opened wide with the realisation, that he had been lied to. Angrily he punched the mattress several times, and with each punch, he exclaimed just one single word.

'Celeste.'

'Oh I don't think she's had much to do with it Lattimer. Did you not see the state she is in? When I found her at the house, she was already close to death and certainly not fit to do anything to anyone.'

Maitland looked at Lattimer, 'But then again, people do recover from such things and, invariably, always want their little piece of revenge, don't they?'

A breathless Lattimer suddenly looked tired and worn out as he sat on the bed, surrounded sheets soaked in his own blood.

To Maitland, the 'all great and powerful' Lattimer was nothing more than a sad excuse of a man, but he also knew that the ideals Lattimer stood for, were a more powerful adversary.

'OK Lattimer, so tell me, why is this merchandise of yours so damned important to you, that people are dying left, right and centre for it?'

Lattimer laughed a little.

'You are kidding right? You really don't know what we're doing here?'

Maitland shrugged. 'Is there any reason why I should know?'

Lattimer returned a dumbfounded look. 'Well no, I don't suppose someone like you would know anything really.'

'Someone like me?'

'You know Maitland, a loner, a selfish thug, who has a real problem with authority and who is only interested in what you want, your needs, your requirements. Ever heard of 'for the greater good' Maitland?'

Maitland smiled at the show of audacity.

'Maybe you can fill me in Lattimer. Perhaps of all the people I have met, you are going to be the one who is going to teach me what it is to be human. Perhaps it's going to be you, you who would kill a man, just because he said no to you and put his family first? So, come on you arsehole, I'm waiting, show me the error of my ways.'

'Maitland, you've got me all wrong, I only want what is right for the people of this town.'

Maitland's eyes showed the disbelief he was feeling.

'Yeah, that's right Jon! Look, why don't I show you? Come on, what do you say?'

'You sanctimonious bastard, I don't need any lessons from you, or anyone else like you. I've met a thousand tinpot leaders up and down the country and you're all the same, all of you trying to look after 'the greater good'.'

Maitland turned and he caught a glimpse of his own dark, misshapen reflection in the window, he ignored it and turned back as he continued.

'You know something Russell, the reality of it is they couldn't give a shit about anyone, but themselves and the power they have over others, just like you.'

'No Maitland, I want to get us all through the gateway into Kernow, I want every last soul to be saved.'

'Through what gateway? The last time I was here there was no gateway and believe me, I would know.'

'You see how much this place has changed Jon; already you don't know what you think you do?'

'OK then Lattimer, come on, we're going for a walk. I want to see what all the fuss is about. I want to see this Kernow Gateway for myself.'

The suggestion seemed to cheer Lattimer up slightly.

'Good, good, but first I need to get cleaned up, we can talk more in there, where it's a little more comfortable.'

Lattimer pointed to the living room.

'Sure, why not, but be quick about it.' Maitland folded his arms and stood in a stubborn immovable stance.

'You can wait outside, you know Maitland.'

'No it's OK, you don't have to be shy in front of me, it's not like it's the first time you've been naked in front of another man is it?'

The outraged Lattimer got out from the twisted bedding and walked slowly toward a closed door, which led to the shower room.

'Where do you think you're going?'

'I need to shower.'

'No, no shower, just get dressed.'

The instruction and the tone in which it was delivered, annoyed Lattimer. Maitland could see that on his face, as he obeyed and moved to the wardrobe.

'Wait.' Maitland shouted and waved the gun, gesturing for Lattimer to move away.

Naked and chilled Lattimer raised his hands in surrender and moved away from the wooden cupboard, his frustration building to unbearable levels.

Without taking his eyes, or aim, from his prisoner Maitland used his bullet-punctured arm to open the wardrobe door. Blindly he reached inside and grabbed whatever came to hand.

He took hold of something that felt like material and on retrieving the garment from the darkened storage unit, he saw the blood from his hand had begun to soak into it, adding a splash of colour to the white cotton fabric.

He threw it at Lattimer.

'That will do, now put it on.'

The leader was getting more and more aggravated with all the instructions, he had so far received from this man. A man who, after all, should have been his prisoner, but Lattimer also knew he had little choice but to obey Maitland's orders, for now at least.

Lattimer begrudgingly put the suit on and as with Maitland, his blood began to seep into the soft smooth cotton.

'OK?' Maitland questioned.

Lattimer only stared at him.

'Good. Now get in there.' Maitland issued another of his orders, whilst again waving the gun, as he followed Lattimer out of the room.

As the two men entered the room Celeste was already sitting behind his desk. He watched as she raised her gun and pointed it at him. This, and the fact that she was in his chair, finally made his tolerance fail him. He sped across the room shouting as he tried to attack her.

Maitland was just as quick in his reactions and with a swift kick to the feet of the runaway, as he was in mid stride, he tripped him.

Gravity took over, forcing the running man to fall hard on to the white floorboards. The memory of Lattimer doing the same to the escaping woman earlier, played out somewhere in his brain as he landed. There was no funny side to it this time, as he came to a stop, ironically in the same place, where he had felled Robert Garforth.

Celeste still had her gun primed, keeping it pointed at the fallen leader. It wavered a little when she couldn't help but snigger at seeing the poor oaf form a sprawling, undignified mess on the floor.

Lattimer was far too busy to notice the blood that had dried between the gap in the floorboards; it was blood that had not been cleaned away properly, blood that was from the body of Robert Garforth.

Lattimer moaned, as he peeled his freshly grazed face from the floor and sat a little dazed. He looked around to see Maitland and Celeste staring at him.

'Well, well, well. Look at you two all cosy.' He forced an evil smile on his blood soaked face, his eyes staring up at them while he sat, defeated and deflated.

'I knew it, you two are working together.'

Maitland stood and watched Lattimer, as he pulled on something that was around his neck.

'OK Lattimer, enough. Now on your feet, you're going to take us to this Kernow gateway, and you can lead the way.'

'You know, I'm sure I know you Maitland, when did you say you were here last?' Lattimer asked as he slowly stood and limped towards the door.

Maitland pressed the gun into the small of Lattimer's back.

'I didn't, now shut the fuck up and move.'

All three walked out of the castle and across the well maintained gardens, towards the Kernow Gateway.

Chapter Twenty

They arrived at their destination.

Lattimer did not need to be a mind reader when he saw the look of utter surprise on Maitland's face and, feeling a little vindicated, he managed to give Maitland a smile. 'You see Jon, the gateway to Kernow.'

'Lattimer, is this it? Is this really your gateway to a new life?'

'No, I mean yes... wait, let me open the door, the actual gateway is inside, this is just a gatehouse.' Lattimer agitatedly searched for the key, while Celeste and Maitland looked at the rickety wooden structure.

'You're kidding, right?' Celeste asked.

'But it's a garden shed, with a small flagpole on the top.' Maitland added with a laugh.

Lattimer flashed the key while shaking his head.

'No Maitland no, come on, take a look inside, the gateway is in there I promise, come on let me show you.'

Lattimer hobbled to the door and put the key into the lock. He turned it, working the well oiled mechanism easily. Lattimer pulled the door wide open and gestured for Maitland and Baker to enter.

'Oh no Lattimer please, after you.' Maitland still had the gun and waved at the sweating Lattimer to move inside.

'As you wish.' He shrugged and as he hobbled inside Lattimer stumbled and at the same time he felt the pain of Maitland's gun barrel being pushed into his back. It was a reminder to Lattimer that it was Maitland who, for the moment at least, was in charge. As they entered, their movement activated some sort of motion detector and as if by magic, the room lit up.

He had electricity in there and the acrid smell of charging batteries, was thick in the air. Maitland looked around and saw cables climbing the wall in one corner and exit through the roof. These must have been solar panels connected to the battery charging unit placed on the floor.

A moment later a timorous Celeste followed them in.

Since her childhood, all Celeste had ever known, was that one day, she would be walking through here, to emerge on the other side in Kernow. The nerves she was feeling, were kept company by the excitement she was trying to contain. This was to be the first time she had ever seen the gateway, the entrance for herself.

'Welcome to my gateway to Kernow.' A gushing Lattimer said, while Maitland and Celeste looked to where Lattimer was indicating with an open hand.

Maitland then turned to Celeste.

He saw then the look of complete shock and utter disappointment on her face.

He turned to him.

'OK Lattimer, if this is your gateway, tell us how it works?'

'What do you mean you oaf, how does it work?'

'What's not to understand about the question, tell us how it works? Show us how you get into Kernow from here and through that Gateway.'

Lattimer looked around and moved quickly to a white sofa placed in front of the gateway. He sat down, nervously wringing his hands and avoiding the stern gazes of his guests.

Sweat ran down his face and body, as he became more and more excitable.

'Surely it's simple, even for a numbskull like you Maitland. We will sit here and wait for the guards from the Kernow side to come and open the gate.' He pointed and again Maitland looked to the direction of the pointing finger.

Celeste hadn't moved from the shock that was making her stand and stare at the incredible sight. She simply could not believe her eyes, for fixed to the wall was simply a poster.

A poster, showing a life size image.

It was a large poster, that was once used to advertise Launceston as a holiday destination, in the time before the old one-two, but the words had been erased with paint.

The poster showed a photograph, just a photo of the old wooden doorway to Launceston Castle, the same doorway they had used to get into the castle, to get Lattimer from his bed.

Lattimer continued, 'I just sit here and I wait to be taken over. They come and unlock the gate and allow me to enter. Then they escort me to wherever I want. When I am finished, they bring me back here.' He giggled a little and leaned forward to whisper, as if he was privately sharing information with the others.

'I have to admit though, it does get really boring here, you know, waiting for the guards to arrive. So I take one or two of these.' His hand disappeared down the edge of the cushion and Maitland immediately trained his gun on him, ready to shoot.

Lattimer retrieved his closed hand, then placing it tight to his chest; he covered it with his other hand.

He furtively looked around, again checking that they were still alone.

He nodded gently to himself, then held out his hand.

Slowly he opened his palm to reveal what was nestled in his hand. Four roughly shaped, jade green pills sat in a cluster; the colour was dissolving into his sweaty skin, discolouring his skin.

'I got Annie Archer to make them for me; they're to relieve the boredom.'

Celeste turned to look at what he was offering.

With a pathetic smile, Lattimer looked at her.

'After I take one or two of these, the guards soon come to open the gateway and we go on our merry way.'

He waited for a reaction from either or both of them.

When he had had enough of the silence, he continued. 'Oh Celeste, you of all people would marvel at the sights they have over there.'

She could no longer contain her anger and explosively she allowed it to finally erupt.

'What? What did you say? Do you mean to tell me that everything we have done here, everything you have promised us, has been based on a drug fuelled hallucination?'

Lattimer looked up at Celeste, confusion settling on his face.

'A drug fuelled hallucination, what the hell do you mean girl? Look, there's the damned gateway there, can't you see it? These, these just help me with the boredom.'

Finally, the truth started to unravel and it was all too much for her. She rushed at him, her flaying hands slapping hard on his face.

Lattimer had to reel his hand in quickly, clutching the closed fist hard to his chest, while attempting to block her attack with the other. He was more interested in protecting the pills in his hand, than what was being said at that point.

'You bastard! You lying, cheating bastard! The things we've done in the name of the freedom you've promised us! Don't you know we believed in you Lattimer, don't you realise that despite everything, we trusted you with our futures!'

'No Celeste no, I'm not lying. Look, why not take one, go on take one, sit here with me and keep looking at the gateway. You'll see, soon the guards will come and take us all to Tintagel, or maybe Newquay, in that electric car of theirs. Oh I'm sure you would both love it there.'

She was crying through the anger she was feeling, and as her strength began to subside, an exhausted Celeste, halted her attack on him and collapsed to the floor.

After a moment of sobbing she sat herself up, not really sure even now, why Lattimer thought he was telling them the truth.

'You disgust me Lattimer you know that! You have lied to us for all these years and for what? A poster! A damned photograph!' As she looked at him she could feel a new rant brewing in her. 'You've forced us to steal and made us kill for this? A freedom that doesn't exist, except in your doped up reality!'

Deep in thought, the battered man opened his palm and looked at the clover leaf green tablets as she continued.

'Lattimer, why can't you seem to understand what you have done? I mean when this gets out.' Celeste became exasperated, 'don't you know what you have done? Don't you realise you have destroyed everything we have tried to achieve.'

All three people remained silent, all sharing glances, all thinking of what was going to happen next.

Lattimer looked down at the four pills.

Maybe she was right, could it be these pills were making him think he was in Kernow? He thought hard, clearing the haze of the drugs and somewhere in his head, he heard a voice say 'yes, of course she's right,' but he ignored it.

For the moment his focus was on the pills, because if she was right, it would be so easy for him to take them all in one go, bringing him eternal relief from the pain and suffering of his skin complaint. He would then be free, from his responsibilities as the Elite Enforcer, free from any blame that would befall him, as the web of deceit he has weaved becomes untangled.

Yes it will end, here and now, but by his own hand. There is no way he would let 'The Reaper', Jon Maitland, have the pleasure of gaining another notch on his belt.

Lattimer quickly glanced at Maitland, who was still holding the gun, but had become distracted with Celeste and not aiming at anything.

Looking down at the four leaf clover of death, he opened his mouth ready to receive the tablets.

From nowhere, Maitland slapped his hand hard onto Lattimer's. It was the loud crack of skin on skin that startled Lattimer, more than the searing pain he felt.

'It's not going to be that easy for you Lattimer; you've got a lot of explaining to do.'

'Explaining, explaining about what and to whom?' He looked at Maitland with a defiant and conceited air. 'Don't you know who I am Maitland? I'm a God here and Gods do not have to explain to anyone, ever.'

Maitland leant forward, putting his face close to the madman and pointed to Celeste, who was now pacing.

'Well your Godliness, look at what you have done and then look at her. You need to explain to her, you have to tell her and the others, why you're worshipping the image of an old doorway!'

Hearing that he was being blamed for the actions of this disillusioned young woman, the truth finally began to affect Lattimer. He looked up at them and tears rolled down his cheeks.

He was crying.

'No Maitland, it's not a picture, it's real.'

When Celeste's frustration erupted again, she stormed over to the image and quickly scanned it, looking for a tear which she could pull with both hands; she blindly took hold of the paper and pulled.

The tearing noise, was covered by the panic stricken screams of Lattimer's protest, at the destruction he was witnessing.

'No Maitland, not again you bastard, not again.'

Lattimer sat back, exhausted and defeated. He was breathing heavily with mucus streaming from his nose.

Glaring at Celeste, he turned his attention to Maitland and pulled out a locket to nervously toy with it.

A wide eyed Maitland stared at Lattimer, taken aback by the outburst and he raised his left eyebrow, while a quizzical look danced on his face.

His gaze moved from Lattimer to Celeste and then back. Something vague began to scurry and jump around in the mind of the confused Reaper.

Twisting his head from side to side, in an attempt to clarify his recollections, Maitland kept his gaze firmly on the locket. Lattimer followed his opponents' line of sight down to the locket.

Fortunately, his own memory was a little better than the man standing above him and he recalled that it was back at the Penthouse this proverbial light bulb started to glow and now it was fully lit, as memory flooded back to Lattimer's mind.

'My god it's you!' He exclaimed. 'How the hell did I miss that? You know I wasn't sure until just now.' Lattimer stopped crying, he wiped away the tears from his face and the snot from his nose with his sleeve.

He started laughing quite loudly.

'Maitland! You are Jon Maitland. The stubborn, Chief Engineer of the Kernow Wall Company.' Lattimer remained seated as he laughed heartily, slapping the side of his leg.

'I thought I remembered that name. It's you, it's him.' He was now pointing at Maitland as he addressed Celeste. He stood up while pointing at Celeste. 'There's you, with him. Well now this is a real turn up for the books and I couldn't have planned this any better.' Lattimer was laughing so much; more tears ran down his face.

Maitland and Celeste looked at one another in utter confusion, as Lattimer continued his hysterics.

'I'm sorry, honest I am,' He calmed down with a final high pitched wail. 'You've forgotten haven't you Jon?'

Maitland remained quiet, trying to decipher his own thoughts and make sense of what the damaged man was saying.

'Understandable I suppose, I mean considering the hell you must have been through over the years. I guess everything is a bit foggy eh? Come on Jon, you must have suppressed or forgotten a lot, surely.'

Lattimer returned to what was near normal for him; he then looked back and forth at the two of them.

'I suppose it was inevitable, just a matter of time before the two of you met up.'

'What do you mean Lattimer?' Celeste asked.

'All in good time my dearest Celeste. Firstly, I want Jon here to remember. For his own sake, he does need to remember, everything.'

Lattimer sat down again and the two men locked stares. He removed the locket from his neck and pushed it into the empty hand of the stunned Maitland.

Maitland looked down, wondering why he had not noticed it in the penthouse and vaguely he became aware of the importance of the dented, yellow metal object.

Without warning, he jumped at Lattimer, pulling him to the floor, grabbing his face in both hands and began smashing it several times, hard against the grimy pine, tongue and groove flooring.

After the fourth painful collision, Maitland pushed down as hard as he could onto Lattimer's skull, it was as if he was trying to burst a nuisance balloon, but when that didn't work, he pulled Lattimer up to a seated position. His victim's limbs flew about like a doll, as he landed punch after punch to Lattimer's face, and finally landing one to his throat. He then let Lattimer fall backward to the floor again and continued to inflict even more damage.

The beating was relentless.

Blood, sweat and spit began to mix and pool on the floor and as Maitland felled the dictator once more he grabbed hold of Lattimer by his clothes, holding him as his giant hands began to throttle the life from him.

Lattimer was gasping for breath.

'Where the hell did you get this from you bastard?'

Celeste had seen the same look in Maitland's eyes before, at the house when he had killed the punisher.

'Maitland what are you doing? What is Lattimer talking about?' Celeste jumped up and grabbed at Jon's arm, trying to pull him away from her old boss, as he pulled Lattimer toward him to look into his eyes.

'Jon you have to stop it, let him go, don't kill him. Not yet.'

Maitland suddenly let go of him, her softly whispered command entered his ear and he obeyed.

Lattimer fell to his knees, gasping for air as he held his throat.

'Come on Jon think, what happened here, you can remember,' he croaked after regaining enough strength to talk.

Maitland looked down at the beaten man. He was as close to death as he cared to be and needed a way of stopping the onslaught.

Maitland then looked over at Celeste.

'You want to know what this pathetic excuse for a man is talking about.'

Maitland was shaking, with anger raging through every fibre of his body.

'He's talking about me, about how I became what I am.'

Lattimer slapped his thigh, cheering out loud as he sat, breathless on the floor.

'Yes Jon, that's it, tell us what happened, you can remember?'

Maitland walked around a little.

'You see Baker, I used to live around here, about seventeen or eighteen years ago.'

He looked at the wall, walked over to it and gently stroked the cold, hard concrete. There were marks where someone had tried to cut into it and on the floor lay a club hammer next to a bolster chisel. Both tools were covered in dust and concrete chippings. They were pathetic tools, used for a pathetic job, that couldn't be done and were now abandoned.

'I was in charge of finishing this damned wall,' his face was drawn and he seemed suddenly deflated as he turned to look at her, 'it was in the final stage of construction and that evening, while I sat at home, reading a book, I had been given by a friend, I could hear the giggles of my wife and small daughter throughout the house. The two most beautiful, precious people in the world to me were playing, as they prepared the evening meal.'

Maitland found a chair and collapsed into it and to Celeste his voice echoed the strain shown on his face.

'The two of them had cooked a wonderful meal and like I said, the house was filled with laughter, but all too soon, it was bedtime for my baby.'

Lattimer and Celeste looked on in silence, as Maitland stared into space for a moment, recalling for himself that his child's bedtime was something he always enjoyed.

'That night I had promised I would read to her, it was to be her favourite book, 'The Wonderful Wizard of Oz,' she loved to add her own characters to join in with the others, that lived on the pages.'

To remove the lump forming in his throat, Maitland had to swallow hard from his dry mouth.

'Her imagination was amazing, it ran wild and as we read, we laughed, all the time we laughed. We used to make up silly names and spoke in funny voices to bring the story to life and we always lost track of time. It wasn't until my Laura came into the room to remind us of the time and that our child needed to settle down and finally go to sleep, that I stopped. She happily hugged us both tightly as she said good night and always with a million kisses.'

Maitland sat back and breathed deeply as he allowed more of the hidden memories to resurface.

'As we left the room, we always made sure her door remained slightly open and I returned to the living room, while Laura made some fresh coffee to have with some of the buns they had made for me to take to work the next day.'

He looked up and noticed the others were listening.

'We sat there relaxing and chatting about many things and started to make more plans about our forthcoming move over the wall into Kernow.'

He nodded as if to confirm his thoughts.

'But like all good things, the evening came to an end, far too quickly. Funny really, I remember telling Laura, I had to be on the site early next morning to supervise the last slab going into place. It would have completed the wall. It was just a few hours away, that's all, just a few stupid hours and we would meet with the helicopter to start our new life in Kernow.'

He stood up and walked around for a while, silently being followed by the eyes of the other two.

'I suggested to Laura that she should go to bed and she suggested that I should clean up from the evening.'

Maitland smiled at this thought.

'Laura giggled; perhaps it wouldn't hurt for me to know what the kitchen looked like from the inside. You see Celeste, we enjoyed one another's company, we were happy together and we both laughed as though it was the first time we had heard that joke and then we went in our different directions.'

'Ah, the perfect family, eh Maitland?' Lattimer whispered. 'Just you, the little woman and the kid!' The words said with more than just a hint of jealousy.

Maitland raised a finger to his lips and shook his head, as he eyed Lattimer with a reproaching look.

'Do you want me to go on or not, you idiot?' He said while unblinkingly staring at him.

'Oh please do Jon; it's important that you do.'

Maitland looked over to Celeste, who seemed so intent on his story, she was visibly annoyed at the interruption.

'As part of our nightly routine, I checked that the locks on the doors and windows were secure. Then about fifteen minutes later, I freshened up to join Laura in the bedroom. The evening didn't quite end as I had thought. My beautiful wife was still awake and I happily fell into bed and into Laura's open arms. We cradled one another for a while, completely silent and feeling one anothers hearts beating their different rhythms.'

He was silent again, savouring the memory.

'I remember we simply laid there, in complete silence and then we made love, for what was to be the last time.'

Maitland looked down at his hands.

Once more looking at the lost and forgotten locket, but with grief and loss. He could still hear himself speaking, as the shed with Lattimer and Celeste disappeared.

He looked around.

The bedroom was just as he remembered, with his jacket hanging from the wardrobe. His eyes fell to his wife lying on his chest, his arm gently resting across her arm.

The clock on the bed side cabinet showed it was the early hours of the morning and he knew he would be soon woken by Emily screaming.

He carefully pushed his wife away and she remained sleeping as he got up and rushed into the child's room on hearing her scream out.

'It's OK honey, Daddy's here, what's wrong?'

'Daddy I heard someone moving in the hallway, I'm scared.' She sobbed as she held out her arms to him. Hiding a smile, he walked over to pick her off the bed. Maitland gently kissed her head, as she snuggled into his chest and with her still sobbing and breathing heavy in his arms, the protective father strolled back to his wife and placed the now resting child next to her mother. Instantly they both cuddled one another and he left the room, closing the door behind him.'

As he turned to walk away, he was back in the shed.

'I decided to sleep on the settee.' He added.

Maitland looked up and noticed Celeste had sat on the floor, in between him and Lattimer, she seemed to be becoming sadder and more troubled as the vigilante's story unfolded.

Lattimer looked at them.

He smiled to himself, enjoying the misdirection he had conjured, allowing himself to take a rest from the beatings and he relaxed a little.

'That's right Jon, you keep talking, just get it off your chest' Lattimer whispered as he wiped yet more of his blood from his pounding, throbbing face and spat some of the liquid from his mouth.

A completely disgusted Maitland stared down at the bloody bubble of phlegm, which had been deposited onto the floor and ignored the comments.

Maitland looked back to Celeste, was she strong enough for him to carry on?

'Anyway, I was wide awake now and decided to look around, just to make sure it was a bad dream, but there was no-one that I could see, so I went to the cupboard under the stairs and pulled out the spare blanket and pillow. I threw them onto the sofa and decided to make myself a cup of tea.

Celeste hadn't taken her eyes from him. The story he was telling mirrored her own and so many others of her age. She watched his face go blank and knew that even though his lips moved and words came from him, he was back there, reliving that night.

On his return to the living room, he placed the cup down on the floor and from the corner of his eye something moved on the stairs. He remained still for a moment, his heart pounding with apprehension as he peered into the darkness.

It happened again; yes, something fluttered. No not fluttered, there was a definite movement and he jumped over the sofa and ran blindly up the stairs and into what felt to him like a concrete fist belonging to a very large Enforcement Officer.

He fell backwards, rolling down the stairs followed by the large man dressed in black. In one move the intruder bent and picked the stunned Maitland up, he was then dumped onto the sofa. His hand hit the cup, toppling it over and spilling the tea everywhere. Maitland lifted his hand to his face and it was wet. He knew it was blood pouring from his now broken nose, rather than the tea on his hand.

The smug walking mountain moved from his view to somewhere behind him. He held him down and he watched helplessly as his beautiful wife, who was intensely hugging their innocent child, was escorted down to join him on the sofa. It was then he became aware that several other Enforcers had entered the room. One of them, who seemed to be the leader, came into view as he sat on a chair in front of Maitland and with his wife and child sitting next to him, the family were reunited.'

The image stopped there, like someone had hit the pause button while watching an old DVD.

'Jon, what was the name of your daughter?' Celeste interrupted softly.

'Her name? Her name was, no, no… her name is Emily.' Maitland looked at Celeste and his eyes glazed over.

'I used to call her Em& M.' Maitland sighed at the thought of his loss, 'oh Em' he cried placing his hands on his face.

'Jon, continue if you want to, please don't let us stop you,' quipped Lattimer.

Maitland thought for a moment and saw that Celeste also wanted him to go on.

'Anyway the leader of the group nodded to someone behind me and I had to witness my screaming little baby being brutally ripped from the arms of her hysterical mother. I tried so very hard to stop them from taking her, but they held me down and I couldn't move, I just couldn't move.' Maitland began sobbing, 'that was the last time I saw her.'

Celeste stood and approached him, she saw in his face the pain of lost years and of lost love. She opened her arms and he let her cradle him, just like a child, just as he described what he had done to his child.

'You do see don't you, I just couldn't move.'

Tearfully Celeste nodded.

'It's OK Jon, no one is blaming you.'

Maitland looked up at her, he suddenly realised her arms were around him and he pulled away from her embrace. It felt wrong; it felt to him as if he were being unfaithful to the memory of his family.

Wiping his face, he stood and crossed the room and then continued.

'Where was I? Oh yes, the Leader looked at me smiling. 'Well Mister Maitland' he said calmly, 'it would seem you will not capitulate to the Elite Enforcers wishes for a gateway to be placed in the wall and to be frank, after tomorrow, it will, unfortunately for you, be too late!'

I looked at him, 'Is that what this is about?' I was angry and scared, tears rolled down my face for the loss of my beloved Emily, the guilt for dragging my family into this trouble, when all I had to do was to agree to this one simple wish.'

Celeste returned to where she had been sitting as Maitland looked at her, his eyes begging for her to understand.

'But that would have been wrong, I would not have been able to live with that on my conscience, just as I cannot live with this.'

He looked saddened when she didn't respond. He had hoped that someone, anyone would say it was all ok.

'The leader shrugged at me. 'Maybe it is, but no matter though, we do have other ways of getting our will carried out.'

The man gave another nod and a sudden darkness painfully engulfed me, as I fell into unconsciousness.

I have no idea how long I was out for, but when I came to, I was in a chair; my head was sore and immovable. The light in the room hurt my eyes, but I couldn't close them, I couldn't even blink, you see they had glued my eyelids open.

My heart was racing, pounding to escape the cage of my chest, not only because of my fear of what was happening to me, but because directly in front of me was Laura. My beautiful wife was crying, she was naked and being held down on our sofa by at least three men. I tried to shake myself free from the bonds, but again I couldn't. I was stuck there, helplessly looking at Laura as she mouthed 'I love you Jon,' over and over again.

He covered his eyes with his arms and screamed out, making Celeste jump.

When he stopped, he was breathless and water dribbled from his mouth. He wiped it away on his sleeve and looked at Lattimer, again his face went blank.

The leader came into his sight and smiled at the trussed Maitland. 'Ah good, you're awake and just in time for the fun to begin too.'

'No,' He kept screaming, 'you can't be serious, you're going to do this to my wife because I refused to do what you asked? No, you can't do this.'

The leader just smiled. 'There's that 'no' word from you again Maitland.'

'What? I mean OK, I'll put your damned doorway in the damned wall, just give me back my family, you have to let them go and keep me. I beg you.'

The Enforcer put his face in front of mine.

'Sorry, I can't do that because it's our turn to say no Mister Maitland, our turn to refuse you your command. Are you beginning to see how this works now Jon?' He moved away and raised his arm.

'Allow me introduce to you to our new man.'

A naked man walked into view, his embarrassment was lost on the terrified Maitland as the man's chewed and flaking skin gave rise to an additional horror.

'Although he is what, about thirty seven, do you know he's never had sex with anyone before, Jon! So by way of a little initiation ceremony for him, I thought I would let Russell here have a go first. What do you think Jon? Do you like that idea?'

Maitland could only scream as the punishment he was forced to watch began with the naked man, covered in sores and flaking skin moved toward his wife while the other animals cheered him on.

The last thing I remember the lead enforcer say to me was, 'Now keep watching Jon' and the men began to take it in turns to defile my beautiful wife, in our home and on the sofa we had made and where Emily had been conceived. Emily! How could I have forgotten about my beautiful, sparkly eyed Emily?'

He held his breath for a moment, stemming the stream of tears that were trying to burst from his eyes.

'Had the same fate befell her little body too?' I thought, but that was so horrific, it was just too much for me.

350

With Laura screaming time and time again for me to help her, I simply blacked out.

Time passed and I woke to find the men drunk and they were slowly falling asleep where they had fallen and with a final burst I found myself free and I rushed over to Laura. I pulled the sleeping man off her.

'Laura, Laura it's me Jon. Laura.' I turned her battered bloodied face to me. 'Laura I'm sorry, it's my fault this happened to you. I'm so very sorry.'

She began to realise it was me who had at last got to her. She raised her hand to stroke my face and she shook her head. 'Jon I don't blame you, but you know I can't live with what's happened to us. Emily maybe dead, or worse. You know what you have to do, don't you? Jon, don't you?' She weakly whispered.

I kept shaking no as she nodded yes.

'It's OK Jon you have to, neither of us can carry on after this, please Jon I am begging you, do it for me, I love you Jon; I love you.'

She guided my hands to her neck.

'I love you Laura.' I spluttered.

She nodded, smiled and as I grabbed at her throat I began to squeeze.

At first I couldn't do it, but hearing her telling me how much she loved me, I found the strength to do what I had promised. I looked into her eyes, watching them roll back as the sparkle drained from them, all because I was holding her down, choking the life out of her.

That night she died by my hand and in my arms.'

Maitland looked up at Lattimer, who sat smugly nodding and then looked across to Celeste.

Tears were falling from her face.

'I cried all that night while watching over my wife's dead body, making sure that they would not defile her any more. I saw they had taken her wedding ring and her locket, this locket. They had taken her dignity and I had taken her life.

I then looked around to see the drunken scum lying about asleep, I remember I wanted these bastards to be stopped, I was not going to allow them to be free to commit such a crime again and I wanted my revenge, they were going to pay.

It was then I remembered, under the stairs was a canister with just one litre of petrol, even a litre was a rare commodity. I had hidden it some weeks before, in case of an emergency. Well, here was that emergency. So I got up and walked to the cupboard.

No one stirred as I moved about the room, stepping over the bastards to get to the under-stair cupboard. I opened the door, stepped inside and found the green plastic vessel and some matches that I was looking for.

When I retreated from the dark space into the bright room, I released the lid and I began to splash the fume filled liquid over my dead wife, allowing it to soak into her skin and into the floorboards. I continued spraying the rest around the room, covering as many of the animals as I could while they slept.

My coughing from the fumes might have woken them up. I had to walk out into the hallway. I struck the sulphur tipped wooden stick and watched as the fizzling spark became a flame, instantly igniting the gases when I threw the hot match into the room. The explosion that ensued pushed me out into the street and once again I returned to unconsciousness.

Feverishly, Lattimer clapped his hands together. 'Well done Jon,' he mockingly said, 'you've remembered almost all of it perfectly.'

Suddenly, there was a connection in Maitland's memory. A spark flickering between Lattimer and that night forcing Maitland to jump to his feet. He picked up the gun and pushed the barrel deep and hard to the side of Lattimer's head.

'You shit, it was you. IT WAS YOU, you bastard.'

'No, Jon wait, you need to remember it all. Jon, I was there, I was, but remember Jon, remember. It was me that set you free.'

'No, you... you were the first to... You were the one who... my wife. You with your skin, the sores, I remember.'

'Maitland don't you pull that trigger,' Lattimer was shouting, 'you need to remember all of it Jon.'

Lattimer was trying to remain as calm as he could while he began to negotiate with the maddened, revenge fuelled gunman.

'I cannot deny they tried to get me to do what you said, but I couldn't do it Jon, you have to remember I couldn't get an erection and they laughed and teased me.'

Both men were sweating heavily, as the gun was pushed further into his soft temple and Maitland saw it hurt Lattimer which encouraged him to push even harder.

'Maitland you must remember,' Lattimer was shouting, 'you have to remember the other men. They all stood there laughing at me. What you saw Jon, what you saw was me pretending to have a go. Back then, that sort of violence was too much for me.'

Maitland slightly released the pressure from his gun, as he began to search his memory, verifying that the words from Lattimer were indeed the truth.

Seizing the opportunity, Lattimer began to speak again, but a little more slowly this time.

'I was pulled away from her Jon and then the others took their turn. I know it's no consolation, but I also had to watch as they all sickeningly took turns, it was like she was just a plaything.

Jon, I found myself disgusted with what they were doing and I was as helpless as you, so I waited until they were all asleep.

Maitland, that night we both changed and as I watched you through the window pouring the petrol, I didn't want to stop you. I watched and I knew that through you I would get my revenge on them all and I let you get on with it. The rest you know, but I thought you perished in the blast, until now of course.'

Lattimer moved his eyes to look at Maitland, who now had an unsure look about him, as he continued to search his memory.

'For what it's worth, Jon I am so sorry for all that has happened to you.'

Maitland quietly retreated, he was so tired.

'Jon, I also made a promise to myself that night, I promised that I would make sure your daughter, Emily, was going to be looked after and be kept safe,'

Maitland looked at Lattimer, who had a sincere smile.

'I kept that promise Jon, I didn't let you down.'

Maitland collapsed to the floor on hearing the news.

'Emily? Alive?'

Lattimer looked over to Celeste with Maitland following his gaze.

Celeste shook her head. 'What? Me?'

Maitland stood and walked across the room meeting her halfway and they examined one another, intensely looking to see anything that would trigger a recollection.

Celeste looked into Maitland's eyes, as he searched her face. It was as if it had been the first time they had looked at one another. Was there anything on her face that would help him remember or connect her face with that of his little 'Em & M?'

Could it be true that this battered and bruised, young woman standing in front of him, was his long lost daughter? Or was Lattimer playing yet another sick joke on him?

He looked deep into her brown eye; he studied her bone structure and softly touched a tuft of her badly cut hair between his finger and thumb.

It could be her. The hair colour was how he remembered it, dark brown but so much shorter. He remembered how his Emily caused a fuss every time she had to have it washed or brushed because of its length.

He moved his hand to her face and his soft touch sent a shiver down her spine. He stroked her lips and then touched her eye patch.

Celeste raised her hand to meet his and guide it in slowly lifting the protective material from her damaged eye, but with the light pouring into the uncovered optic, a heavy pain seared through her eye, forcing her to automatically bow away from him.

Placing his hand tenderly under her chin, he lifted her face to examine the wound, as well as look at her face.

He gasped, his hold on her arm becoming tighter, he saw that beneath the cover was hidden one beautiful eye, ice blue in colour.

He pulled her to his chest, holding tight with one arm behind her back and the other resting on her shoulders. She embraced him with both hands and held on for dear life as eighteen years of cuddles, of lost love and getting to know one another, hit them both squarely in their hearts.

It was the moment they had both been searching for, but it did not last very long, as Celeste pulled away from Jon Maitland.

She was filled with a lifetime of hatred and Maitland could see it on her face and in her eyes as their hands finally parted. She moved back to the bare wall where the poster had been only minutes earlier. She then began hyperventilating before collapsing to the floor, vomit spewing from her mouth.

Lattimer laughed and giggled at the sight of this unexpected reunion.

'Yes Jon, Celeste used to be Emily, Hehehe. Oh Jon, this is so good you know, so very wonderful.'

Maitland was holding out his hand to help his daughter to her feet. Once he made sure she had settled into her chair again, he stood over her, stroking her hair.

After a while watching the touching interaction between the two, Lattimer interrupted.

'Come on Jon, the least you can do is thank me for saving your daughter. After all, you might have killed her in that explosion too if she hadn't been removed from the house.'

An entwined father and daughter ignored him, as they entered a world of new discovery together, both full of doubt and trepidation. The real world disappeared around them, parent and child once more touched one another's face. Both amazed at finding one another, trying to understand the surreal situation they found themselves in.

Then they separated, with Maitland smiling at her, he wanted to continue his story, now more than ever. He needed to attempt to fill in the gaps for her.

'I woke to find I was lying on a mattress, looking up at a ceiling of blue plastic material that rippled in the wind, like the surface of a pond would in the rain. I managed to sit up a little and look around, but I had no idea where I was or how I got there. I didn't even know how long I'd been there. All I do remember is drifting in and out of consciousness.

I remember I was alive, but I did not want to be. My hands and face had received some minor burns in the explosion which my 'saviours' had treated. I looked at my bandaged hands, then lifted them to my face and nose. I drew in a large breath, the pain shot through me at my touch. I choked on the smell of the ointment, it stank to high heaven. I tried slowly to stand and unsteadily moved to the mirror.

My reflection showed me a face that was scarred with burns, it was dirty and unshaven and my eyelids were damaged where they had been glued. I remember thinking so clearly, that I was a million miles from my well organised, happy life, I shared with my girls. Oh god the girls! That first memory hit me hard and physically forced me back, I collapsed back onto the bed and all I could do was cry, just thinking about Laura and you.'

He saw a reaction in her face and stopped the story.

'Do you remember your mum, Emily?' He used her matriarchal title for the first time and her face fell into her open hands.

'No, Maitland, no I don't,' she lifted her head and through wet eyes she looked at him, 'I don't really remember you either.'

Jon Maitland nodded that he understood.

'It's OK Emily, it's not important, I'm sure you will over time. Anyway, the days turned into weeks and over time the psychical pain returned to my numb body. It was a constant, nagging pain telling me that my physical wounds were healing, but my mind, my heart and my soul were the real casualties. Emily, I hope you can understand the events of that night; the things that happened to us changed me. I also made a promise that the change would remain with me until I died and for weeks I laid about all day. Resting at first then becoming restless.' As if to emphasise the point, he stood up to continue.

'Helping around the commune didn't distract me from my loss, nothing could. I missed you and your mother far too much and I so wanted to die, to join you both in whatever life there may be in the beyond. Yet my broken heart still pumped an unwanted life force around my body, keeping my system going, keeping me alive. My mind forcing me to relive that night, each and every time I closed my damned eyes, even to this day.'

He looked over at Lattimer who was still sitting on the floor. He was covered in blood, his face swollen beyond recognition. He was holding himself in agony, unable to move much, but he was still laughing to himself.

Maitland continued, 'I decided I simply couldn't cope any more with this amount of pain and sorrow, so I looked around the compound and I found a small knife that was used to prepare vegetables and meat at meal times. That day, my mind completely cracked. I was crying all the time; I couldn't sleep even though I was exhausted; I couldn't eat. Then I noticed small, insignificant things started to really irritate me. I hated the heat and the cold, the noise and silence, but mostly I didn't like the fact that everyone else around me was going about their business as normal. They didn't seem to understand me.

They didn't understand that my wife and child were dead.'

Globes of water fell from his eyes, the room blurred and as he looked around, he finally let out a sob from his chest, but still he continued.

'I was eating a small meal of something, when I heard a child calling for her dad. I looked around at her, I was expecting to see you, my little Emily, but it wasn't you and I could take any more.

I picked up the blade.

I examined the shining, ground edge and I ran my thumb down it and watched as my skin opened up, releasing blood that trailed down my hand. The knife was razor sharp and without a second thought, I plunged it into my up-turned wrist and began to pull it up my forearm. More blood began to spurt from the open arteries, as the metal sliced through the soft, weak internal tubing.

I calmly lifted my arm to look at the results and do you know something Emily? I felt absolutely no pain what so ever.'

I was dazed and vaguely recalled screaming children and women who watched as I sat there ripping open my skin. That was the only time I have begged to any God, who may have been listening, to take me there and then, just so I could be reunited with my girls, to once more be a husband and father.

Until this moment, I thought that no God heard my plea, but somehow I survived this and all the other attempts I have made of suicide since.

Eventually I gave up trying altogether and instead I decided to travel around, what was left of this sad country, in search of someone who would do the job for me.'

Maitland was now relaxed when he turned to his daughter, only to see her getting more upset as he finished his story. He smiled, indicating for her to stop her tears.

'You see Emily, in life we encounter so many circles and being back here, home with you, I have just found another.'

His account was again interrupted by a laughing Lattimer.

Celeste spun around to look down at him as he had moved to the settee.

'What's so funny?' she bitterly asked.

'Don't you see Maitland, I am that God who heard your prayer; it was me, me who kept my promise to you. I looked after her, your Emily, look at her Jon; doesn't she look like her mother?'

She gasped as Lattimer pointed to her.

'You're no God Lattimer. You're a sick bastard, an evil twisted monster. How can you call having me punished like that looking after me? You have the audacity to sit there and think that taking me away from my family, the people I needed and loved, was keeping me safe?'

Yet another shot rang out.

Maitland's body jerked as Celeste blinked and fell backward in her chair.

Lattimer's laughter turned to screams, as his left knee exploded as the bullet impacted his bone. He writhed about in pain, the like of which he had never known.

She stood. 'You did this to me; you did this to us, why? What the hell did we ever do to you?'

Lattimer was still screaming in pain, 'No Celeste, no!'

'Don't call me that, I'm Emily, Emily Maitland, now tell me why you bastard, why?' She shot at him again hitting his right arm making his screams increase.

Four bullets left.

Emily became hysterical once more and again and again she fired the gun, twice more, missing each time.

Two bullets left.

She remained angry, her face white, her eyes filled with tears while her hand was shaking uncontrollably.

'You're no God Lattimer, you're not even a proper man, shall I tell you what you are Lattimer?'

The hammer on the gun clicked, 'Yeah?'

Her finger moved. 'You're a cunt!'

She squeezed the trigger to fire her penultimate bullet just as Maitland pulled her arm away. The gun still fired and a fraction of a second later, the small metal bullet flew from the barrel, straight and true, albeit aimlessly soaring through the air.

It made a sudden impact with the side of the discarded club hammer, causing dirty residue to erupt. The collision between the tiny pellet and the square club of the tool caused a deflection in the bullet's trajectory, sending the tiny speck of metal spinning wildly in a different direction.

The velocity and size of the projectile penetrated clothing that didn't even slow the thing down, nor did the skin stop the bullet as it tunnelled through the thin elastic dermis. It then quickly moved inside the body, looking for a place to damage or stop its journey, if it could and not even a rib cage could stop it as it shattered through the bone, scraping the heart and finally embedding itself into the lining of the left lung of Jon Maitland.

He collapsed holding his chest.

'NO!' Emily dropped the gun while grabbing at her fallen Father as she screamed out to him.

For the first time in eighteen years he heard his daughter say the word.

'Daddy, no! Please not like this, not now, not here.' She sobbed.

Maitland smiled. 'Thank you Emily, I have wanted to hear you call me that for so long now.' He coughed and a little blood exited from his mouth, running down his cheek.

'Dad no, don't go, I need you.' She was still crying.

He held out his hand and brushed her face.

She grabbed at his fingers with both hands.

'Emily, you mustn't cry, not in front of him.'

'But dad I need you, here with me.'

'No you don't, you're going to be fine. You've grown into a strong, capable and beautiful woman. You must forget the past and move on with your life'

'But what do I do?'

'He's right you know. You are so much like your mother, strong willed and beautiful, you will carry on and you will find your way. Take the lead; give these people a real purpose in life and not the false dream of a madman.'

He pressed the locket into her hand. 'This was always going to be yours. Take it and remember us.'

She held it tight and watched as her father slowly lost his final fight and Jon Maitland got his wish and joined his wife, her mother in another, maybe a more wonderful life.

Lattimer was muttering, moaning and giggling. 'Oh Celeste, the irony of it! Your father killed your mother, now you've killed your father.'

She finally gave in to her hatred.

She picked up the gun and aimed it at Lattimer.

'No Lattimer, I've already told you once, my name is Emily Maitland, daughter of The Reaper, Jon Maitland. He didn't kill my mother; it was you, you and your kind who killed my parents, just as it was you and your kind who killed this world.'

Her hand stopped shaking as her anger subsided, her aim becoming stable.

'I'm not going to allow you to control us any more Lattimer. No more will you be able to oppress us. We will build a life, but without you and your damned lies and it all starts with your death.'

The final bullet sped from the chamber and directly hit Lattimer in the centre of his head, the back of his skull exploded in a spectacular spray of skin, bone, blood and brain. His body went into a spasm where he sat on the settee, his arms settled, outstretched along the backrest and his feet had crossed, one over the other.

He became silent, no more laughing came from him, there were no more orders, because there was no more Lattimer.

He was dead at last.

Emily lent over and kissed the cheek of her dead father, as she gently laid his head on the floor.

'I love you daddy.' She whispered.

She stood.

Looking down at her hands, one filled with hate and revenge, while the other held the secret of her past. Emily Maitland threw the gun at the body of Lattimer and with it all her feelings of anger finally ebbed away.

She lifted her hand and looked at the dented locket. She pressed on the protruding clasp that released the two halves of gold from one another.

She pressed her fingers to her mouth in surprise. She was too scared to open it further, frightened that she would finally find what had been missing for all of these years.

Within the small gold hiding place, so cherished by her parents, were the roots of her past and placing her forefinger on the edge she began to prise it open.

The tiny fragile hinge was stiff through years of damage and non use, she had to carefully increase the pressure; not wanting to break it, until eventually the hinge gave way revealing to her the secret that was hiding inside.

For the first time since she could remember, Emily Maitland looked at a faded and damaged picture of a woman on one half and a baby on the other.

The pictures were old, but the woman was young, young and so very beautiful. All she could do was stare at the picture of the most beautiful woman she had ever seen, her mother.

For what seemed like ages she studied the pictures. She realised that the baby picture must have been of herself and so in the locket, Emily Maitland not only found her roots but she literally found herself.

Lifting her head up, she closed the trinket in her hand and walked out of the shed leaving her father Jon Maitland,

the deranged Russell Lattimer and Celeste Baker all dead, as
she headed toward the penthouse.

Chapter Twenty One

The square was heaving with as many people the Reverend Mike Spencer could gather in such short notice. He promised the people that if they turned up today, they would be given some important news, news about the move to Kernow.

Everyone was excitedly chatting with one another, speculating on why they had been called and what the news could be.

The time approached for Lattimer to appear on the scaffold and silence fell on the crowd, as the French doors opened.

A figure appeared from them, somebody dressed in a flowing red outfit walked out. The outfit rippled in the warm gentle breeze, its cloak billowing behind her, as the wind pushed against the loose clothing accentuating her curves, revealing the figure as that of a woman.

She walked to the edge and looked down.

A gasp ran through the crowd, as people began to recognise the figure of Celeste Baker.

She opened her arms and began to speak.

'People of Launceston I have some news for you all, the vigilante Jon Maitland is dead.

Three of a Kind

'I have killed The Reaper, Jon Maitland!'

The crowd cheered wildly, while Reverend Mike Spencer looked on confused.

'During the skirmish with The Reaper, Russell Lattimer also died.' The people fell silent except for the Priest, who punched the air making a 'whooping' sound.

'Lattimer took with him his dream of opening the gateway to Kernow for us, but it doesn't end there. Today, the subject of this sermon is truth and lies and although what I have just told you is the truth, behind it is a stack of lies; lies that have been told to you all, by Russell Lattimer.' She looked down, licking at her dry lips before continuing, 'so what is the truth? I am the truth; just as you all are the truth. Today I found out who I really am and where I belong. You know me as Celeste Baker, an Enforcer and puppet of Lattimer, but here I stand before you as Emily Maitland, daughter of The Reaper, Jon Maitland.'

She thought she felt the scaffold vibrate as the crowd went wild, shouting and calling to her.

'What do you mean, Celeste?'

'What are you playing at Baker?'

'Baker, did you kill Lattimer?'

That last question caused her to react.

'Yes I killed Lattimer.'

She stopped as the guards drew their weapons; there was the sound of many rifle hammers being pulled back. The gathered crowd began to become terrified at the sight of the guards' reaction.

'NO,' she shouted. 'Do not take up arms against your own. Put down your guns, NOW.' At first, the guards ignored her order, but the Priest moved toward one of them and pushing his hands out he slowly grabbed the weapon and took the gun from the female guard. The others soon followed the lead and relinquished their weapons.

'Thank you Priest. Now go, open your Churches; pull down the barricades. You Sir, have your miracle.'

A bright smile appeared on his face as he quickly hobbled passed the guards and out of the courtyard.

'People of Launceston, listen to me. Lattimer had to die. His lies were his empty promises. His promise was his truth, in that your hard work would finally get us into Kernow.'

She threw down to the people what was left of the poster. 'This is his truth, this is his gateway.'

Hands rose from the crowd, catching the fragments of coloured paper and she watched, as some people tried to match pieces together.

'Today the lies will stop. Today you are free. Free from the tyranny and shackles of the oppression that was Russell Lattimer.'

Emily Maitland retuned to the office from addressing the crowd below the balcony. She sat behind the desk and thumbed the gouge in the wooden top made by Lattimer. She sighed deeply, then, resting her elbows on the hard wooden surface, she placed her face in her open hands.

'What the hell have you done Celeste, I mean Emily.' She corrected herself as she spoke aloud. Removing her hands from her face she spoke to herself again. 'You'll have to get used to that name my girl.'

She looked around the room.

It remained the same, as when she saw it yesterday; the only difference was her. It was around an hour before a knock on the door interrupted Emily Maitland's thought process. Dread jangled at her nerve ends, as she stood to welcome the group of twelve people, which included Mike Spencer.

As they walked in, she noted they looked as nervous as she felt. Emily smiled, hoping her nerves were not so apparent to them.

'Please, come in everyone, it seems we have a lot to talk about.'

The room had already been set out for the meeting, but there were too many chairs, she had expected more people. Emily sat with the group, instead of sitting behind the desk, she was not in control of the town, they were and she did not want them to feel as though she was planning to take over from where Lattimer had left.

'OK, where do we go from here?' She immediately asked them, as soon as they were seated.

Ben Fuge, a forty seven year old Enforcement Officer stood around six feet tall, anger in his eyes, directly aiming his vision at Emily Maitland.

'What do you mean? You're going to prison for the murder, by your own admission, of Russell Lattimer.'

Emily had remained calm as she looked around at the faces. They looked lost and scared, this man had obviously taken the lead and without knowing the facts, he was doing what he was trained to do.

She looked into his emerald green eyes; somehow his stare unnerved her.

'Ben, I didn't murder Lattimer. Oh, I killed him alright, but it was an act of self defence, it was a mercy killing if you like, but not a murder.' She was soft spoken and calm.

Emily did not know if his face reddened through rage or embarrassment, but he remained quiet as he listened to her.

'Ben, he attacked me, he lied to me; he lied to all of us.' She stood up to face him. 'There is no gateway into Kernow. Go, have a look for yourself. You'll see that the people have worked hard and died for nothing, but a lie.'

He wavered a little in his stance and as she pointed out the window, Ben Fuge's gaze automatically followed, but he could not see what she was pointing at.

'Here take the key, go look for yourself,' Emily looked around at the others, 'and anyone else for that matter. Go, I will wait here for your return.'

She held out the key and tentatively, Ben Fuge accepted her challenge, leaving with two others.

Emily again sat with the others.

'Would it be OK if we continue once they return, I think it would not be fair to leave them out?'

Those who had stayed nodded their approval and Emily smiled as she lowered her gaze. She was feeling a little disappointed, she had hoped there would be more people and more of a spark in them. These all seemed to be acting like the robots they have been programmed to be.

Within an hour Ben and his friends returned to the Penthouse. Emily remained seated and looked at his face, it was pasty white, but she didn't know if it was the rage of finding out about the lie, or the shock of finding Lattimer's corpse with its head blown apart.

'Well?' she asked him.

'Well you certainly made a good job of that, if the rumours are right about The Reaper, then you really are your fathers daughter aren't you.'

Emily didn't feel he was trying to compliment her, but she gave a little smile anyway.

Ben Fuge clapped his hands together.

'Right, now this is what we are going to do.' His voice was surly, his demeanour angry and stern.

Emily stood up to confront him.

'Err... what do you mean Ben, this is what we are going to do?'

He smiled at her, it wasn't a friendly smile.

'Celeste,' she put her hand up ready to correct him, but he stopped her, 'OK Emily, you do not seriously think for one second that I am going to be taking orders from a woman in the first place and secondly, I don't think a mere child is suitable to carry on the great work of Russell Lattimer.'

Emily Maitland became exasperated.

'Carry on his great work,' her face screwed up in disbelief. 'Ben, did you not see? There is no work to carry on; there is no gateway into Kernow. It was all a lie and you want to carry on?' She turned around to face the crowd, an attempt on her part to gain support.

They seemed lost, unable to decide what they should be doing. They were too used to being told what to do and what to think.

Mike Spencer was the only one who she could rely on, but for now he remained silent with his hand reassuringly caressing the black rubber covered handle of the cricket bat resting between his legs.

Emily turned back to Ben.

'Well what do you propose Ben?'

He smiled a broad smile.

'Well, I think I will be in charge now, after all I am an Enforcement Officer. I will carry on exactly as Lattimer did, babysitting these worthless bastards, while they feed me with everything I want.'

Ben was pacing up and down in front of the gathered. Placing his hands behind his back was a mistake. He couldn't move them quick enough to block the swing of the Reverend Mike Spencer's cricket bat.

The sound of willow making contact with a skull was blood curdling, but Ben didn't hear it, he was out cold by the time he hit the floor. Spencer stood over him and made the sign of the cross, blessing himself after which, he winked at Emily.

The crowd gasped and Emily tutted at the priest, 'Now Father, is that anyway for a man of the cloth to behave?' She gave him a broad smile before turning to the other people in the room.

'This is not what I want, as you can see it only leads to more violence. Haven't we had enough of all that under Lattimer?'

Still, only blank faces looked back at her. The frustration was beginning to show. Slumping down in a chair she looked around the room.

'You know this room could do with brightening up, I'm fed up with the white,' She said aloud. 'I think I might have some reds and browns, you know autumn colours splashed about.'

The people looked at one another in confusion, then one voice echoed out.

'I didn't come here to talk about decoration Maitland; I want to know what we are going to do. I demand that you tell us what you expect from us.'

At last, a reaction.

'Why should I tell you? I'm not in charge, I'm no leader. Ben was right, I am too young to lead this town.'

An elderly woman raised her hand slightly, she had a wrinkled but soft face; her dark hair didn't seem to match her ageing features.

'I remember you, Emily Maitland, daughter of Jon and Laura Maitland. You all lived in the Kernow controlled part of town and your mother made the most delicious cakes.'

Surprise crossed Emily's face.

'You knew my parents?' she asked, 'Who are you?'

The old woman gently closed her eyes, as she slowly nodded.

'I am Pandora, keeper of records, I know everyone and everything.'

The room fell silent.

A stunned Emily didn't know what to make of this information, someone knew her parents; someone could fill in her past.

'You know me?'

Again the old woman nodded.

'Pandora, will you stay here and tell me what you know?'

After seeing another gentle nod from her, Emily asked the others to leave and take the unconscious Ben Fuge to the infirmary.

'Please think about what has happened here, think of how, not just me, but we, as a town can build a future based on truth.'

Mike Spencer held her hand.

'Do you want me to stay Emily?'

She touched his arm and smiled.

'No thanks Mike, I'm fine, but we need to meet later, OK?'

He nodded, tucked his bat under his arm and followed the rest out, closing the door and leaving the two women alone.